Sleep Forever

I0556764

A Wes and Oz Mystery

Their Sixth Adventure

By

S. B. Biddinger

Sleep Forever

If you have not had a chance, please check out these other Wes and Oz Mysteries on Amazon. (Paperback, Kindle, Kindle Unlimited)

Death of a Trailer Queen

A Mechanic's Worst Nightmare

Two + One = Murder

The Chrome Canyon Killer

Death has No Sorrow

For the latest updates on future mysteries and other exciting news, please visit my website.

www.sbbiddinger.com

Table of Contents

Chapter 1

"I'm going to kill him!" I screamed as my eyes flew open. The guys, a name which I had given our four-legged family members Oz and Annie, raced out of our bedroom as their earsplitting bark echoed throughout the house. I cursed the day Marti's damn brother, Chris, moved to the valley. The man knew no boundaries. I glanced over at the clock as my feet hit the floor. "Two A.M." I muttered under my breath so as not to wake up the love of my life. He had no common decency or respect for our privacy and if he didn't take his finger off the doorbell soon, I'd happily break it. With each step, the madder and madder I got. He was about to get a mouthful of Wes. But when I flung the door open and shouted, "What the hell is wrong with you..." My voice trailed off. Instead of Chris with his finger frozen on the doorbell there stood a frightened, frail Carrie, our next-door neighbor in her late sixties. Her small frail old body was shaking violently, and she looked as if she had seen a ghost. The panicked expression on her pale face meant something had frightened her. We had been close friends since the first day I moved in next door, and I had never ever seen her in such a state. Usually, she was a spunky little old lady in her late sixties filled with lots of energy, but not tonight.

"Wes, Wes, Wes," she stuttered as I helped her inside. After taking a couple of deep breaths to regain some sort of composure. "Wes, there's someone in my house."

"Did you call the police?"

"No, I was too scared. I heard a noise in the den and went to investigate. I had just left my bedroom when I saw a flashlight was moving around and fearing the worst, I raced out of the house and came over here."

I was about to call the police when Marti, my partner in crime and loving wife, staggered out of the bedroom wearing nothing but one of my T-shirts that went down to her knees. She wiped the sleep out of her eyes and froze when she spotted Carrie shaking like a leaf. Marti rushed over and tightly wrapped her arms around Carrie's frail body. Carrie's body collapsed into Marti's as she started to cry uncontrollably. "My poor dear, what's going on? Did something happen to Jack?"

Jack was her boyfriend or as Marti and I would jokingly say, "Her boy toy". A retired schoolteacher and one of those throwback hippies of the sixties with long silver hair in a ponytail. You never saw him without his tied dyed shirt; Birkenstock sandals and a peace sign around his neck. Jack was one of the easiest going people we've known. He split his time between houses, only spending a couple nights a week at Carrie's. Her voice shaken and frightened struggled to say, "Wes, there's a stranger in my house. What am I going to do?"

While I called the police, Marti brewed up a fresh pot of coffee and Carrie explained for Marti's benefit her harrowing story seeing a flashlight moving around in the den. She began to cry when she brought up Dolly, her little four-legged friend and companion who passed away four months earlier. "This wouldn't have happened if Dolly was still here. She was a good watch dog. I miss her so much." Oz and Annie put their heads in her lap letting her know they missed their friend too.

While the ladies talked in the kitchen, I went out front to wait for the police and see if I could tell if the intruder was still in her house. A light danced off the walls as whoever was inside moved from one room to another. I stormed to our bedroom and grabbed Ruthie, my Louisville Slugger baseball bat. I still remember the day my dad took me to a New York Mets game. If you look close enough, you could still see some of the players' signatures, although over time they had somewhat faded. Both Marti and Carrie questioned in unison, "What are you doing?"

"The intruder is still inside her house. I don't want the jerk to get away before the police get here."

"Wes, this is crazy. Put the bat down and please wait for the police." Marti pleaded.

"I'll be careful; besides I have Ruthie and I am packing Oz." Oz was my tricolor, smooth collie. He had been my buddy and protector ever since he was a pup. I'm not one of those macho type men, but with Oz at my side, I felt more confident for such encounters. Lately, Oz had to come to my rescue more times than I wanted to admit as some nasties wanted to physically harm me or even worse, kill me. Oz's pearly white teeth and his eighty plus pounds of muscle made him a force you didn't want to tangle with. Besides, he didn't like anyone messing with his meal ticket.

When I saw the moving light coming from Carrie's bedroom, I started to have second thoughts as I approached. But Oz and Annie, our border collie, sensed danger and were already in attack mode. I was hoping to hear sirens, but nothing yet. After taking a deep breath, I was about to open the front door when something out of the corner of my eye caught my attention and I stopped. Marti and Carrie were frantically waving their arms for me to come back. The look on Marti's face suggesting she wasn't too happy.

The door creaked, sending fear throughout my body. I whispered to Oz as this little voice in the back of my head said, "This is not smart, maybe we should wait for the police." But both Oz and Annie had different ideas and bolted inside barking. From Carrie's bedroom came a blood-curdling scream. "Wholey shit! Where in the hell did you come from? Get away from me! Stop biting and back off!" I was about to see what was happening when the intruder scream filled the house. "Son of a bitch that hurt!"

7

I was standing in the middle of the living room when I heard our criminal type person's body slam into the hallway wall as he tried to escape. With Ruthie posed I was ready as the dark shadow stumbled their way down the hall toward me. For a moment I thought I was shaking worse than Carrie had been standing at our front door. Fear and anxiety raced throughout my body. As the figure moved closer, that little voice in the back of my head said, "What if they have a gun?" I froze, that was something I hadn't thought about.

I was about to retreat outside when this person's body slammed hard into mine. Stars flashed in my eyes as I fell backwards and hit my head on the wall. "What the hell did I just hit?" The uninvited guest shouted. As he tried to get up off the floor, Oz let out a deep guttural growl, as if to say, "I dare you to move."

I reached over and flipped on the overhead hall light switch. I was still seeing stars. At first, I had to squint until my eyes adjusted to the brightness. The frightened man had placed his hands over his head and moved his body into a fetal position fearing for the worse. Oz's face was inched from the man's poised to attack. Our prowler's frightened eyes stared at Oz's pearly whites daring him to move. "Please mister, call off your dogs. I promise I won't move. Just please call them off. I'm bleeding from where they bit me. Could you please call off your dogs?" Annie had grabbed ahold of his pant leg and started pulling as she growled.

Now that my eyes had gotten used to the light, I could see white and red flesh from where the guys had ripped into his black clothing. When I called for Oz and Annie to come by my side, I could see the intruder's face. He looked to be in his early twenties. For a moment the young man breath a sign of relief but quickly covered his head as Oz moved closer daring him to move.

Feeling confident he wasn't going anywhere, I smiled. "Buddy, you picked the wrong house and the wrong dogs to mess with."

Sirens and flashing lights filled our quiet street as two patrol cars screeched to a halt out front. With guns drawn, two offices raced through the front door and came to an abrupt halt. The lady officer turned to see me holding Ruthie and screamed. "Drop the bat! On the floor! Now!"

We were both hand cuffed and shoved out into the cool night air. Oz, not happy seeing the way the officers pushed, pulled and twisted my body was about to attack. I tried to explain but the officer was oblivious to my words as she was more worried about what Oz was planning to do. The other officer dragged the intruder out of the house, the whole time he was screaming that he lived here and I was the one who entered his house and turned my dogs loose on him. He was threatening to press charges. The female officer smirked and rolled her eyes as if she believed him.

When the lady officer opened the back door to her squad car, Marti shouted from our front door, "Officer, that is my husband!"

Carrie also spoke up, "Stop! That's my neighbor."

She leaned me up against the side of the patrol car. "Don't move! I mean it!" she said in a stern and harsh tone as she went over to talk to Marti and Carrie. The young man sat slumped in the back seat of the other patrol car.

More patrol cars appeared with their lights flashing. I watched as the officers huddled around the cruiser with Carrie's uninvited guest inside. While the lady officer who had handcuffed me went and talked to Marti and Carrie, the other officers kept a close eye on me.

Both Oz and Annie sat next to me warning the officers to keep their distance. A curious officer walked over, he shined a light in my face and shouted, "Jane, don't you know who this guy and his dogs are?"

She gave the fellow officer a blank look as if she didn't have a clue what he was talking about. "This guy is a buddy of the Detective Rod

Miller and Captain Ross. I've seen them down at the station a couple of times. He's some kind of private cop and busted that drug ring and killing spree at the junkyard." He pointed at Oz and continued. "This dog is a hero for saving Miller's life one other time." The officer got down on one knee and gave Oz ear scribbles. As soon as Annie saw this, she pushed her body between the two of them to get some loving.

"Hey, how about you undo the handcuffs?" I asked.

'Oh, yea, sorry." Now free, Oz, Annie and I joined the others at our house. Inside Marti served coffee and my stash of Betty's fried deliciousness apple fritters while both Carrie and I gave our statements. On office hauled the young intruder to the station in his patrol car to be booked.

It was close to four when they left. Marti suggested Carrie spend the rest of the night in our guest bedroom, which she gratefully accepted. The police had left Carrie's front door open, so Oa, Annie and I went over to lock it up. Just before I closed the door, I stopped and swore I heard a noise coming from the back of the house. I panicked when the hairs on Oz's back stood on end. He picked up a scent, his ears perked, and he froze. This was not a good sign, not a good one at all. He slowly proceeded down the hallway, his back legs ready to pounce while showing his pearly whites.

When he let out a low guttural growl, I wanted to turn around and run, fearing for the worst. He disappeared into Carrie's bedroom, and a shriek filled the house and Oz started barking. I screamed as a tan and white cat raced out of the bedroom, hissing and crying out in fear. Somehow it must've come through the front door looking for a warm place to spend the rest of the night until we disturbed it. The scared cat ran through my legs and out the door. Oz tried to follow the feline intruder between my legs, but there wasn't enough room and I went crashing backward onto the floor. Oz and Annie were in a hot pursuit barking their heads off as they chased after the cat down the street. I quickly locked the front door and went home. I had had enough excitement for the night. Thankfully the cat had eluded them and   returned home with their tongues hanging out.

Before I stepped into the bedroom, Annie leaped onto the bed and nestled her body between Marti's legs, and Oz placed his head on my pillow. I squeezed into the only open space, closed my eyes and thought, "What a morning".

The bright sunlight filtered into our bedroom. The smell of coffee brewing filled the house. When I stepped into the kitchen where Marti and Carrie were sitting at the counter, I could tell Carrie was relieved that her nightmare was over. Her spunkiness had returned. "It's about time you showed yourself." Using my masterful detective skills, I spotted warm fried deliciousness in a box on the counter from the Whole Bakery Experience. Betty, the owner and where Marti's brother Chris worked made the best apple fritters in town. "I was the first one in the bakery this morning. I wanted to replace the ones we ate last night," Carrie added.

She slowly sipped her coffee and started to giggle. "Are you going to let me in on the inside joke?" I asked.

She looked over at Marti who was also snickering. "When I told the story to Betty on what happened last night, your brother-in-law, Chris overheard and just about had a fit when he realized he had missed out on all the action. He said he would be by later this morning to discuss why I hadn't called him to assist. He claimed to be my partner."

'He's not my partner!" I shouted before I took a large bite.

Chapter 2

My name is Wesley Johns and I reside in Idaho's Treasure Valley with my beautiful bride Marti and our two four-legged kids, Oz and Annabelle. Whenever the State of Idaho Workman's Comp Department or private insurance companies suspect someone has filed a fraudulent claim, they reach out to me to investigate. Lately, with the increased population, there's been no shortage of cases. The leaning stack of files on my desk threatens to bury me one of these days.

After stuffing myself with another apple fritters, I gathered up my usual surveillance equipment and supplies. I was almost out the front door when the back patio door opened and Jack, Carrie's boyfriend, lover and part-time roommate stepped inside. Carrie hurried over into his arms. Marti whispered, "I sent him a text before we went back to bed."

After the two love birds left, Marti dashed into the bedroom and before I finish loading my gear in the truck, she stepped outside wearing her dark blue airline uniform. Her long auburn hair was tied in a ponytail sticking out the back of her uniformed baseball cap. Until a year ago she spent most of her time traveling around the country as a flight crew member, but she didn't like being away from home, especially whenever I had gotten myself into precarious situations which was happening a lot lately. Thankfully, Oz was there to make sure nothing serious happened. Marti thought it was best to stay close and keep an eye on me. She now works at the terminal as a customer service / ramp agent.

My mind flashed back to when we had first met. She and a friend were at the park checking out the classics at a car show. They came upon my nineteen fifty-eight Ford Thunderbird, which I had nicknamed the Bird, and stopped to pet Oz. At these shows he sat out front on guard duty while receiving plenty of attention from onlookers as well as getting his picture taken. I rushed over with my camera to take a picture and when I looked into her beautiful eyes, I was in love and wanted to spend the rest of my life with her. When she mentioned how she loved my car, I offered to give her a ride. She took out a piece of paper and wrote down her address and phone number. What happened next caught me totally off guard, her parting remark, "See you at seven. Don't be late." I stood there in shock as she and her friends walked away. This had never happened to me before. When she looked back and winked, my heart began to race. That evening with her was magical and we've been living the dream ever since.

Back to reality and after a quick peck on the cheek she climbed in her SUV and drove off down the street. Suddenly the SUV's came to a squealing halt and shattered the neighbor silence. I turned around in time to see her brother waving his arms and walking in my direction. I quickly sped off in the other direction. I smiled as I glanced in the rearview mirror to see Chris trying to get my attention. "Phew! That was close," I remarked to myself.

I had been working on this fraud case for over a month and still was unable to prove one way or another my suspect had committed any wrongdoing. When I first re-read the file from the State Insurance Department, I couldn't believe what I was reading. I had to call Gerald Baker, the department head, to confirm that this wasn't a joke. He assured me it was "No joke". An employee of a paranormal team claimed that while working at an old bar/hotel downtown, an entity caused his injury.

My suspect's story was that as the rest of his team worked in the basement setting up their equipment, he had gone upstairs alone to one of the so-called haunted hotel rooms. Supposedly, in the late eighteen hundreds, a client murdered a prostitute, then hung himself in the same room." To this day, they say they've seen him and heard him stomping around the room. The story was that my suspect had finished setting up his ghost hunting equipment and was waiting at the top of the grand stairway for his co-workers to join him when his accident occurred.

What happened next set the hairs on the back of my neck on end. He reported he heard a woman's voice screaming from the bedroom and turned to go investigate and before he could take one step, someone or something grabbed his shoulder from behind and forcibly pushed him down the stairs. After his body came to a halt at the bottom of the grand staircase, he yelled out for help. In the report, he said he was in pain and couldn't move. Since the rest of the crew were still in the basement, no one heard his cry for help. It was only after he hadn't responded to them on his walkie-talkie that a crew member went to investigate. They found my suspect wincing in pain and babbling on about how someone had pushed him from behind. He was taken to the hospital for an evaluation and spent the night under observation. The doctors concluded that the fall had sprained his back and he was sent home with Ibuprofen, ice packs and instructed to take bed rest. The ER doctor explained he'd be fine and could return to work in a couple of days.

It had been over a year now since my suspect had his so-called paranormal encounter and had not returned to work. While at the hospital he contacted one of those ambulance chasing lawyers, and the next morning, the lawyer filed a lawsuit claiming his employer had failed to provide a safe work environment. All this time waiting for his day in court, my suspect, Markus Wright, has been living off the state.

The reason Gerald wanted me to move this case to priority was that they had received an anonymous tip that Markus had been seen at the water park enjoying the slides and playing water volleyball. After re-reading the case file for a third time I decided to name this investigation, "The Case of the Pushy Ghost."

For the last three weeks I'd been camped out down the street from Markus's house waiting and watching hoping he would slip up like other fraud suspects had done in the past. Markus was twenty-seven, single and lived with his girlfriend. After my first sighting of the man, I thought I had found Sasquatch. He was six foot eight and weighed about three hundred and eighty pounds. His long brown hair cascaded down his back and a bushy beard covered most of his face.

Since my investigating was coming up blank, I reached out to his previous employer, "Ghosts R Among Us" hoping they would be able to provide me with any other information that might help. I talked to Markus's boss, Sam Michaels. Sam sounded like he was in his late fifties by the tone in his voice. During our conversation he spoke highly of Markus's work and attitude up until the night of the so-called accident. But his voice change to discontent and ill feeling as he spoke about Markus's claims and that he was going to sue. I asked Sam if he would show me around the old hotel and bar, but instead he suggested I attend their next ghost hunt. He insisted I'd get a better understanding and feeling of the accident if I was there at night. Reluctantly, I agreed to meet him and his crew Sunday night at ten at the old building where Markus's encounter had happened.

I wasn't thrilled at the prospect of spending the night in a dark bar/hotel searching for evidence and maybe encountering the alleged ghostly thingy that pushed Markus down the staircase. It looked, however, as if I had no choice up to now, I had nothing to show if he was committing fraud or not.

I parked in my usual spot two houses down the street waiting and hoping to get a glance of Sasquatch today, I watched a few videos posted on "Ghosts R Among Us" website. Chills raced up and down the back of my neck, making me to rethink whether it was a good idea or not to join Sam's crew Sunday night. It didn't help but while watching one of them, my phone rang. I ignored Chris's call for a third time and hoped he would stop sending me texts begging for me to come get him.

Markus stepped out of his small bungalow style home and I quickly reached for my camera. He slowly made his way to the street where his van was parked. He opened the sliding door and brought out a small binder, then disappeared back inside his house. "Damn" I commented. I was about to leave when he reappeared with his girlfriend who looked to be one-fourth his size. She had a very pale complexion, long dark black hair that hung down to her waist and wore bright red lipstick and glasses. They disappeared into the small garage next to the house. This had been their routine from the start of my investigation. I'd like to know what they were doing since they spent most of their day inside with occasional flashes of bright lights filtering out from under the two old wooden garage doors.

To keep the local busy bodies happy while I was parked on their street, I placed magnetic signs on my truck doors. "Valley Road Monitoring Service" and a yellow light bar on the roof, a prop making my being there more official.

My body was getting stiff from sitting so long so it was time to stretch. I walked to the small mom and pop store just down the street to get a snack and something to drink. The building appeared to have been an old neighborhood grocery store back in the fifties and sixties. It was nestled between two old brick apartments.

When I got back to my truck, Markus and his girlfriend were sitting in lawn chairs they had placed on their front patio. Punk rock music blared out the open front door. Not my taste in music. I waived as I walked by, neither one of them returned with a wave, and their heads followed me while watching through their dark sunglasses.

The rest of my day was a bust. Markus, his girlfriend and a few friends sat around drinking beers and eating delivered pizza. I had to smile when I saw the delivery driver from one of those national chains where the pizzas were cheap, the toppings were sparce and had no flavor. I wanted to walk over and suggest they try ordering pizzas from Donavan's, that was real pizza. Nothing else in the valley compared, but I didn't want to blow my cover. Just to make the day feel like it was not a total waste, I clicked off a few pictures when Markus disappeared inside and returned with a six pack.

Oz and Annie danced around my feet when I reached for their leashes and we drove to the dog park. While they played with their friends, I sat under my favorite tree and thought how best to close this case and move on. After weeks of investigating, I couldn't prove if the man was a fraud or not. One thing for sure, I didn't want to spend the night in the old hotel/bar encountering who or what pushed him down the stairs. If there wasn't enough evidence to prove Markus Wright had committed fraud that night, then it was time to shelve this case for now and move on to another.

Something good filled my nostrils the moment we walked through the front door and the guys raced over and drained the water dish. Marti was at the stove stirring something in the pot, I gave her a kiss on the back of her neck and tried to peek at what she was stirring. She spun around and wrapped her arms around me and gently pressed her soft warm lips against mine. She then turned back toward the stove and said, "Dinner in ten, counter or TV?"

It didn't matter how much I fed Oz and Annie it was never enough. Their sad brown eyes suggested they hadn't eaten for months and would appreciate a small morsel. I almost wished I had chosen the counter instead of sitting in front of the TV. Our taste in entertainment differed, I enjoyed old westerns, cop shows, and action movies. Marti on the other hand was big into reality shows. We flipped a coin and I lost. I had to suffer through two episodes of some reality housewives in New York. All they ever did was bitch about one and other. Fortunately, Marti wasn't even close to being like any one of them.

For dessert I offered to make an ice cream run, hoping not to suffer through a third and possible a fourth episode. Since Annie was content to rest her head on Marti's lap, Oz joined me on our road trip. The ice cream shop was quiet, which meant a quick in and out. To my surprise, Markus Wright and his girlfriend were sitting in the corner and recognized me since I had been staking out his house these past weeks.

When we returned, the TV was turned off, and Marti was in the hot tub. Her eyes were closed as she allowed the warm swirling water to dance around her body. As soon as she heard the patio door slide open, she opened one eye and reached for the cup of ice cream. A slight grin crossed her face when she commented, "The service at this spa has something to be desired. How do you expect your clients to eat their ice cream without a spoon?"

"Lady," I remarked, "Take it up with the management or else you could wait for it to melt and then you could just drink it instead."

"Oh really? I want to speak to manager of this establishment."

"He'll be with you shortly with a spoon." As I started to walk away, I added, "Until the manager returns with a spoon, use your fingers."

After giving both Oz and Annie their frozen treats, which they wolfed down in seconds, it got me thinking, "Do dogs get brain freeze like us?"

Just as I returned with a spoon, I noticed half the ice cream was gone. Marti gave me a devilish grin, "It's about time! I have a complaint about one of your employees."

"You do? The staff here at the Johns' Spa and Retreat pride ourselves on pampering our clients. How can I make it right?"

"I know a way," she seductively commented. No sooner had I slid my body into the warm swirling water than I pulled her in close and gently kissed her. "That's a good start but, I'm still not sure if I want to give this place a four-star rating on Yelp." By the time we retired to the bedroom for the night, the John's Resort and Spa received a five-star review.

Chapter 3

This morning, I sweet-talked my lovely wife into trading vehicles so Markus wouldn't get suspicious and realize he was being watched. His house showed no signs of life, but then again, it was early for him to show himself. I was in the middle of scanning through his social media pages when a light appeared in his front window. The front door opened and his petite girlfriend walked out. Her long black hair fluttered ever so slightly in the light breeze. The skintight black T-shirt with ghost figures barely covered her body and when she raised her arms to stretch, she didn't look embarrassed revealing nothing underneath even though someone might be watching. After a few more stretches, she disappeared back inside and returned sipping something hot out an extra-large red coffee mug. When she sat, she placed her feet on the small brick wall and began to mess with her phone.

Thirty minutes later, Markus stepped out only wearing red and black plaid boxers. When he bent down to give her a kiss, I clicked off a couple of pics. Their first kiss was tentative, but it soon turned into something more. A passerby on a bike yelled out, "Why don't you get a room?" Markus lifted his girlfriend in his arms and carried her inside. Click, click, click my camera sounded as I pushed the button. These photos would help substantiate fraud but they weren't enough to close the case yet.

It had been three hours and there was no sightings of the happy couple. My legs started to cramp up and I needed to stretch. I had just walked past Markus's house but on the other side of the street when I stopped to talk to one of his elderly neighbors walking his tan and black wiener dog. The man was at least six-foot tall with salt and pepper hair, matching mustache and had on a red plaid vest, white shirt and red tie. He introduced himself as Chester Stanley and his four-legged buddy as Officer Rex. When I asked how long he had been living in the neighborhood, he replied, twenty plus years, and began rambling on about how the neighborhood had changed over the years and not in a good way. He pointed toward Markus's house and a few others while his face showed some discontent.

I asked him about Markus, and he started to ramble on how he had no respect for others in the neighborhood. I was caught off guard when he abruptly stopped talking, yanked on Officer Rex's leash and quickly walked away. Both Markus and his girlfriend stepped outside with drinks in their hands. Markus shouted in a snarky tone as soon as he spotted the old man, "Hey Chester! You're late today and missed Jade's morning free peep show. What happened, your old lady kept you inside until it was over?" Markus and Jade broke out laughing. Jade added, "If you'd like, I'd be happy to give you a quick peek to get your engine started." They laughed and continued to taunt Chester and Officer Rex as they walked away.

Listening to how abusive Markus was to his neighbor, I swore I'd make it my mission to prove he was a fraud. No sooner had I stepped inside the convenience store, the young cheerful looking clerk said, "Welcome to Gas and Go. Today's special is two hotdogs for the price of one." How could I resist a deal like that.

When she started to ring up my bottle of water, a jar of peanuts and two hot dogs, each loaded with mustard and relish I asked, "I guess you know everyone who lives in the area."

She snapped her gum a couple of times, "Yea."

"Do you know Markus and his girlfriend, Jade?"

She smiled, "Yea, they're a cool couple. They come in here often. They promised to take me ghost hunting soon."

"Wow, I've never heard of anyone who hunted ghost." I was hoping she would take the bait, and she did.

"Oh yea." She snapped her gum a couple more times which was getting annoying. "They're leading experts and have seen real ghosts. He showed me around his garage once where he keeps all his equipment. I really want to see a ghost." Her gum snapped and popped again. "They're so cool, they let me and my boyfriend come party with them sometimes."

The line started to grow behind me and a ladies voice sang out, "Hey girl, coming to the party Saturday night?" In line was Jade holding onto a twelve pack of beer. That was my cue to leave.

I had just finished my last hot dog when a tap came from the passenger window. There stood Chester. I lowered the window. "Mind if I join you?" He asked.

Nothing was happening across the street and maybe his company would help pass the time and I could gather some additional intel on my suspect. "Sorry, when we met earlier, I never introduced myself, my name is Wesley Johns."

He smiled, "I know who you are."

Not sure where he was going with that I replied, "Do you?"

"You don't work for any traffic surveillance company. I made some calls and my guess is you're interested in my neighbor over there and his girlfriend. Don't worry I won't blow your cover." After a long pause, "I'm a retired Provo Marshall for the Air Force. I called my buddy, Captain Ross. He and I play golf every Thursday. He said you and your dog," Chester stopped and looked in the back seat, "had solved a couple of homicide crimes together. So where is your buddy?"

"Oz is at home today. It's just me."

"So, what has our neighborhood trash done to warrant you spying on him?"

I explained I was a workman's comp fraud investigator and Markus was under investigation. He broke out laughing when I told him the full story. From time to time, I glanced toward Markus's house to see if there was any activity, but nothing.

The next two hours Chester talked my ear off about when he and his wife had moved on this street twenty years ago and how things had changed. By the time he left, he had eaten most of my peanuts and drank my water. His parting comment was, "See you tomorrow."

I was in the middle of debating whether I should leave or not when Markus and Jade disappeared into the garage. From previous history they'd be there for hours. That made my decision easy and I left.

I was deep in thought about how I was going to break the news to Marti that we were going ghost hunting. She wasn't a fan of those paranormal shows. In fact, she didn't enjoy watching anything scary. Just saying the word "Boo" now and then caused her to jump and scream. I started to open our front door when someone from behind shouted my name.

"Hey, Wes," Marti's brother followed me inside before I could close the door. "Hey Partner, I have the next couple of days off, so we can do some investigating."

"Chris, how many times do I have to tell you before you get it through your thick head, that we're not partners?" I regretted the day Marti's younger brother came to visit. It was only supposed to be for a week, but after a month plus of freeloading off of us we had to call his mom to come and get him. Instead of leaving, he went and got a job at Betty's bakery, then he met Denise, his girlfriend and rented a house down the street. It was like he never moved out of our house because he was always here. What makes my life miserable is that he insists on helping me with all my investigations, which never failed to turn into a disaster.

"So, what kind of case are we working on?"

"Chris, there is no we. Why don't you go back home? I thought I heard Denise shouting your name."

"Nice try. Sis has invited us over for dinner." I rolled my eyes as my nice quiet night at home was quickly going down the drain. No sooner had we walked through the front door, than he went straight to the fridge looking for something to eat. Marti came into the kitchen and slammed the door closed on his head. "Christopher, you'll have to wait until dinner is ready. Now get out."

After feeding the guys and Marti and I were alone, I asked. "What's up with inviting them to dinner?"

"Mom called me this afternoon at work. Chris had called her and whined about how you don't ask him to help with your cases." I opened my mouth, but she placed her fingers on my lip. "I know, trust me, I know. So, I thought the least we could do was to have them over for dinner. Look, I'll make it up to you after they leave. I promise."

I pulled her close again and was about to kiss her when the front door opened. "Hey, hope I'm not late!" Denise was holding a large pink box. "Christopher, you forgot to bring the cake from the bakery. Luckily, I saw it on the counter." I was never sure what she saw in Marti's brother. Denise worked for my mechanic, Willy, along with three other women. They knew their stuff and were the only ones I trusted with the Bird. Marti raced over and gave her a hug.

Since it was a beautiful summer evening, we ate out on the patio. The guys put on their best act for handouts. They knew from past meals that Denise was an easy mark. Chris kept badgering me to let him help with my current investigation and it was Marti who brought up the subject that I was investigating ghosts. Chris turned a little pale, but Denise pleaded for me to tell them more.

Once I finished, Chris blurted out, "You can count me out on this one. I don't do ghosts!"

"Darn," I gave him my best disappointment look. "I signed us up for a paranormal investigation this coming Sunday night." Marti gave out a slight smirk, that was until I explained she was coming along.

To my dismay, Denise said, "Count me in." I had only purchased two tickets and hadn't planned on them joining us.

Marti offered to let Denise go in her place, but Denise insisted the four of us should go. She'd pay for their tickets.

Marti and Denise were in the kitchen cleaning up after dinner as I sat in silence on the patio. Chris did nothing to help but planted his body in front of the TV as usual. Denise stepped out onto the patio and looked behind to make sure Marti was still in the kitchen. She closed the door and said, "We'll have everything finished a week from Friday."

I smiled from ear to ear. "Yes, I have the following Saturday circled on my calendar."

"What time should we meet?"

I thought, "How about six?"

"Perfect, I'll be there." When the patio door opened, we both jumped. "What are you two talking about?" Marti questioned. It was Denise's quick thinking that brought up the ghost hunt and how excited that we were all going. For a moment I thought I saw the love of my life turn a little pale but instead it was me when she placed the Scrabble board on the table. I gave her a reluctant glance. I hated this game. I held the world's longest losing streak. At the beginning of the game, we would write out a wager on a piece of paper. The loser would have to do whatever the winner's wager was. I have been to the store late at night picking up ice cream, hiking in the mountains and curtain shopping to name just a few wagers I had lost.

After everyone played their first tiles, I thought, "Oh crap." It was like three tigers fighting over a piece of meat, me, the lamb as they yelled, screamed and argued throughout the game. Whatever happened to a friendly competition was not in this house between the three of them. Coming in last as usual, I read the bet and cringed. "Oh, no." Right now, I wished it was climbing up the side of the mountain or something like that. This is the worst bet I had ever seen. I went inside to sulk and to tell myself how I hated that stupid game. I wished we played something different, like Monopoly where I had a chance. The three of them went on playing one more game. They were yelling and screaming so loud I thought the police would show up for disturbing the peace.

After the second game, I smiled when Chris came and sat next to me, the losers' place. When I asked what he had to do, I thought he was going to break down and cry. He showed me the piece of paper and all I could say was, "That's brutal".

Marti and Denise served up large slices of carrot cake from Betty's and we sat around watching a cop show. I was happy to see them finally leave. I was ready for some peace. As Marti joined me on the sofa, I pulled her close and suggested we retire to the hot tub but she just wanted to veg out in front of the TV. Once she changed the channel to one of her reality shows, I went and got another slice of cake and headed to the bedroom. I was still sulking over losing and having to pay off the ridiculous bet.

I was almost asleep when I was rudely awakened. "What do you mean you signed us up for a paranormal event!" Opening my eyes, there stood Marti looking down at me. I rolled over and pulled the blankets over my head. "Wesley Johns, I am talking to you." She tried to turn me back over and when she couldn't, she walked around the bed and climbed in on her side, staring into my eyes. I pulled her close and kissed her. "No changing the subject and don't try to sweet-talk your way out of this. You know I don't like those kinds of events. They give me the creeps and nightmares."

An evil grin crossed my face. "Okay, let's make a deal. You don't go to the ghost hunting event with the three of us and I don't have to pay off on this crazy wager."

There was a long period of silence as she considered my proposal. She then pulled me in close and whispered in my ear, "Not on your life. I will go with you on this stupid ghost thing. I'm not letting you off the hook that easy."

I kissed her back and pulled her T-shirt over her head. "That will not work." She said before kissing me back. The ole Wes's charm was working and maybe she'd relent and make the trade. But after we made love, instead she seductively remarked. "You know your sexy secretary is going to need a new outfit."

"A new outfit?"

"Yes, an expensive one."

Chapter 4

It was well past my bedtime when I climbed out of the truck. The downtown core was like a tomb, and the only other vehicles parked in front of the old bar/hotel besides my truck and Denise's Jeep belonged to the ghost hunters. Marti looked sharp in her new ghost hunting outfit: skintight black pants, a black shirt with a ghostbuster's ghost on the front, as well as her black baseball hat. However, the expression on her face showed she wasn't thrilled to be here. As for Denise, she was as giddy as a five-year-old on Christmas morning. When Chris stepped out into the light, the tone of his skin matched the white shirt and pants he was wearing. "Oh my God!" I jokingly remarked. "I think I see a ghost." Marti slapped me on the arm for me to stop teasing her brother. "Okay, I didn't see a ghost but how about the Stay Puff Marshmallow Man instead?" Denise got a chuckle at my comment but Marti wasn't impressed.

The logos on the two black panel vans that were parked out front read, "There's Ghosts Among Us." The crew was dressed in black with the company logo printed in white on the back of their shirts. The owner of the business, Sam Michaels, came over and introduced himself to Marti, Denise and Chris. Sam was a tall middle aged looking man, clean shaven head and a long brown handlebar mustache. "Glad you could make it. I'm hoping tonight you'll have an experience with a couple of the entities we have discovered still haunting this old building." A frightened expression appeared on Marti's face. Sam quickly added, "Don't worry, they're mostly harmless." Marti squeezed my arm so tight that my fingers went numb.

While the crew finished setting up their equipment, we stood outside in the cool night air out of their way. "Wes, my brother doesn't look so good. See he's nervously pacing in circles and rubbing his hands. It might be a good idea if I take him home and you and Denise continue trying to find additional information that might help you with your case," Marti remarked. When I looked into her eyes, I could see the fear and apprehension about tonight's investigation.

"Nonsense," Denise commented. "He'll be okay once we get inside. All he talked about on the way here was how he was working this fraud case with you."

Marti asked, "Chris are you sure you'll be, okay?"

He hesitated for a moment and stared down at the concrete sidewalk before saying in a somewhat shaky voice, "Sis, I'll be fine. Wes and I are partners and wherever my partner goes so do I."

I started to say, "Chris how many..." Marti stopped me by saying, "Wes, this is not the time." She then grabbed my hand and squeezed it tight.

Sam introduced the rest of his crew and gave us a short talk about what they expected to see tonight. The more he explained the more nervous both Marti and Chris became. Slowly and with some hesitation the three of us stepped inside the semi dark bar, only being lit by a few low voltage lights along with the crew's computer equipment. I sneezed from the dust, which caused Marti to jump and Chris to let out a scream. I overheard one of the crew members whisper to another member, "I think we have found our patsy for the night." They both chuckled under their breaths and glanced over at Chris. I started to feel sorry for him, but that passed quickly since he was the one who insisted on butting into my investigation.

With each step the creaking floor creaked gave an eerie vibe. Marti's grip had tightened on my wrist and my fingers again went numb as we approached the staging area by the bar. Sam was about to give out the do's and don'ts when we all glanced up at the ceiling after hearing footsteps. Marti leaned over and whispered, "Give me the truck keys. I'll make it up to you in the bedroom when you get home."

Sam noticed the tension in Marti's face and calmly said, "That's one of my crew members finishing setting up equipment. We're going to divide into teams. Wes you will come with me. We are going up to the second floor." He then pointed toward Chris, "Follow these two to the third floor."

"Chris quickly asked, "Can't I go with my partner?"

In an assuring voice Sam added, "Don't worry, you'll be in good hands. As for the two beautiful ladies, you'll each go with a tech, as one will go to the basement and the other to the kitchen."

Before we separated, Marti whispered, "You owe me big time, Buster."

The glow from the computer screens added an eerie element to the room. One of the crew members commented, "Boss, there was some activity on the second floor and basement." That's when I started to have second thoughts also and wanted to turn and leave.

Sam smiled, "Let's go find us some ghosts."

I heard Chris's obnoxious voice echo throughout the building, "Do we have to climb the stairs? Isn't there an elevator?"

I joined Sam and Lynn, one of his employees, at the base of the grand staircase. Lynn handed me a flashlight as Sam explained this was where they found Markus crying out in pain. He moved the light to the landing on the second floor and said. "He said he was standing right there when he claimed someone or something pushed him."

The floors creaked above us as Chris and the other two employees climbed up to the third floor. I was starting to question if this was a good idea or not and thought, "Why couldn't we've done this during the daytime where there'd be sunlight coming in through the dust filtered windows. I wished I had brought my bodyguard. Oz would've scare off any ghost with his bark.

With each step, the old wooden floors creaked under our feet, sending chills up my spine. For the first few minutes I don't think I blinked once. Moving my flashlight around the grand staircase, I marveled at the magnificence of its size. Each step must've been at least eight foot wide. Slowly, we climbed the first ten steps and stopped at the large center landing. From here you could proceed either to the right or the left to the second floor. Sam and Lynn each held little machines in their hands and explained they were EMF meters and the lights would show a change in the electromagnet field. If any lights would appear, it would be interpreted that ghost activity was close by. I looked down at the dark units and swallowed hard.

The landing was large enough for all three of us and more. Sam looked down at his little device and remarked, "It's pretty quiet so far. Wes, we only have one light showing, but if they all light up then we have company." A knot formed in my throat when I tried to remark, "Great."

We continued up to the next landing, which was in the middle of the staircase. From here you could see down into the hotel lobby below and most of the bar area. Again, we stopped and waited, nothing. We were almost to the second floor when from the third floor came a blood-curdling scream followed by a loud thud. Sam's and Lynn's walkie-talkies squawked. "Sam." The voice on the other end jokingly said. "This Chris fella just passed out." Lynn broke out laughing. "They must've pulled the fake skeleton arm gag by placing it on your friend's shoulder. I think this is the first time we've ever had anyone pass out. Most of the time they just run out of the building screaming."

"Is he okay?" Sam asked in his walkie talkie.

"Yea, he's coming around. We'll take him downstairs and get him some water," one of the crew members half-laughing commented.

When we stepped onto the second floor Sam commented, "Wes, Markus was standing right here when he claimed someone or something had pushed him down the stairs. None of my crew were with him at the time. He claimed that he felt a presence and a cold blast of air which caused the hairs on the back of his neck to raise. Before he could turn around, he was falling."

I quickly stepped back a couple of feet from the edge of the stairway before moving my flashlight up and down the massive staircase and its landings. Per the case file and comments from both Sam and Lynn, "How could Markus have rolled down to the main floor. The worst case would've been a ten-step tumble to the landing below which was large enough to stop his progress. But to roll all the way down to the bar floor would've been next to impossible with two massive landings and having to do a right turn.

Using my low light video camera, I cautiously made my way down each step hoping not to fall or be pushed. I stopped at the first landing, then proceeded to the grand landing before making my way down the final steps to the bar's floor. Lynn shouted down from the second floor. "So, Mister Private Eye, could you please explain to us how anyone could've fallen from here and land where you're now standing? They couldn't. I had to agree, he was right. Even with Markus's massive body, he would've stopped at the first or at best second landing, let alone make a right turn and tumble down to the main floor. It just didn't add up as Markus claimed.

I regretted not waiting until we finished whatever they wanted me to see on the second floor before I made my trek down to the bar floor. By the time I climbed the magnificent staircase for a second time I was out of breath. Maybe Marti was right, I should cut back on enjoying Betty's fried apple fritters.

No sooner had I joined the two men, when Lynn's EMF thingy lit up like a Christmas tree. The three of us quickly stepped away from the stairs.

I followed the two men down a dark hallway, using my flashlight to highlight the floor where I was stepping. As we entered the hotel room, I flashed my light overhead and saw the number thirteen. At first it was pitched black. The windows had been boarded up, blocking the light from outside. Sam turned on the overhead light. A single low-wattage bulb cast an eeriness throughout the room. I had seen enough and was ready to leave. In the center of the room was an old wooden table and four chairs. Sam and Lynn each sat in one. I hesitated before joining them. Lynn explained, in nineteen twenty-five, four men were playing poker. Things started out pretty civil until one accused another of cheating. A fight broke out and one of the men was stabbed in the chest and was left to die on this very table. The three men ran out of the room, closing the door behind them. It wasn't until the next day that someone discovered the body. By that time the three men had vanished. If you look closely, you'll see where blood has soaked into the wood. To this day, the victim still haunts this room looking for his killer.

After taking a deep gulp, I asked, "What was his name?"

"No one knows."

Sam pulled out a deck of cards and started shuffling. The lights on both of their meters lit up, and they both carried on as if it was no big deal. I was starting to get a bad feeling about what was about to happen. Sam placed the deck in the center of the table. The room became silent until it sounded like someone or something wrapped their knuckles on the deck. I almost fell over backwards in my chair. Sam smiled and started dealing out the cards. I looked hard around the room to find someone else, but there was nobody.

Sam and Lynn each picked up their cards. After a quick glance at my cards, I kept my eye on the empty chair, not sure what to expect next. Lynn commented he would take two, I said one, and Sam took two. We all waited, looking at the empty chair. If I hadn't seen it with my own eyes, I wouldn't have believed it. Two cards flew off the table. Sam dealt two cards from the stack and placed them on the remaining three in front of the empty chair. We all turned over our cards and Lynn turned over our so-called visitor's hand. Lynn remarked, "He's never lost a hand." This spooked me out and I was so ready to leave. I had whatever evidenced needed to know Markus was committing fraud, now it was time to prove it.

The lights on their meters went dark. We played another hand, but our ghostly poker player had left.

By the time we joined the others in the bar area. Chris was sitting slumped in an old wooden chair with his head between his legs. One of the techs was telling him to take deep breaths. Marti appeared out from the kitchen smiling, the tech she was with said they had no encounters. We all watched the monitors as their computer guru played back the video recording of our poker game. Marti clung onto my arm and held on tight as she watched for a second time. "Wes weren't you afraid?" she asked.

I smiled and with a joking remark I said, "No. I was just disappointed I didn't win." On the outside I was playing it cool not to give away that my insides were a plate of scramble eggs.

Denise came screaming into the room all excited. "I saw one! Well, I actually didn't see one but we did have a visitor. We turned off our flashlights and placed them on a table, then one by one they lit up. Then I place a quarter on the table and we watched as it moved. Oh my God, this was a blast. How do Chris NS I join your crew? I can't wait to do this again."

Marti remarked, "You better do it without him." She pointed toward her brother.

"What happened?"

"He fainted," one of the crew members said.

While Chris was still trying to get back to reality, we all stood around the monitors and watched as Denise and the crew turned off their flashlights. One by one they turned on. This caused Marti to tighten her grip on my arm and the pain shot throughout my body. When the quarter moved across the table, she whispered, "Wes, I would like to leave now."

It was close to one o'clock when we stepped out into the cool night air. Chris was stable enough to stand but only as long as Denise held onto his arm. I only wished I had my camera out when Denise told him they were going to join the ghost hunting team. All the color drained out of his face.

The two ladies escorted Chris to Denise's SUV while I talked to Sam and his team. I wanted to get his crew's opinion on Markus and what they thought about him. Not one of them had anything good to say. Lynn went as far as to call Markus a fake and even joked he thought of himself as an expert. Sam and his crew hoped I had enough evidence to prove the son of a bitch was a fraud.

As Marti and I started for my truck, Lynn asked, "Wes, are you going to join us out at the old pen next week?"

"Thanks, but I'm busy."

Denise shouted from her SUV, "I'll be there, what time?"

They didn't say what night and I didn't say why I was busy but we all knew my ghost hunting days were over. I expected the guys to come and greet us but instead, after some investigation, we found them asleep on our bed. I returned to the kitchen and removed the lid from their snack jar. Before I could turn around, they were at my feet waiting anxiously for their treat.

After I climbed into bed and snuggled my body next to Marti's, she asked, "Wes, do you think there are any ghosts in our house?" She gave me a peck on the cheek and in seconds, she was snoring away. As for me, my eyes were wide open and with every creak or noise, I worried my poker playing buddy might have followed us home.

Chapter 5

After spending a chilling night in that old hotel/bar with Markus's employer and crew, I was convinced there was no way the events happened the way he claimed. But unfortunately, the past two days of surveillance yielded nothing to substantiate that he had committed fraud. Each day, right at nine, Chester appeared and spent hours reminiscing about his time in the military.

However, today I promised Marti, against my better judgement, we'd attend one of her favorite charity events. Last year I was the laughingstock and the brunt end of many jokes, but love makes you do silly things and I told myself it was for a good cause.

The guys were wolfing down their breakfast when Marti stepped into the kitchen looking amazing, with her pink golf style shirt and very short and tight white shorts which accented her long, sexy legs. "How do I look?" she asked as she adjusted the white baseball cap so her long auburn hair would cascade down the opening in the back.

"How about we stay home and play around instead?" I suggested with an evil grin.

"Maybe later. Are you ready? They're waiting for us out front."

Bruce and Sue, members from our little classic car group, were waiting for us in their vintage Ford Falcon. No sooner had Marti stepped outside, Bruce blew out a wolf whistle, followed by, "Hubba, Hubba, Hubba." I chuckled when Sue whacked him on the arm.

When I opened the passenger door of the Bird for Marti, I asked. "Are you sure you want to do this?"

"What's the matter, are you afraid I'll beat you worse than last year?" She smiled and kissed me on the cheek.

"No, but remember what happened last time."

"How can I forget. Now hurry up or we'll be late."

Between the two of us, Marti was the most competitive as she tried egging me into a little wager. But I knew better, because I'd end up doing something I'd regret. The parking lot was filled with good old Detroit steel classics with their chrome bumpers glistened in the bright sunlight. A young girl decked out in a bright green t-shirt saying "Event Team" showed us where to park.

All giddy and excited, Marti leaped out and started bouncing up and down on her toes, impatiently waiting for me to open the trunk. With the click of the key, the trunk lid sprang open. Bruce walked up, placed his arm on my shoulder and commented, "Wes, for all our sakes, please don't do it." I just gave him one of my Wesley Johns patented glares of disgust.

I was just about to lift the objects out when a female's voice sang out over the PA system. "Welcome to the Third Annual Children's Hospital Putt and Cruisin' Car Show." Last year the event raised over twenty thousand dollars, and this year we hope to do even better.

Under my breath, I said, "And yours truly was the largest contributor." Good thing it was a tax write off. The way it worked was you donated three dollars per stroke, and after eighteen holes, I contributed the max at three hundred and fifty dollars. By the end of the day, when you include the entry fee, lunch, the game, club and bag rental, and auction, I wrote out a check for just over sixteen hundred dollars.

Little did I know Marti wasn't going to be denied when the bidding started on his and her set of golf clubs and matching bags. Not only did I try to discourage her but so did others, mostly for their own safety. I cringed when the auctioneer banged his gavel, pointed at Marti and said, "Sold, for eight hundred dollars!"

No sooner had the trunk lid sprung open than Marti leaned in and grabbed her set of clubs. She rushed over to show them off to Sue. Those in my inner circle of friends knew sports weren't my thing. In bowling, I'm known as the "King of Gutter Balls". We tried Pickle Ball, I got the title, "Pickle me not", just after one game. The racket had flown out of my hand a couple of times and almost hit our opponent's head. Last year after attending this event, everyone started calling me "The Wreck on the Course". Bruce, our self-appointed car group leader wouldn't let it go and kept telling everyone how I almost killed him not once but twice. Each time he told the story it kept getting more and more exaggerated. Every time he brought it up, you would've thought he was an expert and played every weekend and that Sue was a golf widow. But it was Sue who spent most of her time on the course, while Bruce just drove the cart and kept score.

I made an executive decision and closed the trunk lid. I'd watch from the clubhouse drinking glasses of cold, frosty root beer while others would chase little white balls around the course.

Marti shouted from the putting green, "Wesley Johns, you open that trunk and take out your clubs! I didn't win them for you to look at!" I shuttered at the thought about how this was going to be another long, agonizing day.

Bruce yelled, "The Wreck of the Course is here. Quick everyone run for cover."

The PA system squawked, "Everyone, please gather around the stage for instructions." A young, very attractive woman wearing a bright green t-shirt with her long blonde hair in a ponytail stood on a makeshift stage explaining the rules. "This year instead of three dollars a stroke we have raised it to five. Just a reminder, all the money raised is going to the local children's wing at the hospital." I did the calculation in my head and thought it would be better and safer for all of us if I just wrote out the check now.

Since people watching was one of my hobbies, I noticed the small group of men all ages clambering for her attention when our hostess stepped off the stage. Marti leaned over and whispered, "The wolves are on the prowl." My eyes followed them as they made their way to the first hole. Out of the corner of my eyes, I spotted a scruffy looking young man somewhat hidden in the trees. His eyes were glued on someone but I couldn't tell who. He looked so out of place with what used to be a white T-shirt and jeans that needed a good wash or tossed into the trash from the dirt and numerous stains. The man's long scraggly brown beard and hair which covered most of his upper body needed a wash and trim. The out of place man looked as if he hadn't bathed in days or even weeks. I reached for my phone and when he saw me point it at him, he quickly disappeared into the trees. That was strange, I thought.

They paired us up in groups of four. With so many people attending, some would start on the first hole and others on the tenth hole. Jack, Carrie's love interest and also a classic car owner as well as a member of our little car group walked up and said, "So, Wes, are you going for two in a row and win. "The World's Worst Golfer Trophy?" I didn't have the courage nor the desire to place it on the shelf with my other two classic car trophies. It was out in the garage collecting dust.

I turned to Marti. "You know it's not too late. It would be in everyone's best interest if I sat out on the patio watching you play and downing a couple of cold frosty root beers." The look in her eyes told me no.

Bruce wisecracked, "Wes, that's not a bad idea. It might save someone's life, like mine."

"Honey don't listen to him. It was an accident. I'm sure it won't happen this year." Marti said, while giving me a kiss on the cheek.

You should've seen the look on Bruce's face when the event lady announced that he and Sue were paired with us again. He quickly blurted out, "I object, I want a recount." Everyone broke out laughing. A few walked over and patted him on the back to give him their condolences. He yelled, "I'll contribute a thousand dollars if someone changes places with us." To his dismay, there weren't any takers.

Since the organizers thought it would be best if no one went before our group, we were the first to tee off. It was a safety issue. Last year when I teed off the first hole, the ball bounced off one of those marker things and hit Bruce in the chest. He was even standing behind me. Two holes later, my ball hit one of those things again and hit Bruce in the thigh. This year, they instructed me to tee off in front of those markers, making sure that wouldn't happen again.

We watched as Bruce teed off and his ball went straight down the fairway. So did Sue's and Marti's. Out the corner of my eyes I saw people scrambling for cover when it was my turn. "Haw, haw, haw, you're all so funny," I shouted.

I connected with the ball on my second swing, and surprisingly enough, I out drove everyone. Maybe my new clubs really would make a difference this year. Feeling pretty confident, I carefully lined up the club with the ball for my second shot and with the swing of a professional, I smiled as the sound of the club connected with the ball. To my dismay the ball only moved about ten feet. After five more strokes I was on the green with everyone else. The foursome following behind couldn't help but laugh. One commented with each of my swings, "There's another five dollars to help the kids."

I putted out after four attempts. Marti was kind enough to let me know that I was on track to contribute paying for one of the specialized medical equipment the hospital needed. Unfortunately, at my expense, Sue commented, "Wes, at this rate you'll surpass last year's total donation before we finish the front nine."

The next three holes things got a little better, but not by much. Someone from the group behind us commented, "At this rate, it'll be dinner time before we even finish the front nine and it's going to be dark before we get in all eighteen holes." One onlooker even went so far as to say, "My ninety-year-old grandmother could outplay you and she lives in a nursing home".

Using my quick wit, I fired off a couple of my snappy Wesley Johns comebacks like, "I'm doing my part to help the kids. How come you aren't?" Or my favorite was, "Charity begins at home, so why aren't you there instead of here?"

Just three more holes and we could break for lunch, but before me was the dreaded seventh water hole. Last year I contributed four balls into its dark murkiness. I watched when Marti's, Bruce's and Sue's balls cleared the water and landed on the green. After a deep breath, I pulled the club back and with a swing Tiger Woods would've approved of, the club came in contact with the ball. The next thing I heard was a splash. I placed another stupid tiny ball on the water's edge and was about to swing, when Bruce walked over and handed me one of his old golf balls. "Here, use this one. I would hate to see you lose another one of your new balls."

"Thanks for the confidence," I sarcastically replied.

I whispered to myself, "You can do this." With one swift swing, the ball flew in the air and landed in the middle of the pond. Sue and Marti, as well as the peanut gallery behind me, broke out in laughter. Someone yelled, "That was your best shot of the day and it still landed in the water. Are you going to play it there?" I turned to the group and took a bow. They all cheered and applauded.

After struggling through the seventh and eighth holes, it was a welcome relief knowing just one more hole before lunch. I was ready for a break and hoped to convince the others to play the last nine without me, I'll just match the strokes from the front nine and write out the check.

Before we teed off, Bruce turned to the now gallery of golfers waiting their turn and remarked, "He's in line to take home the 'Worst Golfer of the Year Trophy', for a second year in a row." Some applauded and others made jokes about it.

Marti said, "Wes dear, don't let it bother you. It's for a good cause. For your birthday, I'll buy you lessons."

Great, that's all I needed or wanted. To spend more time out here hitting these stupid little balls. The sign said par three, which meant about ten strokes for me. Marti was jumping up and down and screamed when her ball landed a few feet from the hole. The crowd cheered and whistled. Sounds of thuds and cracks echoed as my ball veered off to the right into the trees.

You'd think a stupid little orange golf ball would be easy to spot, but no. The tall grasses, leaves and trees almost made it impossible. Marti came over to help search and I was about to tell her to forget it when she let out a blood curdling scream. I raced over to where she stood frozen and staring down at the ground. My first thought as I ran to her was that she had found a dead animal or worse a live snake. Her face was pale and she had placed her hands over her eyes. When I saw what she was looking at, I jumped back. It wasn't an animal but a bloodied woman's body.

I gently moved Marti off to the side and bent down to look for any signs of life. A large gash was on the side of the lifeless body's head, her long blonde hair was stained a crimson red. Her amber, green eyes stared blankly up at the trees. There was a trickle of blood flowing down her chin. Bruce came up from behind to see what all the commotion was about and after seeing the lifeless body shouted, "My God, Wes! Did you kill her!"

Sue pushed past me and looked down at the still body and remarked, "She got what she deserved." I gave her a funny glance. She just shrugged her shoulders and walked toward the green.

Someone from the peanut gallery remarked when they joined us, "Who did Wes hurt this time?" As soon as they spotted the body, they screamed, "Oh my God, that's Madison Quinn." I took a closer look and realized she was the person who was running the event. Another spectator ran back to the fairway shouting, "Someone get a doctor! Hurry! Madison has been hurt."

A tall, good-looking young man pushed through the crowd, claiming to be a doctor. There was a brief hesitation when he looked into her eyes. He had paused as if he knew her. After checking for any vital signs, he announced, "She's dead."

Still in shock and with tears streaming down her cheeks, Marti commented, "Wes, it wasn't your fault. It was an accident. You didn't mean to kill her."

"I didn't kill her," I rebutted.

"How can you say that? That man just said she's dead." I pulled her in close and wrapped my arms around her frightened body. Using my right arm, I pointed toward the bloody club about ten feet from the body. Struggling to get the words out she said, "Does, does this mean she was murdered?" She buried her head into my chest, her body shaking violently as she sobbed hysterically. Her tears soaked my shirt.

The middle aged and slightly overweight golf course manager appeared and screamed, "What the hell!" She bent down to take a closer look at the body and suddenly her face turned green. She covered her mouth and rushed to the back edge of the woods and lost whatever she had eaten that morning. After gaining some composure, she punched numbers hard into her phone and we all heard her say in a panic tone, "Hurry, send the police to the Spring Green's Golf Course. We found a bloody body."

It wasn't long after when two police officers rushed through the woods followed by EMTs. After inspecting the lifeless body, an officer called for the homicide officer on duty while the other herded everyone but Marti and me toward the club house. He asked us to stand at the edge of the woods so his partner could ask us a few questions.

Yellow crime scene tape circled the scene as more police arrived. I had just finished giving my statement when out of the corner of my eye I saw this tall, slim attractive middle-aged woman strutting her way down the fairway as if she owned the course. She walked with confidence and an air of arrogance. Her long, dark hair flowed in the light breeze. The light tan pant suit and white shirt buttoned two thirds of the way up accented her light brown skin.

 She came to an abrupt halt before us, lowered her large, dark rimmed sunglasses just enough to look over the top and glare at Marti, then me. One of the officers started to open his mouth, but she held up one finger as if to say zip it. She then pointed the long index finger at me and in a gruff tone said, "You, come with me."

"Who are you to give me orders?" I questioned.

She came to a sudden stop, turned and with a sarcastic smirk and using her left hand pulled back her jacket wide enough to show off her badge. "Chief Detective Vera Sanchez. I was told you found the body." Her tone was harsh and I had a feeling us finding the body had caused her some inconvenience. She then grabbed the note pad out of the officer's hand, glanced over his notes and tossed it back at him.

When Marti tried to follow, the rude detective turned and remarked, "Not you. Go to the clubhouse with the others." Marti looked hurt as she was being escorted away.

I stood back and watched as the detective walked around the scene taking her time to examine the body and the surrounding area. Another homicide detective, Eddy, who I knew from a previous murder investigation, walked over and whispered, "We're all going to wish Rod was here right about now."

The brash lady detective shot at him a glared glance that would've even scared a veteran marine. He did a quick about face and disappeared into the crowd of first responders.

I had a bad feeling the officer was right. Last week, Rod and Nancy were married at City Hall and were on their honeymoon in Hawaii. After seeing the travel plans and accommodations Rod had made, Marti quickly worked her magic and upgraded them to first class air fare and booked them in a luxury ocean view suite on the big island for two weeks. Right now, I bet they were sitting on the beach soaking up the sun and drinking some kind of exotic adult beverages with those tiny little umbrellas.

The arrogant lady detective turned and after taking two steps placed her face inches from mine and sarcastically commented. "What makes you think it was murder and not some kind of accident?"

I gave her my patented Wesley Johns smile and answered, "Gee, I bet it was the bloody-broken club over there?" I used my index finger to pointed at it.

"What are you some kind of a wise ass?" She replied in an indignant tone.

I didn't like her or her abrasive attitude and tone. "Yep, you're very observant for a detective. I bet you were first in your class when it came to crime scene investigating."

"Save your weak attempt at humor for someone who thinks you're funny. It's Chief Detective Vera Sanchez, to you. I don't have time for your weak humor. I want a brief and to the point report of what happened."

Unfortunately for her, she was messing with the wrong guy. "I came into the woods and found the body. Is there anything else, detective?"

She quickly removed her sunglasses and stood so close that I could smell the garlic on her breath. Instead of backing away like most would've done, I stood my ground while trying not to gag. She pushed her index finger hard into my chest. "My name is Chief Detective Vera Sanchez, whenever we talk in the future, you'll address me by my full title, not just detective. Do you understand!"

"Really, there's going to be another time? I was hoping we were done and I'd get to finish the back nine." I didn't like her, nor did I want anything to do with her. As far as I was concerned, she could go back to the squad room and stuff herself with some cheap store-bought donuts.

Her nostrils flared and her face turned a shade of red and was about to let me have her full wrath when Captain Ross appeared and remarked, 'Wes, I see you've met Detective Sanchez, she'll be covering for Miller while he and his new bride are on their honeymoon." I smiled when her nostrils flared and she let out a huff for not being announced as Chief Detective Vera Sanchez.

"Excuse me Sir, do you know this man?" She harshly asked. I smiled at the puzzled at disappointed look on her face.

"Why yes. With Wes's help, he and Detective Miller have solved a couple of nasty homicides. I suggest you play nice. You don't want to get on Oz's bad side." We both watched Captain Ross examine the body before walking back to the clubhouse. His parting words were, "I mean it, you two better get along."

The thought of having to work with me was the last thing the brass detective wanted. As I started to walk away, she placed her hand on my shoulder to stop me. "Where do you think you're going?" She commented harshly and in an indignant tone.

I removed her hand and kept on walking. "To get a frosty cold root beer. It's been a trying day, it's not even noon and my nerves are already shot." My real reason for leaving was to check on Marti and to make sure she was okay.

In a huff she shouted, "I'm not through with you yet."

"I'm sure, but I'm through with you." While Eddy escorted me to where they had corralled the others I asked, "What's her story?"

"She moved here from Florida last week. The rumor going around the station was that she found her husband sleeping with a young bartender and in a fit of rage, she beat the crap out of both of them. They were hauled away in an ambulance." The officer paused and we both glanced back toward her. "She was placed on disciplinary leave. Two weeks later we got stuck with her. She's been a real peach to work with." He paused. "There is a secret pool going around the squad room to find out which one of the brass she was sleeping with to get not only hired on, but to also promoted to Chief Detective." Again, after a long pause, "If I were you, I'd keep your distance. She is nothing but bad news."

Marti was being comforted by Sue and a few other ladies when I stepped up onto the overlooking patio. I was immediately bombarded with questions to which I had no answers. Marti pulled me off to the side. "Wes, they took ours and everyone else's clubs and bags. Will we ever get them back?"

Jokingly I remarked, "I hope not." That didn't go well.

"I sure wish Rod was doing the investigating and not that lady detective. I can tell she is nothing but trouble," Marti remarked.

"You and me both. I have a feeling she's going to be a real pain in my you know what?"

We watched as Chief Detective Vera Sanchez strutted her way to the patio where everyone had been gathered. She stopped, placed her hands on her hips and surveyed the group of people. Then she lowered her oversized sunglasses, glared at one couple and using her index finger suggested they should follow her. One by one she pulled others aside and interview them. This went on for hours. After each interview, that person or persons were instructed to leave. I was surprised after noticing the victim had been bludgeoned to death by a club that the detective was allowing them to leave with their clubs.

Not many were left when she finally pointed to us. "How's the investigation going detective? Have you figured it out if she accidentally wacked herself on the head with the club or is it murder," I sarcastically remarked.

"Wes, that's not nice. Hi, my name is Marti Johns. I'm sorry for my husband's warped sense of humor." Marti had offered her hand, but the detective ignored her gesture of goodwill. "Not a wise thing to do," I thought to myself.

The detective's tone was harsh and almost to the point of downright rudeness. As we told our side of what we saw, she would from time to time stop us and make us repeat it over not once but twice. Twenty minutes had passed and I had enough of her condescending attitude. "We have given our statements. We're leaving."

"You'll go when I tell you, you can go. Now go stand over there. I'm not through with you yet."

"Yes, you are. If you want to talk further with us, then you'll have to do it in front of our lawyer. We had nothing to do with that poor lady's death. We just happened to discover the body."

As we stepped away, we heard her comment under her breath but loud enough for us to hear, "What a pair of snotty, rich jerks."

"That was the wrong thing to say," I thought to myself. Marti swiftly turned around with fire in her eyes. She placed her face inches from the detective's and replied, "I don't care if you are the lead detective on this case. Sister, someone needs to teach you some manners. Your tone and attitude needs to be adjusted and if you can't do that then pack up your bags and get out of our town." Marti snorted at her. The few golfers who were still here applauded.

The detective was unfazed by Marti's words. She just stood there, smirking. Wearing those big dark sunglasses didn't help. "Go stand over there with the rest of the people or would you like to spend your time in the back of a patrol car!"

Marti was fuming and I had to struggle to pull her way before they both came to blows. Marti still furious added, "I don't like you and if you ever come near me again with that nasty attitude, then you'll regret the day we ever met. Understand!"

The detective just nonchalantly waved her hand as if to dismiss her.

"Wes, what a bitch. I hope we never have to deal with her again. Promise me, you won't try to investigate what happened to that poor lady. Knowing her, if you solved the crime before her, she'd find a way to throw you in jail for making her look like the fool she is."

The whole time the detective interviewed others, Marti sat glaring at the detective with her arms crossed mumbling what she'd do if she could get her hands on her. I was so focused on what was happening where we had found the body and that I didn't notice Captain Ross had joined us. He was in his mid-fifties with salt and pepper hair. He was trying to watch his weight but I knew his weakness, Betty's fried deliciousness with the sprinkles. He made everyone around the station, including me, promise never to tell his wife.

"Marti, I heard you found the body. Is there anything I can do to help?"

"Yes, get rid of the nasty detective over there. She is rude and doesn't care about anyone's feelings."

He glance back at Detective Sanchez. "Sorry, but all my other detectives are working on other cases. Give her a chance. She just moved here from Miami and is just getting used to our western culture and lifestyle."

"I still think she needs a good kick in the you know where," Marti added.

Trying to defuse the situation Captain Ross asked. "How's my buddy Oz? You need to bring him and Annie around the station one of these days." He tipped his hat at Marti and walked back to the crime scene.

After all the interviewing, the only ones left were Bruce and Sue and Marti and me. We watched Eddy and another officer escorted Bruce and Sue inside the club house, leaving just us alone with the detective. She removed her oversized sunglasses and her brown eyes moved back and forth from me to Marti until she abruptly remarked, "Leave."

"Whatever you say, Detective." I remarked.

"That's Chief Detective Vera Sanchez and don't forget it." Her tone was harsh.

"Whatever, Detective."

Marti giggled and put her arms around mine. "You know she's not going to be happy, you calling her that."

An officer handed me my clubs. I hesitated before placing them under the sign that read. "Donations."

Marti gave me a puzzled look and then commented. "Are you sure?"

"Yep! After today, the last thing I want to see is one of those stupid little balls again," I smiled.

"I agree." She then proceeded to place her clubs and bag next to mine.

Not feeling like cooking we stopped at our favorite drive thru burger joint and picked up dinner. The guys were excited to see us, especially when we gave each a burger. After dinner Marti sat in front of the TV vegging out watching some reality show and drinking out of a wine bottle trying to forget her experience of finding the body and her encounter with the rude detective.

I sat out on the patio enjoying the peacefulness, while trying to understand what happened today. I closed my eyes and listened as the crickets played their evening songs. The guys were asleep on the grass and occasionally a sound would come from the trees above causing Oz to raise his head but he would soon lose interest and go back to sleep.

I was about to head inside when my phone rang. "Mr. Johns?" The soft woman's voice asked.

"Yes?"

Chief Detective Vera Sanchez would like you to be at the station at eight for your formal interview and please bring your wife."

"I can't, I have to be in court." Being a fraud investigator from time to time I had to appear and be a witness and explain the evidence I had gathered.

There was a long pause, "Okay, I'll let her know."

I smiled. I'd like to see the expression on the detective's face when she learned I wouldn't be there in the morning.

I had just crawled under the sheets when Marti asked, "Wes, do we really have a lawyer or were you just blowing smoke at her?"

I bent over and kissed her on the forehead, "Jackson."

A smile grew on Marti's face until it reached from side to side, "Jackson."

Chapter 6

As the aroma of freshly brewed coffee started to fill the house, I sat staring at the blue screen waiting for my computer to come to life. Finally, the photo of Marti, Oz and Annie appeared and I started typing at my usual non blinding speed of hunting and pecking. I had never met or heard of Madison Quinn until yesterday and wished I never had. If this murder was anything like the ones in the past, one way or another I'd be drawn in to investigate. So, I thought it would be best to learn more about the victim.

Marti entered my office and kissed me on the cheek. "Thanks for making the coffee, you'd better get moving, you have to be in court soon. A smile crept across my face at the thought of Detective Sanchez stewing at her desk waiting for me to come to her office.

After dealing with the snail's pace rush hour traffic, I was in no mood to have to testify if called upon. The only space available was the one furthest away from the courthouse's front door. Both Gerald, the department head of the State Workman's Comp Department and Vicki Ann, the state's attorney, stood by the court room door waiting for me.

"We were getting worried you weren't going to make it," Vicki Ann commented. I chose to sit in the back hoping to make a quick escape once the trial ended. Unfortunately, since ours was fourth on the docket this morning, that meant I had to sit through three others. None of them had anything to do with workman comp fraud.

An hour and a half later, it was showtime. My fraud suspect's attorney presented his case. He contended his client's injuries sustained at work were permanent and kept him from seeking further employment. He also tried to convince the judge that his client would need the state's assistance to survive.

Vicki Ann stood up, turned back to give me her famous, "We got this," smile. She started out showing the photos I had collected during my investigation at a local skateboard park. When his attorney remarked, "Your honor those photos don't prove anything. He's just sitting there holding a friend's skateboard."

Vicki Ann proceeded with confidence and went in for the kill when she showed the video. After seeing it for second time, both my suspect and his attorney sat slumped in their chairs. Vickie Ann winked at me, which meant I wasn't going to have to testify. There was a strange hush in the courtroom as we all waited for the verdict while the judge sat pondering over the photos. My phone started to vibrate in my pocket, just as I grabbed it, Detective Sanchez angrily plopped her body down next to mine.

"What are you doing here?" I questioned.

"I wanted to make sure you weren't feeding my clerk a bunch of bull by blowing off our meeting this morning." She was just as neatly dressed as she was yesterday, wearing a black pant suit with large lapels. The blue, three-quarter button-down shirt completed the look. In one pocket were her large frame sunglasses. Draped over the other was her detective's badge.

"I spoke to the captain about you this morning. He says you're some kind of a private copper." Her tone was sharp with some attitude added.

"What else did Captain Ross say?"

"That since I'm new to the area, you'd be a good resource to rely upon." I glanced over and gave her a half-cocked smile. "Well, let me tell you, Mr. Want to Be Copper, that's not going to happen. I demand you appear in my office once you're done here. If you don't, I'll arrest you for impeding my investigation. Do I make myself perfectly clear?"

"I have no intentions of meddling in your investigation. As for being at the station, my wife and I both gave you and the officer our statements yesterday. Like I said, if you want to formally interview us then you'll have to do it in front of our lawyer. So why don't you do your job and leave us alone, Detective?"

I grinned when her nostril flared and her cheeks reddened. "It's Chief Detective Vera Sanchez. Why do you need a lawyer? What are you hiding from me?"

The judge banged his gavel and remarked, "Is everything okay Detective?" His piercing glare was directed right at her.

"Sorry, your honor. Just having a conversation with a witness on another case."

"Well, then take it outside, I won't stand for another outburst. Do you understand?"

"Yes, your honor."

She then glared at me while under her breath whispered. "I'd better see you there ten minutes after you leave this court room!" In a huff she stormed out.

After the judge had made his ruling on my fraud suspect's case, both Vickie Ann and Gerald were all smiles. Ninety days in the state hotel and he must pay back every penny the state had compensated him for his so-called injury.

When I joined them in the hallway, standing by the elevators was Detective Sanchez starring at us. Vicki Ann remarked, "Who's your fan?" She pointed toward her.

"It's a long story. I won't bore you with the details." When they started back to their office, I took the opportunity to duck out through the back stairwell while the detective was busy talking on her phone. Instead of going down I raced up two flights. Just as I thought the door below me slammed open and I heard the detective's heels hastily clicking on the concrete stairs as she raced down chasing after me.

I knew she was not going to let up, so I made a call and we arranged to meet. Down the street from the courthouse was the Dayton Diner and I took the long and back way hoping to avoid you know who. Irene, the owner had moved an old stainless-steel diner from Philly and after some hard work brought it back to life. With lots of gleaming steel and neon lights the place looked amazing. The walls were lined with photos of the history behind the old structure. With business being so good, she found a second diner in desperate need of repair in New Jersey. Even now with double the space there were even times you'd be lucky to get a booth or sit at the counter without waiting.

Irene saw me through the kitchen pass through window and remarked, "Wes, good to see you. Take a seat and I'll be out shortly. A waitress walked over and placed a glass of water in front of me along with a menu before checking on other customers at the table behind me.

I smiled when Irene sat down next to me. "This is the first time today I've been able to rest my tired feet. It's been a zoo this morning and we're a little shorthanded. You must've smelled the fresh peach pies I had just taken out of the oven." Each day of the week, Irene made a special pie, today was peach and tomorrow is chocolate cream. Peach pie was one of my favorites.

"I wish. Just got out of a successful court case and now I'm here to celebrate with one of your trucker specials and a slice of you know what."

"I'll send a whole pie home with you as long as you promise to share it with that lovely wife of yours."

"I'll not make any promises," we broke out into laughter until a dark shadow appeared at my booth. Towering over us was the one and only, Detective. "I thought I told you to be at the station." There was fire in her voice.

Irene, feeling the chilly confrontation, quickly got up and shouted, "One Trucker's Special, large chocolate milk and slice of peach pie." Before sitting across from me the detective rudely remarked, "I'll have the same."

Irene forced a smile and in a non-descript tone mentioned. "Wouldn't you rather see a menu? You don't know what's included with the Trucker's Special."

The Detective flashed Irene her badge all the while harshly demanding. "Now, now leave us alone. We have business to discuss."

I've known Irene for a long time and one thing about her was, she didn't take crap from anyone. Not even snotty arrogant detectives. "Look Sister, I don't like your tone of voice. You don't come in here and insult me or my customers. Do you understand and if you don't, you can lift your sorry excuse for a police officer's butt out of that booth and leave by the way you came in. Got it!"

Unfazed by Irene's remarks, Detective Sanchez smirked, "I'm giving you a warning, if you don't leave us alone, I'll make a call and have two officers here in five minutes to arrest you. Now do your job and get our food!"

Irene was fuming. "That's it, I don't care if you are the President of the United States, no one comes in here and talks to me or my customers that way." Irene pulled out her phone and within seconds, she said, "Donnie, I have one of your detectives in my establishment being rude and disrupting my customers. She won't leave when I asked her." Irene handed her phone to the detective and smiled, "Will that be one order or two?"

Shortly after placing the phone to her ear, Detective Sanchez's face turned pale and her arrogant attitude vanished. She turned to Irene and said, "Please, excuse me for my rudeness. I'm sorry for the way I acted, it won't happen again." She then handed the phone back to a smiling Irene.

I remarked, "She's good friends with the chief of police. He comes in here at least twice a week for her pancakes."

The detective in a defeated tone said to Irene, "A Trucker's Special would be great with coffee. Thank you."

I looked up at Irene and remarked, "Better make that three specials." This caused the detective to shoot me a puzzled look.

"Jerry, two more Trucker's Special to go along with the first order and two cups of Joe." As Irene walked away, what patrons that were in the diner all broke out in applause, congratulating her on the way she handled the detective's big city disruptive attitude.

After sulking for a few moments, the detective demanded, "You need to change me places, I never put my back to the door." Unfortunately, the rude detective I came to despise was back.

"No, instead how about you move to another booth, like the one at the front of the diner so I can enjoy my meal while not looking at your face."

"Do you always show this kind of disrespect to other police officers?"

"No, just the ones who come into our town with a big chip on their shoulders like you."

There was an uncomfortable silence while we waited for our food. I was relieved when the waitress placed four plates on my side of the table and two in front of the detective. She remarked, "Jesus, are you going to eat all that?"

"No." Just then a salt and pepper looking man dressed in a three-piece suit slid down next to me. "Great, you ordered for me! I'm starving."

Detective Sanchez gave him a suspicious once over before asking, "Who are you?"

Jackson responded with, "And you are?"

"I'm Chief Detective Vera Sanchez investigating a murder and you're interrupting my interrogation of this witness. Now will you take your plates of food and go sit somewhere else?"

Jackson finished swallowing a mouthful of pancakes when he reached into his vest pocket and pulled out a business card and handed it to her.

She glanced down at the card and in an indignant tone remarked. "You called a lawyer?"

I nodded my head and kept on eating. Begrudgingly the detective sat and sulked while attempting to eat everything before her.

Stuffed and with still enough food left on my plates, I remarked. "I bet you don't have a lot of friends."

"What makes you say that?" Her tone was abrupt and snarky.

"Just an observation."

"I have plenty of friends. Now that you're done eating you can accompany me to the station."

"Jackson, do you have time to join us?" I asked.

This caused an uneasiness in Sanchez. I could tell the last thing she wanted was to have to deal with Jackson. "Maybe Captain Ross thinks you're some kind of super star, but I want to let you know; I don't care! This is my case, I'm warning you to keep your nose out of it! If you don't, you are not going to like being on my bad side and will be spending a long weekend in an eight by ten cell with an unfriendly roommate!"

"Are you threatening my client?" Jackson calmly questioned.

I followed up with, "Don't worry, detective. I'll gladly keep my distance."

"I insist you address me as Chief Detective Vera Sanchez and not detective."

"No." I replied.

She abruptly stood up and started to leave when Irene placed a piece of paper in the palm of her hand. The glare from the detective to Irene would've melted ice cream on a cold winter day. She reached in her pocket and pulled out a wade of cash and shoved it in Irene's hand before storming out of the diner.

Once Detective Sanchez was out the door, Jackson asked, "Do you mind telling me what that was all about?"

I went on to explain what happened yesterday at the golf course. I also told him the lady detective recently moved here from Miami and was handling the case since Detective Miller was on his honeymoon and that she had a large chip on her shoulder. After a brief conversation we both agreed, the detective wasn't going away.

When Irene placed the boxed warm peach pie in front of me, Jackson took a deep breath and asked if she had another one for him.

After a brief conversation, Jackson had to get back to the office and I went home to check on the guys. They happily pranced around my feet waiting for their treat. Before I could put the pie on the kitchen counter Marti raced over and grabbed it out of my hands. "What are you doing home? Aren't you supposed to be at work?"

"I got to the airport and we were overstaffed so my boss sent me home with pay. How did your court case go?"

She fished for a spoon out of the drawer and started eating the center of the pie. "It went great. I didn't need to testify."

"Other than the case, anything else happen?" She sheepishly questioned.

Once I could see the expression on her face, I knew. "You told the detective where to find me didn't you?"

She quickly shoved a large mouthful of pie in her mouth, buying her time to come up with an answer. When I went in to tickle her, she muffled, "Sorry, it kind of slipped out."

"What slipped out?"

"Some guy from the police called and wanted to know where they could reach you. I knew after a court case you always went to the diner to celebrate the victory. I didn't know he was calling for her?"

"That explains how she knew I was at the diner. She was totally upset when Jackson joined us."

"What? Who invited him?" Marti muffled with a mouthful of pie.

"I called him before leaving the courthouse. I had a bad feeling my encounter with the detective in the court room wouldn't be my last one today."

"What did she do?"

"She demanded that he leave not knowing who he was at first. But then when he gave her his business card, well the expression on her face was priceless. Unfortunately, I wasn't quick enough to take a picture."

"Oh my God, I wished I was there to see that. Hopefully, she'll get the message now and leave us alone."

"Fingers crossed, but I don't think that's the last we've heard from her." I then took the spoon out of her hand and commented. "Now, let's address the issue of my sexy secretary telling the police where I was."

Marti's eyes bugged wide open. "You wouldn't dare." The grin on my face told her I would. The one thing about Marti was that she was very ticklish. She leaped off the stool and raced to the bedroom, closing the door behind her.

By the time I joined her she was already in the shower. I thought about joining her but someone was at the front door. I thought about not answering, fearing it was you know who, but when they began banging on the door and the guys were aggressively barking, I begrudgingly went to see who it was. Instead of the detective it was two of Marti's girlfriends. "Hey Wes, is she ready?" one of them asked.

Before I could invite them inside, Marti blew past me, leashed up Annie and blew me a kiss. "See you boys later."

After the door closed, I looked down at Oz. "What the hell just happened?" Since it was just us boys, I packed some water and treats. "Okay, let's go to work big guy."

On the first drive by of my suspect's house I spotted a large black panel truck parked in front. Oz and I settled in my usual spot and with my camera poised we waited. It hadn't been ten minutes when a tapping on the passenger side window caused Oz to leap out of the back seat and onto the front to investigate. His sudden reaction and pearly white teeth caused Chester to back away.

After having to coax Oz into the back seat with a snack, Chester hesitantly climbed in the front. "Wow, he's big. Does he bite?" Worried lines appeared on Chester's forehead when he glanced back at Oz.

"Only if he doesn't like you." This didn't keep Chester from worrying.

 "Wes, I'm glad you showed up. That big truck showed up and two men got out. Then, see those two cars?" He pointed at them. "Three people got out and they all went into the garage. About ten minutes later the new people started carrying stuff out to the truck. Something is going down tonight."

"How do you know?"

Chester let out a smirk. "I took Officer Rex for a walk and we happened to stop by when they were loading the big truck. I asked what was going on and one of the men said, 'Ghost hunting.'"

The two of us watched and waited. It had been an hour when two men, dressed in black appeared and climbed in the cars and left. Markus and his girlfriend came out of the garage with two women dressed in black. After a short conversation the women climbed in the truck and left leaving both Markus and his girlfriend standing on the sidewalk.

A look of fear shot across my face when Chester leaped out of the truck and started walking toward them. The stupid old man was going to blow my cover. I watched in panic as he approached them. They talked briefly. By the expression on Markus's and his girlfriend's faces they were having a good laugh at Chester's expense. Once they went inside, Chester continued to walk down the street and turn the corner.

Ten long minutes had passed before Chester returned and opened the passenger door. He was slightly out of breath. "It's going down tonight." He struggled to say.

"What's going down?" I questioned.

"Tonight, they have their first ghost hunting investigation at Lancaster Fine Furniture."

Chester begged me to let him come along, but I worried since some of my previous investigations had turned somewhat sketchy. I thought it would be best if I stopped by in the morning and briefed him on what went down tonight. He reluctantly agreed.

By the time Oz and I returned home, Marti was in the kitchen getting out plates for the pizza she ordered from Donavan's. As we ate, I explained that both Oz and I would be working late tonight at the Mitchel's Furniture store. It was a relief when she didn't offer to join us this time. She said she had invited Chris and Denise for a rousing game of Scrabble so I quickly inhaled two slices of pizza, grabbed my equipment and Oz and I made our escape. The last thing I needed was to have her brother come along.

The last time he tried to help with my investigation I ended up with a damaged truck among other things.

Oz and I parked across the street from the furniture store where I had a good view. Now we just had to sit and wait, which was about eighty percent of what this business was all about. Oz was asleep and my phone came to life when I started to receive texts. Marti must've told Chris I was on a case. He wanted to know why I didn't ask him to come along. My phone beeped and now it was a text from Marti. "Sorry, I let it slip. I promise to make it up when you get home."

Ten minutes later Chris's truck, which used to be my old truck, came barreling down the street and came to an abrupt stop behind us. Chris banged on the passenger door which woke Oz and caused him to bark. "Wes, let me in. I'm your partner. Come on! We're a team."

I tried to ignore him until the large black panel truck and Markus's van parked in front of the furniture store. Afraid Chris might blow my cover I quickly unlocked the door and told him to get in and shut up. I was trying to concentrate on what was going on at the store but he went on and on about how I had left him out of this investigation. When I told him we were going ghost hunting on our own after my suspect left, his face turned white at the thought. He then leaped out of the truck and drove away without saying a word. I looked at Oz and commented, "I'll have to remember this for the next case."

An older looking man, with a hunched back and cane walked out of the store to stop and talk to Markus and his crew who were dressed in black. After a brief conversation, the old man gave Markus his keys and walked to the back of the building. He honked his horn as he past the ghost hunters in his car. Headlights came around the corner and another van parked next to Markus's.

I turned on my low light video camera and was poised with my thirty-five-millimeter digital camera to click off a shot at a moment's notice. Everyone disappeared inside but soon returned and started unloading the large truck and vans. To my disappointment Markus stood and watched. I became worried tonight would turn into a bust. I so wanted to close this case.

My lucky break came when a crew member struggled to pull out a large heavy looking footlocker from the truck and almost dropped it onto the ground. In one swift move Markus stepped in and with one arm lifted it up onto his shoulder while with the other arm grabbed his girlfriend and did the same. Click, click, click, click; I had fired off shot after shot as fast as my camera could process each frame. A few minutes later when Markus and others returned, I pressed the button on my camera, it sounded like a rapid-fire machine gun, click, click, click, click as Markus carried out four rolls of thick black cable that looked heavy. He tossed one to a fellow ghost hunter who almost fell over from the weight. But the smoking gun that really sealed the case for me was when two ghost hunters struggled to move a large cabinet on wheels. Instead of pushing the cabinet, Markus grabbed both ends and carried it inside. I said to Oz who was asleep in the backseat, "He is so busted."

I was about to leave when what looked like another crew member showed up on one of those electric unicycles. To my surprise, both Markus and his girlfriend stepped out from the furniture store and after a brief conversation, Markus lifted his girlfriend onto his shoulders and together they rode the unicycle down the street. With these photos and the video, I hoped the judge recommended Markus spend time in the state hotel for committing fraud.

Chapter 7

The garage walls vibrated when the Bird's engine fired on all eight cylinders. Marti and Annie were off hiking with her friends, leaving Oz and me to attend the car show in the park. The weatherman predicted a cloudless sky and temps in the low eighties. Oz rode with his head out the window sniffing in the smells and checking out the sights.

I still remember the day when a friend of mine asked me to come over and check out her new litter of pups. Oz walked over, lifted his little chubby body on his hind legs and begged to be lifted. Once I picked him up, I knew we were meant to be together.

I marveled at the line of pristine Detroit steel classics neatly parked in a row in front of Betty's Whole Bakery Experience. No sooner had I parked the Bird that Oz leaped out and raced over to Mike's open arms. To Mike's dismay, Oz's massive body slammed into him, sending his body backward onto the sidewalk. Before he could recover Oz was licking his face. They'd been buds since the first day Mike gave him ear scribbles. Once Mike even threatened to take him home.

It looked like a few of the car show regulars wouldn't be joining us today. I scanned the parking lot looking for Bruce and Sue with their Ford Falcon, but it was nowhere in sight. Bruce, our group's self-appointed leader, never missed an event.

Looking through Betty's windows I could see a line. She was the queen of fried deliciousness and her apple fritters where the best in the valley. Not only was she an amazing baker, but she was also mother to three Bassett Hounds named: Moe, Larry and Curly. She always made sure to have plenty of freshly baked treats for her two-legged customers as well as her four-legged ones. No sooner had I stepped inside than my stomach rumbled at the enticing smells. "Hey, Wes, the usual?" She asked from behind the glass counter.

"How about adding an extra fritter and treat for both Oz and me?"

Just as I stepped outside with our bag of goodies Mike shouted, "Let's fire up those engines." I had just closed my door when a voice screamed, "Wes, wait for me. I'm coming with you." My whole body cringed. Now that Marti's brother, Chris, worked here, I regretted the group chose to meet at the bakery before our events. I had hoped I could've escaped before he noticed. The last thing I wanted was to have him tag along with us, nothing good ever came of it. Once he broke the mirror off the Bird and don't get me started on the other few times he came along.

"Chris, what are you doing?" I asked as he pushed his way past Oz and climbed into the backseat.

"My shift is over and when I talked to Sis last night, she said you would be alone at the car show today, so I thought I'd join you."

After digesting what he had said, my mind translated it into what she really said to him. "Chris, Wes wants to be alone at the car show tomorrow so don't tag along." Giving him a quick glance in the rearview mirror I asked, "You're not going to wear that are you?" He had on his white baker's uniform which was decorated with various colors of icing and smelled of grease.

"Naw, Denise is going meet us there with some other clothes."

I cursed the weatherman under my breath with his forecast of a cloudless day, instead there was a dark cloud over my head. It was Chris. "Hey, how did our case go the other night? I would've stuck around and helped but I had to get up early to work. You know me, I need my beauty sleep. Were you able to get enough on our perp to prove he is a fraud? I can come over tomorrow and we can start working on our next case, Partner," he asked. I was wrong, not a dark cloud but thunderstorms with high occasional gusts of winds. When I get home, Marti and I'll have to have a serious talk about her brother and what it meant for him to give me space.

Chris wouldn't shut up and when I increased the volume of the radio almost to ear shattering, he continued to shout over the music. No sooner had I parked the Bird than Oz leaped out of the open driver's window and took his usual place in front. As for me, Chris followed me everywhere babbling on, the man wouldn't shut up or stop to take a breath. When I opened the trunk to set out my chair, Chris immediately plopped his body into it and started messing with his phone. Finally blessed silence.

My favorite thing about attending these events was watching the circus unfold before me. I enjoyed watching the classic car enthusiasts busy themselves making sure their pride and joys gleamed in the sun. As for me, it was a quick once over with a feather duster and I was good. I had just finished when Mike and Marsha displayed a large black stuffed gorilla, wearing a Hawaiian shirt and straw hat. Mike placed him in a chair in front of their Dodge Coupe holding a sign. That was sure to catch everyone's eye. I jokingly remarked, "Trying to keep up with the Jones's?"

"We'll see at the end of the day who takes home the trophy," He replied. I never went in for trying to win a trophy. After a week all they ever did was collect dust.

The band's opening song blasted out from the stage and the smell from the food trucks filled the air. Time to sit back, enjoy a fritter or two and relax, especially now that Denise had shown up and dragged Chris off to change his clothes.

No sooner had I reached into the bag for a fritter that suddenly another dark cloud blocked the sun. When I glanced up, their stood none other than Detective Sanchez. She wore a dark green pant suit with a lime-colored shirt buttoned three-quarters of the way down. Her long brown hair cascaded over her shoulder and she still had on those stupid funky oversized sunglasses. "To what do I owe the pleasure, Ms. Detective?" I questioned.

Before I could stop her, she grabbed the bag out of my hand and reached inside and pulled out a treat. I smiled after she bit off a piece and heard the crunching sound. A sudden look of disgust crossed her face and instead of losing face and spitting out what remained, she swallowed hard. "Tasty?" I commented.

"How can you eat this crap?"

"I don't. That was a special treat the bakery makes for her customer's pets. Oz won't be too happy once he finds out you ate his snack." I then pointed toward him out front guarding the Bird. "Now that you've spoiled my fun, why are you here? I figured you'd be out trying to catch who murdered the lady at the golf course with your rude Miami city style attitude, Detective."

Her nostrils flared as she lowered her oversized sunglasses showing her brown eyes. "That's Chief Detective Vera Sanchez. After yesterday's experience at the diner, I was called into the Captain Ross's office and had to explain my actions. I tried to convince him that you were a prime suspect and that I wanted to arrest you for not coming to the station to be interviewed. He assured me you nor your wife were suspects and that I should be concentrating my efforts on others suspected of committing the crime."

"Well, there you go. So how about you leave me alone and go find who actually killed that poor lady. Also, could you move to the right about two feet, you're blocking the sun and ruining my efforts to improve my tan."

"Yea, always with the smart mouth. I don't have to take your crap. You're lucky I don't drag your sorry ass out of that chair and haul you downtown in front of all your friends right now."

"You can try but you'd be lucky to leave this park alive." I aways felt confident whenever Oz was close by.

She lean down and placed her face inches from mine. "I'm here to tell you that I don't need some private dick interfering with my case. I don't care if the higher ups at the station think you'd be an asset or not. If I find out you're poking your nose where it doesn't belong or even having a casual conversation with any of my suspects, I'll have you behind bars in a New York minute for contempt. Capiche?"

I just couldn't help myself, "I didn't know you spoke Italian?"

"I'm warning you, stay away from my case or you'll regret we ever met!"

"That works for me. So then why are you still here?"

She lowered her oversized sunglasses to where I could see the pupils of her brown eyes. Her voice was getting harsher and louder when she said, "I've just about taken all the crap that I want from you. One more wise crack from you and I don't care what my boss says, I'll arrest you for assaulting an officer."

"The only thing assaulting here is your garlic breath. Now please remove your face from mine and leave."

Fuming, she reached behind her back and pulled out a pair of handcuffs. "That's it, get up!" When I didn't budge her voice grew louder and a lot harsher. "Get out of that chair now!" Her loud harsh voice caused everyone close by to stop doing whatever and waited to see what happened next.

I'd had enough of her crap and leaped out of my chair. "Look, I don't care if you are a detective. You take your high-flying Miami attitude back to Florida. We don't need or want your kind here." Now it was my turn to put my face inches from hers. I glared into her eyes and was about to tell her to get the hell out of here when Chris and Denise showed up at the most inopportune time.

"Did you say something about a case and needing our help?" Chris questioned the detective.

Sanchez spun around and leered at Chris. He immediately tried to backed away but she pushed her finger hard into his chest. "Who in the hell are you, Bozo?" she demanded.

For one of the few times since Chris had moved here, he was speechless. His mouth opened but all he was able to squeak out was, "His partner."

Denise pulled the detective's finger from her boyfriend's chest and placed her body within an inch of the detective's and remarked, "The next time you do that, you'll find yourself lying flat on your back with a black eye. Do you understand?"

"Are you threatening an officer of the law. You know I can arrest you here and now."

"I'd like to see you try it." Denise defiantly said. My money was on Denise if they got into a fight. She was four inches shorter than the Detective. There wasn't an inch of fat on her body and her tattoo covered arms hid the bulging muscles. Denise never went to the gym. She got her work out daily at the shop lifting heavy auto parts all day.

As the two of them stood face to face, neither one flinching or willing to turn and leave, Oz pushed his body between Denise and Sanchez. This caused the detective to slowly back away. "Your damn dog got his stupid dog hair all over my pants." When she waved her finger in my face, Oz let out one of his low guttural growls.

When she turned and looked down to see his pearly whites she immediately moved to the other side of the Bird. "Remember what I said. Stay away from my investigation or you'll regret you ever got involved. And as for you, Bitch, this isn't over yet between the two of us."

"Name the place and time!" Denise shouted as the detective pushed her way through the onlookers.

"Nice talk. We'll have to do it again. Give my regards to Captain Ross and tell him I'll stop by next week," I shouted. I reached down and gave Oz some well-deserved scribbles for a job well done along with one of his treats.

Once the detective was out of sight, Denise and I broke out into laughter. Chris collapsed in a chair with a blank look on his face. Nothing new for him. But the best part was when Lois, another member of our car group, showed up smiling. "Would you like to see the video I recorded?" Denise and I looked at each other and nodded our heads in unison to say, "Yes". It was hilarious.

Now that the excitement was over, since the Detective had taken my fritters and his snacks, Oz and I went to get something to eat. There was a line of six food trucks dishing out their specialties, but only one interested me, "Donavan's Pizza". When Donavan joined our little car group, we decided to hold our monthly social meetings at his restaurant. At his first car event, he realized he was missing out on a great business opportunity to market his pizzas. First it was passing out coupons, then it was taking orders and having pies delivered to customers at the events. Now he and his daughter Rose had taken it one step further and upgraded to a food truck, and by the looks of it, business was good.

"Morning Wes, the usual?" Rose asked.

"No, you better make it two extra-large ones. Marti's brother, the bottomless pit and mooch is here."

She let out a slight giggle. "I know, he already stopped by this morning and asked us to make him a large pepperoni and to put it on your account."

"You didn't let him, did you?" I asked.

"Relax, we didn't. When we explained he'd have to pay, he cancelled his order and walked away disappointed."

"That works for me. How come your dad isn't here?"

"He'll be here pretty soon. We had some issues with the oven at the restaurant and was waiting for the repairman. We'll have your pies out to you shortly."

As usual during these shows, members of our car group set up our chairs in a circle while we ate and talked. No sooner had the pizzas shown up, so did Chris. When he attempted to help himself, I slapped his hand hard. "Go get your own." I said.

"But, you have more than enough to share. Beside look how long the line is, it will be at least an hour before they'll deliver mine. Please let me have a slice?" His begging was worse than Oz's. I caved and allowed him to have one slice but before I could stop him, he had half my pizza in his hands.

The hot topic was about the murder at the golf course. I listened to the few different versions and opinions about what people had heard. It was Lois who asked, "Wes, are you going to investigate since it was Marti who found the body?" Lois was a firecracker for her age. Since I'd got to know her, she had helped me on a few occasions with my cases. "No, the detective has made it perfectly clear I am not to interfere with her case."

Doug, another member of our group chimed in, "That's never stopped you before," as he chuckled.

"Well, this time, I'm staying as far away as I can from the lady detective. She's a real pain in the you know what. Beside I have a stack of fraud cases threatening to fall on me if I don't give them my attention soon."

"Yea, right," Doug commented. "Okay, everyone I'm taking bets, two to one within a week Wes will be trying to find out who killed that lady. Any takers?" No one took him up on his offer as they all knew me too well.

Before leaving, and dragging Chris with her, Denise walked over and whispered, "Willy would like to see you Monday about you know what." I told her I'd be there at nine.

Everyone but me started to get up and go toward the stage to see if any of them had won a trophy. I cared less if I won one or not. I came to relax and enjoy the day, but unfortunately that rude detective kind of soured it for me. I had just closed my eyes when a shadow appeared in front of me. There stood Mike and a few others, each with grim expressions on their faces. "The trophy presentations over all ready?" I asked.

"No," Mike said. "I just got a call from Bruce. He called to tell us that that detective with two other officers hauled Sue down to the police station in handcuffs. They said she was their prime suspect for murdering the lady at the golf course."

Lois who was standing next to Mike added, "Wes, we can't let this happen! We need to do something."

For the first time, I was at a loss. Normally I would've reach out to my buddy Detective Miller, but he was in Hawaii, and I surely wasn't going to call Detective Bitchy Pants. "I'll talk to Bruce, but I'm not sure what I can do."

"It's that nasty detective," Lois commented. "I know she's behind this. We need to do something. There's no way Sue could've or would've murdered that lady. Let's all go down to the police station and demand they release her!"

Once Lois calmed down, Doug suggested we all meet at Donavan's around six to discuss the unfortunate situation both Bruce and Sue were in and possibly find a way to help. Hopefully by then I would have the opportunity to talk to Bruce and have a better understanding on what was happening.

On the drive home, my mind flashed back to the golf tournament. The more I started piecing the puzzle together the more I began to think about the off-the-cuff comment Sue had made after we discovered Madison's lifeless body. "She got what she deserved." Maybe there was a dark side to Sue that we all didn't know about and she and this Madison lady got into it for some reason and Sue actually did commit the murder. But if so, when did she have time to do it? I didn't remember her ever leaving our sight. The one thing I knew for sure was that Marti wasn't going to be so happy if I started to investigate.

Marti's SUV was in the driveway. I asked Oz, "Are you going to tell her, or am I?"

He gave me one of his patented looks as if to say, "You're on your own."

Marti and Annie were asleep on our bed. I left Oz to guard the house while I went next door. When Carrie answered the front door the first words out of her mouth were, "Wes, this is absurd! Sue wouldn't hurt a fly. She didn't even know that lady."

"How did you find out? You and Jack weren't at the car event today."

She smirked, "Guess?"

"Lois?"

"Yes, she called me as they were heading home from the show. Have you told Marti you're going to help and investigate. She's not going to be happy about that."

"No, I was hoping you'd tell her." I jokingly remarked.

"Not on your life."

We sat at the kitchen table, and I asked her if there was anything that she could remember the day of the golf tournament, since she and Jack were the only other ones attending from our car group besides Bruce and Sue.

She gave it some deep thought and started from the moment we arrived. There was a slight hesitation, "Wes, I'm not sure but now I think I remember seeing and hearing Sue arguing with that poor lady before you teed off. Do you really think she did it?"

"Any idea, what she was so upset about?"

"Not really, I was talking to Jack and the other couple in our foursome at the time."

"Well, if you can think of anything that might help, let me know."

I was almost out the door when Carrie stopped me. "Wes, I don't know if this will help or not. I just remembered seeing Sue with a club in her hand when she went into the trees for what I assumed was looking for a lost ball."

"Do you remember what hole we were on?"

"Yes, it was on hole number five which is on the other side of nine. Oh my God! Please tell me she didn't."

"I don't think she did, but until I get all the evidence, I'm not coming to any conclusion. See you at Donavan's."

Marti stood in the doorway with her hands on her hips and a look that could melt a quart of frozen ice cream. "Wes, how could you not call me to tell me that bitchy and rude detective thinks Sue murdered that lady. I had to hear about it from Lois."

"You were asleep, and I didn't want to disturb you. I went next door to see if Carrie remembered anything about that day."

"What did she say?" After I explained what Carrie had told me, she added. "Wes, this is so messed up! What are we going to do?"

"We?" I questioned.

"Yes, we". Let's go or we'll be late for the meeting."

The chatter was loud when we entered the back room at Donavan's. Almost everyone in our car group was there. The room quickly quieted when they saw us entering. It was as if they were waiting for me to tell them the latest news. I had none. Within seconds the chatter picked up and the room started buzzing again.

I sat next to Eric who leaned over and commented, "She," pointing to his wife, "made me stop by the office supply store and pick up some things." He then pointed to the whiteboard on a stand at the head of the room. "I think she's been watching to many police dramas on TV."

I gave him my, "I'm sorry" look.

After everyone had eaten, Lois got up and stood in front of a whiteboard on the stand. Once she started talking, I began to agree with her husband. She had been seeing to many police shows on TV. She listed the victim's name in a bright red lettering across the top. Before she could add any more to the board, things took on an interesting twist as Chris tried to take the marker away from her as if to say he was in charge. We all watched and laughed as the two fought over the marker. Lois quickly put Chirs in his place and he sulked back to his seat to pout. By the time everyone left Donavan's it had been decided by the group, except for me, that I should look into this case.

Oz and Annie were excited to see us, especially once they smelled the pizza. I gave them each a slice and saved the rest for tomorrow. Marti settled in front of the TV to watch one of her reality shows. I was about to go to bed when Bruce called and explained they had been down at the police station for hours being interrogated by the detectives. Bruce pleaded with me to come by their house in the morning and I assured him we'd be there. I turned off the light and looked up at the dark ceiling, "What was I getting myself into again?"

Chapter 8

Bruce and Sue's mid-century home was in the foothills. As soon as you stepped inside you were greeted to a breath-taking view of the city below and the mountains off in the distance. Every time we visited, I'd joke with Bruce about selling the place to me, even though I could never afford it. But I could spend hours sitting out on their balcony enjoying the serenity and scenery.

Bruce looked as if he had aged five years since the last time we had seen each other. The grim expression and the bloodshot eyes suggested he hadn't gotten much sleep in the past couple of day. Sue didn't look much better, with her red puffy eyes and face. Our car club friends looked like hell, and hell is what they had been going through. Marti pulled Sue's body into hers and held onto her tight. Her exhausted body slumped into Marti's and started sobbing.

Bruce and I stepped out onto their balcony leaving the ladies to talk inside. He rested his elbows on the railing and stared down at the valley below. "Wes, how did we ever get into such a mess. I never knew or met that woman, and Sue only dealt with her when she asked for things to donate for the charity event. Now that brash and rude detective thinks we had something to do with the poor lady's death. This is just madness. Just madness! I know you don't want to get involved in our mess, but I'm begging you to help." The more he spoke the more he choked out his words. "Sue can't eat or sleep. She spends most of her time sitting in the living room chair staring at the walls and crying. I don't know how to help her. It's as if all life has been ripped out of her body. What are we going to do? I'm afraid. For the first time in my life, I'm afraid and don't have a clue how to fix this." His head slumped onto his chest and from the back I could tell he was crying.

I put my arm around him and allowed my friend to cry it all out. Once he gained somewhat control, I said. "We're here to help."

Marti and Sue joined us on the patio with drinks. At first, we made small talk, like the weather, the booming building craze that was happening in the valley, and what happened at yesterday's car show. I left the part out about my visit with Detective Sanchez.

Being the designated driver, I had just orange juice while the others enjoyed Bruce's spiked version. I could tell Sue's mood had lightened some, not sure if it was us being there or the alcohol. I took this opportunity to have her give us a play by play of everything she did as soon as they arrived at the golf course. Bruce, being the overprotective husband that he was started to give us his version of her day, but I quickly interrupted him by saying, "Bruce, I need to hear this from Sue. Please let her speak."

Sue started out by saying, I didn't kill her. You have to believe me!"

Marti rested her hand on Sue's. "We understand and we're here help, but you have to tell us everything no matter how painful or insignificant you think it might be. The more Wes knows the better chance he'll be able to help."

Sue looked into Marti's warm eyes and nodded her head. "Yes, I knew her. I worked with her on last year's golfing event seeking donations. This year when she contacted me, I convinced my boss it would be good publicity and together we reached out to our travel partners to make it happen. By the time we finished we had arranged three packages to donate, Hawaii, Las Vegas, and New York City."

Sue got up and disappeared into the house and soon returned with a platter filled with warm, gooey cinnamon rolls. I didn't want to make a pig out of myself and stopped at three.

She took a deep breath and continued, "The day of the event, I presented Madison with enveloped certificates. She hastily grabbed them out of my hands and ripped them open, then proceeded to tear up the flyers we had put inside along with the certificates. Her words were, 'This won't do. It won't do. I won't allow free advertising. People and businesses should be willing to donate out of the goodness of their hearts, not to promote their business. No! It is unacceptable.'" There was a long pause as Sue took a drink of her spiked orange juice. "Wes, I was totally shocked by her behavior. Then she tossed the table- top flyer advertising ours and the others business who made the donations possible onto the ground and started stomping on it as if she was possessed. Her face turned bright red as fire and vile words spewed out of her mouth. 'How dare you do this to me! You stupid bitch! Did you think I wouldn't notice. How dumb do you think I am?'"

Sue paused. I could tell reliving that moment not only upset her but it also hurt. Once she allowed her emotions to calmed down, she continued. "After being called names and on the receiving end the abusive wrath from Madison, I ripped the certificates from her hands and threatened not to donated them. For a brief moment, I thought she was going to hit me or something but then she slightly stepped to my right and stared at something or someone behind me and her face turned white as if she had seen a ghost. When I turned to see what caused her to stop, I saw nothing."

"Did she happen to say what or who?" I questioned.

"No, after that, she apologized and begged me to give back the certificates. I watched as her eyes became watery and tears started down her cheeks. One minute she was ripping into me and the next she stood there sobbing. I didn't know what to think or do."

"How strange," Marti commented. "So, what did you do?"

"I felt sorry for her and handed back the certificates and walked away, but when we were about to tee off with you guys, she walked up to me and said in the same harsh tone when she saw the flyers and posters before, 'I've decided to not use your donations for the auction. Instead, I'm going to save them for another time and event.' That broke the camel's back, I demanded she hand them back but she gave me an evil grin and remarked, 'Too late. I've already made my decision.'"

The look on Sue's face suggested we take a break. She and Marti disappeared inside and returned with bowls of fruit. While we ate, I asked, "What did you do then?"

"What could I do? I was furious and wanted to ring her neck. But there were all these people standing around us waiting and watching for us to tee off. I went over and told Bruce what happened. We both agreed I should calm down and that after we finished the course, I could try to reason with Madison to either give me back the certificates or we could give them out to the top three scores."

Bruce interjected, "I could tell Sue was upset, so I reasoned with her and assured her that we would go together and talk to Madison."

I asked if either one of them had any other conversations with Madison after Sue's confrontation. They both claimed they hadn't. I brought up the moment when we discovered Madison's bloody and lifeless body. I told Sue that I heard her disturbing comment, "She got what she deserved!"

Sue gasped and remarked, "You heard that! I didn't mean anything by it. I was still mad from what happened earlier. I thought I had said that under my breath. Oh my God, Wes, do you think other people heard me? What are we going to do?" Tears streamed down her cheeks as Bruce put his arm around her and pulled her close.

Marti looked over and said, "Wes, we've got to help them. If we don't that nasty detective will try to pin the murder on Sue. I sure wish Rod was here right now. He wouldn't be so quick to label her as a suspect."

"But we agreed after the last case where I almost..."

She stopped me, "I know, but this is different. They're our friends."

I looked into her pleading eyes and turned to Sue. "Sue, I'm only asking this once and I want an honest answer. Did you have anything to do with Madison Quinn's death?"

Bruce leaped out of his chair and looked as if he was going to hit me. Sue quickly pulled on his arm and said, "Bear, sit down." He struggled to free himself from her grip. She repeated, "Sit down." He looked into her pleading eyes and plopped down in the chair, and the fire extinguished inside of him.

Sue stared into my eyes not blinking and calmly and purposely said, "No."

We all sat looking at each other when Bruce asked, "Wes, how are you going to be able to help with that arrogant detective insisting my wife is guilty? She kept grilling Sue over and over last night trying to get her to confess. It was late when they allowed us to leave but that nasty detective warned us this wasn't over yet."

"Wes, Honey, I don't care what it takes. We have to help them and put that bitch of a detective in her place. She has no evidence to pin this murder on Sue. Anyone could've taken her club out of the bag when she wasn't looking. That detective is just looking to close this case quickly to get brownie points with the brass. Your sexy secretary is ready and willing to take notes when we get home."

Sue let out a slight chuckle and remarked, "Sexy secretary? Marti do you also wear dark stocking with a garter belt and a sexy little ensemble to go along with the stockings?"

Marti smiled, "Let's not forget the high heels, the ruby red lipstick and my black framed glasses."

This lightened the mood and both ladies broke out in laughter. Bruce being the good sport that he was let out a, "Grrrr," along with a wink at Sue.

Now that the tension had eased somewhat, I asked Sue to go over her story one more time, including everything that was said and the events that happened at the police station. Much more relaxed, she repeated everything. After she finished, the one thing I didn't understand was why she had left out the part where she met Madison in the woods on the fifth hole. Why leave this out this key element from her story and what was she hiding? Even when Bruce gave his abbreviated version, he didn't mention anything about her leaving our group for a short time. This caused some doubts whether she was as innocent as she professed. I made a mental note to ask around and question anyone who may have seen Sue and Madison together in the woods on the fifth hole besides Carrie.

"Sue, any idea why someone would use one of your golf clubs as the murder weapon?"

She shook her head as to say, "No."

"Were your clubs ever out of your sight?"

Yes, lots of times. I placed them next to Bruce's by the club house door where anyone could've taken any one of them."

"Was there any time you reached for the club and noticed it wasn't there?"

Out of the blue, Sue grabbed the plates off the table and disappeared inside. Both Marti and I shot puzzled looks at each other. When she returned, she remarked in a somewhat evasive tone, "Come to think of it. I remember now, it was strange. It wasn't in my bag when I went to reach for it. I figured it might still be in the garage where I cleaned my clubs the night before. I appreciate you both stopping by and that you are willing to help, but I'm tired and didn't get much sleep last night. I've told you everything I can remember about that dreaded day. I'd appreciate it if you would leave. Bruce will you please show them out? I'm going to bed." Without saying another word, she left.

Bruce added, "Maybe it would be best if you both would leave. This has been such a nightmare and I worried it has put a lot of strain on her."

Before we stepped out the front door, Marti asked, "What does your lawyer have to say about all this?"

"What lawyer? The detective insisted we didn't need one if she was innocent."

"Don't listen to the police. That detective is trying to get Sue to confess for a crime she didn't commit. It would be in your best interest to hire one before you go to the station in the morning. Do you know of any?" I asked.

"No, we figured we wouldn't need one, but now after talking to you, maybe we should. Any ideas?"

I smirked and thought back at the time when Jackson Fritz Pickett joined Detective Sanchez and me at the diner. She looked none too pleased he was there. "Yes, I do." I took out my phone and after a short conversation I said, "Your attorney will be here within the hour. He's good. Be straight forward and tell him everything, and I mean, EVERYTHING." I had emphasized everything, knowing Sue was still not telling us why she met Madison in the woods next to the fifth fairway.

On our drive home, we talked about what both Sue and Bruce had said about the day of the charity event. What still bothered me was Sue not coming clean about meeting Madison in the woods. Why? Was Madison waiting for Sue still fuming about the gift certificates? I had just pulled into our drive when Marti commented, "Wes, I think now I remember, Bruce and I were trying to locate your missing ball on the other side of the fairway. I think, and please don't hold me to this, but for a moment when I glanced back at the fairway, Sue was nowhere in sight."

"Well, if you think she might've gone into the woods, and Carrie claims she saw both Sue and Madison together, then what is Sue not telling us?"

"Wes, do you think Sue might have murdered that poor lady?"

I shrugged my shoulders, "Let's hope not. One thing for certain, they're definitely not giving us the whole story. I don't know what Sue is hiding but it's not good. Sooner or later, Detective Sanchez is going to find out what it is and that will fuel her desire to pin the murder on Sue."

I needed some time to be alone with my thoughts and the best place to do that was at the dog park. I settled under my favorite tree and watched the guys chase their friends around. I thought about what Sue had told us and I couldn't come up with a valid reason for her not telling us she saw Madison in the woods off hole number five. I trusted Carrie, and if she said she saw Sue and Madison in the woods, then Sue had some explaining to do.

The other thing that I didn't understand was if someone else did murder Madison, why take Sue's club and not someone else's? There were over sixty golfers attending the event. Maybe the person who killed Madison saw them arguing over the donations which gave the perfect motive. Hopefully, after Sue and Bruce talked with Jackson, he'd be able to get the truth out of what truly happened and tell me. Especially if they wanted my help.

After an hour trying to put the pieces of the puzzle together, I noticed the guy's tongues were dragging, and they had enough fun for one day.

I was hoping for a quiet night but no sooner had I stepped inside, there was Denise and Marti in the kitchen. Chris was in the living room eating a burger and watching TV. As soon as he saw me, he remarked, "We brought dinner and maybe after we eat you and I can discuss our case, Partner."

That was all I needed, having Marti's brother's nose meddling in my investigation, again. After we finished eating Marti brought out the Scrabble game and I rolled my eyes. Not my favorite game, since I had the world's longest losing streak.

Tonight, Marti and Chris both came up with the idea that our wagers would be just between couples. Lucky for me the Queen of Scrabble was on my team or that was what I thought until Chris blurted out, Wes and I against Marti and Denise. I was doomed. I just prayed that Marti and Denise would take pity on me knowing if we lost, it wouldn't be some outrageous task I'd have to do with Chris.

It was ugly as they destroyed us. When Marti happily read out the wager, I just about fell out of my chair. The four of us were going on a two-day charity bike ride. We would take everything we needed to camp out overnight on our bikes. It had been years since I had ridden a bike and the thought of my sore leg muscles and my rump made me want to cry.

After they left, I questioned the love of my life about this two-day bike ride. It was in September and would supposedly be a leisurely ride through the mountains looking at the fall colors. When I remarked, "mountains?" She commented, "Don't sweat it, we'll have months to get you in shape. Next week we'll go out and buy you a bike."

"Better make it one of those electric ones," I added.

Chapter 9

While waiting for my computer, I made a call and after a short conversation we agreed on a time to meet at the diner. With a few clicks of the mouse and with my not so blinding typing speed I punched in the name Madison Quinn. Madison was twenty-eight and married to Trevor Quinn. On Facebook Madison was an active blogger and posted once or twice a day. Most of the photos showed her with various young good-looking men and none of her and her husband. I tried looking him up on Facebook but came up blank. Searching through the online public records, Trevor Quinn was CEO of Quinn Rentals and I found a photo of him on the company's website. He looked to be more than twice Madison's age. So, who were the other men in her posts?

The further I read and scanned through Madison's Facebook pages, there were a lot of posts dating back for months where she talked about how miserable her married life was and that she was looking for Mr. Right to take her away from hell. The day before her death, she reached out to friends and followers asking if they knew a good attorney, that would squeeze every penny out of her husband's vast fortune when she filed for divorce. That could explain the reason the wolves clung onto her at the golf course.

Besides the doom and gloom posts about her marriage, the only other posts were about the charity she founded, "The Gift of Love" it helped children with extreme illnesses. In pictures she posted about the charity it showed her with doctors and others. In those photos she looked happy and smiled in each one.

Two days before the charity event and her death, she posted a video of her and a striking young gentleman, each showing a lot of affection to each other. The caption below read, "I think I found my knight in shining armor. After watching the video for a second time, something in the back of my head told me I had seen him before, but I wasn't sure where. I froze the video and clicked off a photo using my phone. By the time I finished researching Madison's social media sites, I had taken seven photos of her with various men.

Hours before the charity event, Madison's last post read, "I don't know how much longer I can take this. Last night we had a big fight when I asked for a divorce. He vowed to never let me go."

After going through all Madison's posts, I thought that maybe Detective Sanchez should be concentrating on the husband and not Sue. I closed my eyes and rocked back and forth in my chair trying to recall if I had seen Madison's husband at the charity event. I didn't, but then again there were a lot of people there and I wasn't really looking for him in the first place. I made a mental note to reach out to a business associate for help.

I left the guys to guard the house while I dropped off my report and invoice from my latest fraud investigation, "Case of the Pushy Ghost". Lucy, the receptionist at the State Workman's Comp office, handed me a stack of new cases plus the recent photos of her German Shepherd named Cooper. She also had a stack of new photos of her grandkids. Lucy was in her mid-to-late fifties. I quickly thumbed through the photos while she gave me a brief description of each one.

As soon as Gerald, the manager of the department, waved me over, I quickly made my escape before she was able to start talking about her latest vacation. I never knew what was worse, Lucy's vacations or Gerald fishing tales. Gerald was an avid fisherman and instead of going out for lunch he'd use that time to go fishing in the river that ran through the center of town.

"Wes, good to see you. I take it you've closed another case?" I handed him the thumb drive and was about to make my exit when he suggested I have a seat. "Did I tell you about my latest fishing trip?" I shook my head as if to say, "No." but luck was on my side and when his phone rang, that was my clue to escape. I grabbed my case files and closed his door behind me.

As promised, I went and parked down the street from Markus's house. The house was dark and showed no signs of life. It had been only ten minutes when right on cue, Chester tapped his cane on the passenger window. Once inside I explained to him what happened the other night and that I had enough evidence to prove Markus committed fraud. He smiled before commenting, "I had a feeling you'd crack this case. I'm going to miss our talks. It was the highlight of my day." We agreed to keep in touch and promised to go out for lunch one of these days.

The diner was buzzing with activity as Irene and her crew worked diligently to take care of her customers. I gave her a passing waved and found the only empty booth. It had been maybe a minute when a hush filtered throughout the place as a clown walked through the front door. Everyone's eyes were focused on her as she made way to the back of the diner and sat across from me. I asked, "How have you been?"

"Good. I was surprised when you called. What's on your mind?"

Shawna Patten was one of my previous fraud suspects. She worked on a local television station's afternoon children's show as a clown. I had gotten to know her after reading a case file about her Workman's comp work injury. After proving she had faked her work injury, she turned her life around and was now working for the hospital in the Children's Cancer Ward and terminally ill patient ward. She did her best to ease their pain and fears while bringing them some joy and laughter.

A little girl walked up to our booth and without hesitation Shawna brought out a red balloon and quickly turned it into a dog. The little girl ran back to her parents laughing and giggling as she showed off her new prized toy.

The waitress took our orders and as soon as she left I asked, "Do you know Madison Quinn?"

There was a moment of hesitation. "The name sounds familiar. Is she a patient at the hospital?"

"No, she did some charity events for the children's ward at the hospital."

"Do you have a picture of her?"

I showed her a photo on my phone. There was a long pause. "Yes, I've seen her a few times hanging around the children's ward. Mr. Johns, what is this all about?"

"Call me Wes. She was murdered the other day."

"Oh my God! How awful. Murdered?"

I nodded my head and gave Shawna some time to get over the shock. "Is there anything you can tell me about her?" I asked.

"Honestly, not much but as I said, I've seen her around the ward every now and then."

I showed her the photos I had taken of Madison's social pages and the various men she was with. Shawna didn't have a clue about the men in the first two photos but after taking an extra-long look at the third photo, she remarked, "That's Dr. Lewis."

Then it clicked in my head. Now I remembered he was one of the wolves at the golf course. After Shawna finished looking at the other photos, she had pointed out three other doctors, a Dr. Burns, Dr. Wayne Stewart, and a Dr. Oslow.

The waitress returned with two slices of pie, a coffee for Shawna and chocolate milk for me. We were interrupted when in a loud belligerent voice remarked, "You've got to be kidding me." I quickly gathered up the photos and shoved them in my pocket.

Detective Sanchez strutted down the aisle with long strides and the arrogance as if she owned the place. When Irene started to open her mouth, the detective directed her right hand toward her and with her index finger moved it from side to side as if say, "Don't." Irene quickly closed her mouth.

Shawna asked, "A friend of yours?"

"Not exactly."

The detective removed her oversized sunglasses and glared down at Shawna before rudely commenting, "I can't believe the crap you find on those dating websites. Who's the clown?" She then pushed her frame against mine making me slide over. "So, when did the circus come to town?" She remarked in a sarcastic tone.

I was getting tired of her abusive tone and the condescending remarks she directed toward Shawna. "Leave, this is a private conversation," I demanded.

"Does your wife know you're seeing a clown behind her back or is this some kind of sick fantasy you're having?" The detective's tone was off putting and somewhat rude.

Using my body, I shoved hard until the detective slid off the bench and landed on the floor. She glared at me and without hesitation got up, dusted herself off and tried to sit back down. I refused to move. When she attempted to move Shawna aside, Shawna got up and said, "Wes, I'd think I better leave. I don't want people to get the wrong idea. It's not good for people watching a clown go ballistic and start beating the crap out of stupid people. I'll call you later."

After Shawna vacated the other side of the booth, Sanchez quickly slid her body onto the bench.

"You had no right to be so rude," I said. My tone was harsh and curt.

"I agree," Irene commented as she stood at the end of our table with her arms crossed and a scowl on her face.

"I thought I'd stop by and order me another one of those daily trucker specials," the detective replied in a snarky tone.

Irene glanced over at me, and I nodded that it was okay. She stormed off and stood behind the counter the whole time glaring at the detective.

"What are you doing here?" I asked.

"I wasn't sure you had gotten it in your thick head to stay away from my investigation. We have your friends place under surveillance, making sure they don't do a runner. It just happens I know you and your wife spent time with them yesterday. So again, I'm warning you to stay away from my investigation, or else," she demanded.

"Or else what?" I asked.

 She then took out a pair of handcuffs and dangled them in front of me. "I think I'd be able to get you and your wife adjoining cells down at the stations." She gave me a devilish smirk.

The detective's smirk quickly disappeared when Irene placed an extra-large plate piled with food in front of her. "What's all this?" Detective Sanchez nastily asked.

"You ordered the trucker's special. Well, today our special is liver and onions over a pile of mashed potatoes covered in gravy. Enjoy. I be back shortly with the rest." Irene winked at me as she made her way back to the counter.

"This looks disgusting! Will someone come and get this crap away from face?" Sanchez remarked in a loud outburst. Irene returned with a smug smile on her face and before picking up the plate she asked, "Is there something wrong with the food?"

"Don't expect me to eat this crap? Now, get it out of my sight. Just leave us alone." The detective remarked harshly.

Irene gave the detective a smug smile before picking up the plate and replacing it with a piece of paper. "What's that?" Sanchez remarked.

"Your bill," Irene remarked while smiling.

"You don't expect me to pay for something I didn't eat."

"Yes, you ordered it and it's not our fault you didn't eat it. Would you like us to put it in a box to go?"

"No!" Irene held out the palm of her hand and with everyone in the place watching the detective had no choice but to pay her bill. "This is the last time I step foot in this dump."

"Promise?" Irene said and she walked away chuckling. "Next time you show your face in here, I won't be so gracious."

I quickly tossed a twenty on the table to pay for Shawna's and my pie and drinks."

When I slid out from the booth, Sanchez demanded I sit back down.

"Sorry, but if you want to talk to me, it'll have to be in the presence of my lawyer. You remember him, we had breakfast together the other day."

Irene handed me a whole pie as I walked past her. We both winked at each other and smiled. I was just about to get in my truck when Sanchez followed me outside and remarked, "It was you."

"It was me, what?"

"You're the one who suggested to your friends they needed to hire that attorney."

"Bingo. I wished I'd been there to see the expression on your face when Jackson Fritz Pickett strutted into the interview room this morning along with Sue and Bruce."

Her nostrils flared and I could tell behind those stupid oversized sunglasses her eyes were burning with anger. "Well, it's not going to help them. By time I finish, she'll be behind bars serving a life sentence."

I closed the door in her face and fired up the engine. As I pulled out of the lot, Sanchez stood there with her arm crossed.

My phone pinged and it was a text from Shawna, "What a bitch. I had to leave before I did something I regretted. I'll ask around at the hospital about Madison and I'll let you know what I find out."

I replied with a smiley face.

Willy, my Bird's mechanic, was sitting at his desk enjoying one of Betty's fried treats when I entered his office, "Denise said you wanted to see me?"

He smiled and tossed me a set of keys, "She's all yours."

I raced out of the office and down to the last bay in the garage. There in all its beauty was the secret project I had kept from Marti. It was an old nineteen forty-nine Pontiac Chieftain, which I had nicknamed, "The Lady." I had rescued it from an old junk yard during one of my investigations. Everyone here thought I was crazy when I had it towed to Willy's garage, but I knew Willy and his team of ladies could bring her back to her old glory days. A tear trickled down my cheek. Janice, the shop foreman, put her arm around my shoulder and remark, "She turned out better that I thought."

I agreed and slowly walked around checking each and every inch. The cream and root beer paint sparkled under the lights and the chrome glistened. Janice opened the driver's door and I ran my hand over the buttery leather tan dash and marveled at the updated instruments. It smelled like a new car. Janice grabbed the keys out of my hand, climbed into the driver's seat, and turned the key. When the engine roared to life, I shouted, "Yes!" It purred like a happy kitten. No one was ever going to believe this beautiful classic once sat out in front of the junk yard rusting and falling apart for more than a decade. I couldn't wait to show it off at the next classic car show. I made arrangement with Willy that I'd come to the garage at six A.M. Saturday morning.

I was having a hard time concentrating on my way home. I'd rather be cruising in the Lady but I didn't want to blow the big unveiling. I was surprised that Willy and his crew were able to keep a secret for so long. Especially since Marti's brother was living with Denise.

Oz and Annie wolfed down their treats before bolting out the doggie door to chase after squirrels. Finally, the blue screen on my computer changed to a picture of Marti and the guys. I typed in Quinn Rentals website to do a deeper dive into the company. It was founded by three brothers, Trevor, Robert and Tanner. The company now operated over one hundred retail construction rental locations throughout the western half of the United States and in Florida, mostly in Miami.

The company's humble beginnings started in Eastern Washington working out of the back of Trevor's garage. Four years later they moved out of the small garage and into their first retail location. From there the empire grew to what it was today. Three years ago, they moved the company's headquarters to the valley, claiming it was more centralized to most locations.

Just after they moved the headquarters here, in two thousand and nineteen Robert, the oldest of the three brothers, resigned his position as the company financial adviser and moved to California. This left Trevor and his younger brother Tanner to run the business. I made a mental note to pay them a visit in the morning.

I turned my attention to learn more about the charity work Madison had been doing. It was called the "The Gift of Love", a charity to bring awareness to children's cancer. The charity was founded by Madison Quinn along with two doctors, Dr. Winston Lewis and Dr. Andrew Burns. That explained some of the photos on her social media pages of her with them.

Dr. Winston Lewis looked to be in his mid-forties, tall, blonde hair and very dashing. The photo of him with Madison hinted that there might be more to their relationship than business acquaintances. Dr. Andrew Burns appeared to be younger than Dr. Lewis by about ten years. He was tall with a very muscular frame, his curly brown hair flowed down to the top of his shoulders. Again, the photos on Madison's social media pages suggested they might be romantically involved.

I was deep in thought about whether Trevor had seen these photos of his wife and maybe in a fit of rage was the one who murdered Madison. I felt a hand gently rest on my shoulder and I almost jumped out of my chair. Marti leaned down and whispered in my ear, "Wes, be a dear and open a bottle of wine. It has been one of those days."

Being the good husband that I was, I did what I was told as she disappeared to change out of her uniform. No sooner had I removed the cork from the bottle than she appeared wearing pink boxers and a white T-shirt. She grabbed the bottle out of my hand and took a long swig. "What's for dinner? I'm starving. I didn't get lunch. The computers were down for two hours and the passenger's attitudes weren't very pleasant." She and bottle disappeared into the living room and shortly after I heard two women ranting and cussing at each other, she had turned on one of her reality shows.

I rummaged around the fridge looking to see what to make. There wasn't much since neither one of us had done any shopping lately. After finding some meatballs in the freezer, tonight's menu would be spaghetti with meatballs along with some homemade cornbread. She vented about her day and I told her about mine as we sat at the counter and ate.

I wasn't in the mood to watch TV, so instead I joined the guys in the backyard and tried to process if I had seen Trevor Quinn at the charity event the day his wife was murdered, nothing. I did remember seeing Dr. Lewis and Dr. Burns that day. I had just closed my eyes to reflect on seeing, "The Lady" in all her newly painted body and bright shinny chrome, when Shawna texted, "Madison's Memorial service is tomorrow at ten at the Holy Trinity Church." I thanked her and asked if she was going. She wasn't. Hopefully, attending would give me a better idea of who the players were and who had the motive to murder Madison Quinn. After some consideration, I named this investigation, "The Case of the Death of the Charity Princess."

Chapter 10

The church was packed, so many had come to pay their final respects and say goodbye to Madison Quinn. I used my press pass to gain entrance and was escorted to the choir loft to join the other press personnel. It was a good place to be since I was able to look down in the large chapel.

Thanks to Royce, the editor of the local paper, I had access using the pass he had given me after I proved a previous employee committed Workman's Comp fraud. It saved the paper a lot of money and became to be a useful tool for my investigations.

An expensive looking casket was draped in flowers by the altar along with numerous flower arrangements displayed. The church was filled with the sound of a thousand bees buzzing as people talked waiting for the service to begin.

Trevor Quinn, Madison's husband, sat in the front pew along with a very large man with a buzz cut. Even from here I could tell the man's biceps were threatening to burst out from the skintight suit jacket. In the row behind the two men sat three beautiful women. My camera was the only one clicking. Both Dr. Lewis and Dr. Burns sat together in the back along with what I assumed was hospital staff acquaintances who knew Madison. Standing alone in the back of the church was the same scruffy looking man I saw at the golf course. I quickly took a bunch photos of him and wondered what his relationship with Madison was.

The talking turned into a hush after the music stopped. Catherine, my old friend and local television manager, sat in the seat next to me. She whispered that her news crew were out front, since they weren't allowed inside. Throughout the ceremony she pointed out some of the key players in my investigation. The three ladies sitting behind Trevor were three of his four ex-wives. The man sitting next to Trevor was Jake Toleman, an old military buddy and personal assistant.

After the short ceremony, Madison's casket was lifted and carried down the wide corridor with precision and skill you'd find at a military funeral. Trevor and personal assistant, Jake, followed behind. I had a good view of both men's faces as my camera clicked rapidly with the press of my finger. Instead of heartbroken or a distraught appearance, the expression on Trevor's face was stoic and stone cold. His three ex-wives followed closely behind. Only one looked as if she had shed a few tears. She was very beautiful and looked to be the youngest of the trio. Her long blonde hair draped down to the center of her back, and her petite frame gave the impression she could've been a model.

The other two ex-wives showed no emotion, their faces matched Trevor's cold expression. Catherine leaned over and whispered, "Trevor's trophy wives. Rumors were that once they're past what he considered their prime, they were dumped for a younger trophy replacement."

"How many wives did he have?" I questioned.

She paused for a moment, "five."

I commented as we left the choir box, "Who would've known that Madison touched so many lives?"

Catherine let out a smirk, "Oh Wes, the same old naïve kid I grew up with. These people are not here because of Madison. They're here because of Trevor. Most of them are business associates and employees." I stopped and gave her a blank stare. "You be careful around that man. The rumor around the TV station is that he's not one to mess with, especially with that gorilla that's always by his side."

As we left the dimly lit church the bright sunlight caused our eyes to squint. I pointed toward Dr. Lewis and Dr. Burns and asked if she knew anything about them.

Catherine smiled, "Wes, is there something here you're not telling me? Please, don't tell me if you're here because of some workman's fraud case. Why are you here?"

I explained it was Marti who had discovered Madison's lifeless body, and a friend of ours was under investigation as her possible killer. She smiled and went on to describe each doctor. Doctor Winston Lewis was the leading pediatric physician in the Northwest. The hospital was lucky to have him on staff. He did his residency in New York and came to our city about two years ago.

She then explained that Dr. Burns was considered one of the valleys best pediatric oncology doctors. She then pointed toward a third man standing next to the two doctors. He also happened to be a doctor. His name was Ulrich Oslow. He moved here from Sweden, and his specialty was cancer. Both Dr. Lewis and Burns were single, but Dr. Oslow was married with three children. A brass looking young man joined the trio and Catherine stated he was Dr. Wayne Stewart. She didn't know much about him but promised if she and her team turned up anything she would let me know. When I asked her how she knew so much about these men, she replied, "It's my job to know all these things."

I was about to suggest we go and grab some lunch when a dark cloud appeared on the horizon. Detective Sanchez was storming her way in our direction. Her body language suggested she was none too happy, but then what else was new. I don't think she's cracked one smile since the first day I laid eyes on her. It might be that if she had, it would've cracked her makeup. The first words out of her mouth were loud and caused people to turn their heads. "Hey, Scumbag, what are you doing here? I thought I made it perfectly clear to stay away from my case. Who's this tart?"

I gave her one of my famous Wesley Johns patented smile, "I'm covering the event for the paper." I whipped out my press badge to shut her up.

Before the detective could utter another word, Catherine waved her arm and her news crew rushed over at her beckoning. Catherine reached for the mic and asked, "Detective, could you please give us an update on your case and are you close to solving who murdered poor Madison Quinn?"

The detective looked lost for words with a dumbfounded expression and when she tried to speak nothing came out. She lowered her large brown glasses, glared at me before storming off in a huff. Catherine and her crew broke out laughing. "That was great, don't you think Wes?"

Catherine and the crew then tried to get an interview with Trevor, but Jake placed his body between them with his arms crossed and a stern expression. When Trevor snapped his fingers two of his ex-wives climbed into the limo. I clicked off a couple more pictures but not before I noticed Jake's piercing stare in my direction, he climbed in the limo's front seat before it sped off.

I looked around at the crowd gathered out front hoping to find the scruffy looking man. Unfortunately, he was nowhere to be seen. Since all the key players had left, which included the doctors, I decided the fun and games were over and started for my truck. Then a strikingly beautiful lady in a tight black dress wrapped her arm around mine and suggested we meet at the dog park in an hour. As she walked away, I stood there dumbfounded.

I raced home to change into more casual clothing like jeans and a t shirt and grabbed the guys leashes. As I drove to the dog park,

I tried to figure out why all the cloak and dagger with this mysterious woman when we could've just talked at the church.

It had been almost two hours and I thought she was not going to show. I began to think she played me for a fool by having me meet her here. Then out of the corner of my eye I spotted an extremely large Husky eagerly approaching the play area. Doing her best to keep up the woman commanded, "Slow down Grimm, slow down." But the dog was eager to play with his friends. She stood by the gate making sure her four-legged buddy was accepted by the others before coming over and sitting next to me under my favorite tree. I marveled at her beauty. Her tight white jeans hugged her body and the pink shirt accented her features leaving nothing to the imagination. Her long blonde hair was stylish and flowed down to the center of her back. Not a blemish or mark was on her face. She had a striking beauty that I had seen on someone else but couldn't place who.

We sat in silence watching our dogs play together. She broke the ice by asking, "Which one is yours?"

I pointed out Oz and Annie and told her my name was Wes."

There was a long pause, "I know who you are. I'm Chloe." She paused, "Chloe Quinn."

"You're one of Trevor's ex-wives. I saw you sitting behind Trevor with his other exes." I remarked.

She nervously glanced around the park which started to get me a little on edge. "Yes." There was fright in her eyes as she again glanced around the park.

"What are you so worried about?" I asked.

"It's Trever. You don't know him but he's a very dangerous man." Her words caused me to look around. "I was married to him for three years. I'm wife number four." She took a deep breath. "I know who you are, because the lady from the television said you'd be the one to find out who killed my sister."

"Your sister?" I exclaimed out loud.

Chloe jumped and looked around hoping no one had heard or was spying on us. "Madison is or was my younger sister. Trevor dumped me for her." A tear slowly trickled down her cheek followed by another and another. "That's his nature, he collects trophy wives. He likes them young, beautiful, and blonde. First, he entices you into his web with dining, expensive gifts, trips and offers you a lavish lifestyle. But once married, he puts you on a pedestal for all to see. He controls every part of your life, what you eat, who you can see and when, what clothes to wear. You get the picture. Worst of all, if you try to speak up or threaten to file for a divorce, he lashes out in anger. Believe me after the first time you never want to see that side of him again." Tears now flowed freely as she leaned over resting her head on my shoulder. Grimm must've seen her being distraught and stood at the fence whining and pawing at the wire mesh to get out. She smiled, "He's my baby and protector." She ran over to him and after some ear scribbles and nose rubs, he ran back to play with the others.

Chloe hesitated and looked around before coming back to sit next to me under the tree. "Chloe how did Madison fall into, as you would say, Trevor's web? Didn't you warn her?"

"My little sister never listened to me. I tried telling her to stay away but when Trevor gave her an expensive diamond necklace and took her on one of his exotic trips, it was too late. She had fallen into his trap. Once you reach the big thirty-five, you're out and he's back on the hunt for the next Mrs. Quinn. It was four days after my thirty-fifth birthday when he handed me the divorce papers and gave me twenty-four hours to move out of the house. No matter how hard I tried to convince Maddy to stay away, all she saw was her living the life of luxury and royalty."

"So, you're telling me they fell in love."

"No nothing like that. There was no love between them, just like mine or the others. I guess we all did it for the money. I bet right now he is already showering the future Mrs. Quinn with expensive gifts, high end dinners and trips."

When Chloe glanced around the park for a third time I had to ask. "What are you so afraid of?"

She stood up to leave, "Once you've been married to Trevor, you're never really divorced. He stills controls your life. Ask his other ex's."

"I want you to prove that bastard killed my sister. I've got to go. We have talked too long. Here's my number, but please be discrete if you call. I'm not sure that he doesn't have my phone tapped. Be careful, Trevor is a very dangerous man and Jake gets off on hurting people."

The guys were ready to go home too. I kept glancing in the rearview mirror worried someone might be following us after seeing me with Chloe.

No sooner had we stepped inside than my phone pinged. It was a message from Shawna. "Madison's Celebration of Life is being held at the Riverview Hotel tonight at seven."

I replied, "Thanks. Are you going?"

Her reply was, "No."

Marti stepped through the front door and noticed I had changed into a black pair of dress pants and a blue button-down shirt. "What's the occasion? Are you taking me out to dinner?" she asked.

"Madison Quinn's Celebration of Life is tonight at the Riverview Hotel."

"Give me five minutes and I'll be ready."

After circling the packed lot a couple of times, I was able to snag a parking place. By the door of the meeting room was a large poster of Madison Quinn, posing in front of the Children's Hospital. A long line of people waited to give Trevor their sympathy and condolences. We skipped the line and stood off to the side to watch.

Marti asked who the man was standing next to Trevor. When I told her the brief information I knew about him, she shuddered and clung onto my arm. "Wes, he looks dangerous. Please stay away from him." I scanned the room and pointed out Trevor's three ex-wives. Marti remarked, "Three?" I smiled and explained there was another but I didn't see her here tonight.

We watched as people slowly filed into the room. It was interesting when Dr. Lewis and Dr. Burns entered the room. Both Trevor and Jake glared at the two men. Trevor leaned over and whispered something into Jake's ear, who then nodded his head and his attention was placed directly on them. I explained about their so-called affairs with Madison. She kissed me on the cheek and commented. "Time for your sexy secretary to go to work."

I watched as she graciously weaved her way through the crowd toward the bar where the two doctors stood. It wasn't long after being served her drink she struck up a conversation with the two of them. Chloe stood alone in a corner and looked as if she was afraid. The other two ex-wives where on the other side of the room having a heated discussion. I fought my way through the crowd and at first Chloe tried to play it as if she didn't know who I was. The whole time looking over my shoulder at Trevor and Jake. Her eyes shot wide open and fear replaced her worried look. I turned in time to see Jake pushing his way toward us. Chloe whispered, "Don't say anything about us meeting this afternoon."

Before I could reply, Jake grabbed her arm and pulled her back into the crowd and disappeared. Soon she and the two other ex-wives were sandwiched between Trevor and Jake. None looked too happy.

Marti was talking to three doctors Catherine had pointed out at the service. Dr. Oslow had joined the group. The next time I turned my attention toward the line, both Trevor and Jake were nowhere in sight. Neither were the ex-wives. I wanted to get Marti and leave but I knew she was gathering some good intel. I ordered a double club soda on the rocks with a lemon twist when Chloe appeared with a much more relaxed look on her face. "Trevor and Jake have left." Standing next to her were Trevor's other ex-wives.

Chloe said, "Leah and Ava this is Mr. Johns, he works for the paper." Leah gave me a hesitant look and Ava closely eyed me as if she was looking into my mind and thoughts.

It was Ava who asked, "Mr. Johns, are you here to dig up the dirt on our family?"

"No, this is personal, it was my wife who found Madison body at the golf course. She's been haunted by the expression on Madison's face and I suggested it might be good to attend to help her deal with this trauma."

"Where is your wife now?" Ava questioned suspiciously. I pointed toward Marti and the three doctors. Ava let out a huff and nastily said, "Who let those sons of bitches in? They're the ones who ruined Trevor and Madison's marriage. I hope they burn in hell."

Leah added, "Losen your panties, Ava. They were having a little fun. Or did you forget what it was like being married to that asshole."

Ava shot Leah with a nasty glare and looked as if she was about to take a swing at her when Chloe interjected. "Leah, sometimes you just can't keep your big fat mouth shut."

Leah quickly downed her drink, tapped on the bar for another. "Look, Miss Goodie Two Shoes, Madison wasn't the only one who had to go looking for some extracurricular activity. The man was all smoke and mirrors. Big promises and lots of romance. But once married, it all stopped and we were nothing but his slaves."

Ava dragged Leah back into the crowd but not before she was able to pick up her drink. Leah's parting words were directed toward the bartender. "I'll be back."

There was a moment of awkwardness before Chloe spoke. "Mr. Johns, please don't get the wrong impression. Maybe my little sister did go outside the marriage for some fun, but she didn't deserve to die."

"That bitch had no right doing that. If I didn't know better, she was still in love with Mr. Asshole. Mr. Bartender, Stud, when do you get off work, I have some built up stress that needs to be released," Leah remarked as she scanned the crowd.

Chloe looked around the room for Ava. Leah picked up on Chloe nervousness and remarked, "Relax Honey, she's gone. Now the celebration can start."

The bartender refused Leah's insistent advances which didn't deter her from looking for another victim. Since Trevor had gone, the crowd was beginning to thin out. Marti was now only talking to one doctor, Dr. Lewis. When the bartender announced the bar would close in five minutes, Leah staggered her way through those who were left and demanded a double.

"Any luck?" I asked.

Her words were slurred, "None of your business? It's time for this little bird to get some action. Since the bar is closed here, I'm off to the bar across the street. Do you want to come along?" She sarcastically remarked before weaving her way to the front door. When one of the wait staff tried to pry the glass out of her hand she screamed, "How dare you try to take my drink away! Do you know who I am? I'm the only ex-wife that asshole ever really loved. What did I get for pouring out all my love and passion for the man. Nothing! Now let go of my glass before I belt you."

I couldn't believe my luck when my mystery man from the golf course and church appeared in the doorway. I pushed my way through the crowd to only find he was gone by the time I reached the door. There was something about him that made me think he had something to do with the murder, but who in the hell was he?

When I looked back into the sparce room, I saw Chloe was nowhere to be seen. Marti put her arm around mine. "Ready, to go home? I've got some hot and juicy news for you."

"I can't wait you hear what my sexy secretary has found out."

We were about to leave when Detective Sanchez came strutting down the hall, with her hands on her hips as if she was out for blood. We stepped back inside and I asked the bartender while slipping him a twenty, "Is there another exit door where we can slip out?" He pointed to the door behind the bar and we made our escape.

Chapter 11

I rocked back and forth in my office chair and I thought it would be foolish to get involved with Madison Quinn's murder, especially now that I'd be dealing with Detective Sanchez. Not only had both Sue and Bruce pleaded for my help but now Chloe wanted me to find out who was responsible for her younger sister's death. I just wished Rod would get back here soon, then he could take over the investigation. However, in the end I decided I needed to also know who murdered Madison Quinn. I called it, "The case of the Charity Princess."

It was obvious I needed to find out more about the players and what possible motive they had for murdering Madison Quinn. I reviewed my previous notes and then started to make a list of suspects.

Trevor Quinn: husband and owner of an equipment rental empire throughout the northwest and Florida. He was a controlling husband who demanded his trophy wives maintain the high standards he had set for them.

Jake Toleman: an old military buddy, had a keen eye and was always aware of what was going on around him and Trevor. He was Trevor's enforcer and had the body to back it up. I had been warned to be careful around him. I glanced down at my protection asleep at my feet and smiled. Jake would be no match for Oz.

Trevor had a total of five wives: Jennifer, Ava, Leah, Chloe, and Madison.

Jennifer Quinn: ex-wife number one. She wasn't present at the service or last night's event. The only reason I knew about her was from Catherine at Madison's funeral service. I thought it was strange that at Madison's Celebration of Life that no one mentioned her name.

Ava Quinn: ex-wife number two. At last night's celebration she displayed resentment toward Madison. She suggested all Madison wanted was Trevor's money and didn't actually love him. Her attitude toward Chloe and especially Leah was harsh and abrasive at times. I was caught off guard by Leah's fleeting comment about how Ava was still in love with Trevor. My first impression of her was she was mentally and physically strong and wasn't intimidated by anyone.

Leah Quinn: ex-wife number three. She had nothing good to say about Trevor. I got the impression she had drinking problems as well as infidelity issues while married to Trevor and was the reason behind the divorce.

Chloe Quinn: ex-wife number four. She was Madison's older sister. Of the three ex-wives I've met so far, she gave the impression of being the weakest and the least secure in her life. She appeared to be frightened and suspicious someone was always watching her. At Madison's funeral she was the only one who showed emotion for her sister. From past experience, until I know more about her, she'll remain on my list until I prove otherwise.

Besides the husband, his personal assistant and ex-wives, there were also the doctors Madison had in her life.

Dr. Winston Lewis: rumors were he and Madison had more than a business relationship. Looking at Madison's photos and reading her posts, gave the impression they might be secret lovers.

The same went for Dr. Burns.

I didn't have much about either Dr. Oslow or Dr. Stewart and what their relationships were with Madison, but I intended to find out.

Sue was also on my list. It was her golf club found at the crime scene covered in Madison's blood. She was seen arguing with Madison before and during the event. Plus, her off color remark after discovering Madison's lifeless body was hard to get out of my head. I hated to tell myself but she was to remain a suspect.

Last on my list, was the elusive mystery man. First, he showed up at the charity event, then at Madison's funeral and her Celebration of Life. Judging by his unkept appearance made him out of place from this high society group with his scraggly beard, blondish-looking hair that hadn't seen a comb in weeks and dirty clothing that needs to be tossed in the trash instead of the wash. Who the heck was he and what was his connection with Madison?

I wanted to meet with Trevor, but before doing so, I thought I'd better get an understanding of him by talking to his wives.

Researching public records, Jennifer Quinn divorced Trevor twenty-two years ago. They were married for three years. Two days after her divorce she changed back her maiden name, Stucky. Using the database one of my insurance companies provided me from working previous fraud cases for them, I was able to find her address and phone number in New York City. Jennifer had remarried with four children and worked as a fashion designer.

A young girl answered on the second ring, and I asked her to speak to her mom.

"Mom, it's for you."

"Hello?" A soft and questioning tone said.

"Jennifer, my name is Wesley Johns. I'm a private investigator in Idaho looking into the death of Madison Quinn. I was wondering if I could ask you a few questions about your ex-husband, Trevor, and the time you were married to him?"

There was a long pause. "How did you get my number? I don't want to talk about that evil man."

"I understand, but right now a good friend of mine is being accused of Madison's murder. If we could please talk for a few minutes, it might help me bring the real killer to justice. Please, I just have a few questions."

Again, a long pause. "Okay, what do you want to know?"

"How long were you married to Trevor?"

"Three years of living hell."

"Why do you say that?"

"I should've seen the signs after the first night when he demanded we sleep in separate bedrooms. The whole marriage was a sham. The man was nothing but a monster. He dictated who I could see and who I couldn't, what to wear, and how much makeup I could use. I was a natural brunette and like my hair short, but he demanded I change it to blonde and to grow it out. Every day I had to keep a dairy of my time when I left the house and returned. Do you understand? I had to get his permission to leave my own house! At social events, he planned out what I was to wear, to get his drinks, and smile. Worst of all, I had to stand by his side the whole time and speak to no one. I could only drink water and he monitored what I could and couldn't eat. Each morning, he made me stand naked on a scale before him, and if I even gained one pound, then he forced me to only drink water until I lost it."

"From what you've described of your marriage, that does sound like a living hell," I remarked.

"Do you want to know the worst part? Every night before I went to bed, he made me account for every penny I spent that day. Every damn penny!" Jennifer's tone changed to fire the more she spoke about her life with Trevor. I had to beg for money if I wanted something for me. I felt like I was a prisoner in my own home. Looking back, I should've known after the first night and gotten out."

"If he was so controlling, why did you stay with him as long as you did?"

"I thought about it a lot, but there was Jake. Don't get me started on him. Every time I thought about leaving or asking for a divorce, he'd show up and wouldn't let me out of his sight. It was Trevor's way of making sure I didn't. Then one night he found out I had bought lunch for me and a friend without his permission. He forced me down on the bed and using his belt he spanked me and threatened to do worst the next time I didn't get his permission first."

Jennifer paused, used her hand to covered the phone and whispered something to someone. When she continued. "That was the last straw, no one beats me and I had had enough of this insane relationship. At two in the morning, I snuck out of the house and walked to the bus station and hopped on the first one. I didn't care where it was taking me, I just wanted to get away from him and hell. Unfortunately, two days later Jake tracked me down and dragged me back home. I was locked in my bedroom twenty-four hours a day for two weeks. When he finally let me out, he threatened to kill me if I ever did that again."

The fire that was once in her voice had gone out and was replaced with pauses and sobs. "So how did you get out from under his control?"

"Six months later, he had his lawyer serve me with divorce papers. I had two days to move out of the house or be thrown out."

"Where did you go?"

"I was young and naïve when I went into the marriage. I thought I had found the love of my life and we would spend happy years growing old. I thought nothing of it when he asked for me to sign a pre-nup. I was to get nothing in the settlement except the clothing I had on my back."

The fire ignited in her voice again and I heard a slight chuckle. "Trevor had a safe in his office. From time to time for the first couple of weeks in our marriage he would ask me to get something out of it. The night before I was to be kicked out of my house, I helped myself to twenty thousand dollars from the safe. I felt I was owed it for the suffering and abuse from being on the receiving end of that wicked man."

"Weren't you afraid he would send Jake after you again?"

"Yes, but this time, I used my head. Instead of taking the bus, or any other traceable transportation, I purchased a small motorcycle off eBay and went to my college friend's house in Baker, Oregon. She and her husband, a cop, took me under their protection until the divorce was final. I knew I was safe when I heard he was getting married again. I wanted to warn her about his trap, but I was free and never wanted to have anything to do with that man, ever again!"

"Did the two of you have children?"

"Thank God, no! One of the stipulations to our marriage was that I must be on birth control pills, as if it did any good."

"What do you mean by that?"

She let out a haunting laugh. "It was all a farce. We never had sex, not once. The only reason he married me was because all he wanted was a trophy wife. We never had sex."

"Thank you for taking the time to talk to me. I have just one more question."

"Do you know what caused the falling out between Trevor and his brothers."

"What do you mean?"

"I read there where three brothers who started the business, but now Trevor's the sole owner."

"Sorry, I don't anything about that. Look, I've got to go and take my kids to school. Please, don't call me again." Before I could say anything, the line went dead.

I thought about what Jennifer had told me about their marriage and how it was a sham, and the more I thought about it, the more confident I felt that what Chloe had told me at the dog park was true. I removed Jennifer from my suspect list for now and felt more confident Trevor and Jake were responsible for killing Madison, but now how to prove it.

That left both Ava and Leah. As I read through Leah's social media sites most of her posts were about the tattoos that covered her body, bar hoping and various one-night stands. The photos she did post of herself when she wasn't drunk showed her to be a very attractive woman. After talking to both Jennifer and Chloe, I started to get an understanding of Trevor's lust to have beautiful arm candy and what attracted him to her in the beginning. Leah owned a small glass blowing studio. It opened in twenty minutes.

No sooner had I stepped out the front door than I almost tripped over Marti's brother, Chris. "What are you doing here?" I shouted.

"Hey, Partner, I'm here to help you investigate our case."

"Chris, it's not our case. Why are you sitting on our front step?"

"I'm here so you wouldn't leave without me this time. I tried your truck, but it was locked."

I really wanted to turn around and go back inside closing the door but he'd just follow me. Against my better judgement, I caved and unlocked the passenger truck door. He shouted, "Shot gun. Hey, are we first going to stop to get something to eat? I'm starving."

I ordered two breakfast sandwiches at a drive through, one for each of us. Chris whined when I didn't order anything else. I had only driven a few blocks when I reached into the bag for mine, there was nothing. At Chris's feet were two wrappers on the floor and I watched as he inhaled my sandwich.

Leah's single-story studio was in the heart of an old industrial park and could use a good coat of paint. The large front windows displayed various kinds of glass work. I begged Chris to wait in the truck, but he refused. Outside the temps were in the seventies but when we stepped inside the building I started sweating. It was well over a hundred degrees.

When Chris bumped into a table loaded with glass works, I cringed and so did a middle-aged man watching us. After steadying the table, he asked. "Can I help you?"

Before I could say a word Chris blurted out, "We're investigating a murder, this is my partner, Wes. Man, it's hot in here. Do you know a..." He then turned to me and asked, "Whose murder are we looking into? I forget her name."

"Sorry, my brother-in-law has a wild and vivid imagination. I'm here to talk to Leah."

Chris blurted out, "Do you think I could try blowing some glass?"

A devilish grin crossed my face, "How much to let him work on a piece right now?" Hoping to distract him so I could talk to Leah alone.

The man glanced over at Chris and back at me. He got my drift. "One hundred and fifty dollars." He then pointed toward the back room.

Leah's head was resting on an old metal desk which looked as if it had been there from when the building was constructed. She didn't move as I entered her office. "Rough night?" I asked as I sat on a padded vinyl chair patched with duct tape.

Leah slowly lifted her head and asked. "Who are you?"

"We met at Madison's Celebration of Life last night."

She struggled to focus on me through her bloodshot eyes. "Look, come back tomorrow. I'm sure I'll have the money for you by then. Now can't you see I'm in no mood to talk?"

The sound of glass breaking in the front room didn't cause her to flinch, until a voice shouted. "You stupid fool! Now look at what you've done. It took me hours to make that for a customer." She raised her head again and tried to focus.

"So did you find what you were looking for last night?" I asked.

In a moaning tone, "I don't know what you're talking about. Now leave me alone, I've got a splitting headache."

I smiled, "The last time we talked you were trying to seduce the bartender in going home with you. When he turned you down, you continued your hunt at the bar down the street."

Look Mister, whatever your name is, I promise I'll get your money in the morning. My ex said he'd have the money here by ten. Now will you just get the hell out?"

I could tell this was a waste of time. "Great, I'll be back tomorrow. I expect full payment or else I'm shutting this place down."

That sparked a fire inside her and she leaped out of the chair swaying back and forth trying to get her balance. "Hey, wait a minute, you're not from the city. Who are you?"

I gave her one of my famous Wesly Johns smiles and showed her my press pass. She had trouble focusing but when she did, she screamed, "You're that reporter?"

"Yes. Now that we've got the pleasantries out of the way, how about you tell me about your marriage with Trevor," I asked.

"It's none of your frick'n business. Now get out."

Before I could press her further, glass shattered in the front room and the middle-aged man shouted, "You idiot! Get out before you break anything else."

We peaked out the doorway to see Chris being forcibly escorted out of the building."

"Is he with you?" She questioned.

"Yes, unfortunately. I forgot his leash."

She gave a slight chuckled until she focused on the damage Chris had caused. "Why are you here again and whose going to pay for the destroyed items?"

"I want to know more about Trevor Quinn, your ex."

"I would appreciate it if you would leave!" she demanded.

Leah physically pushed me out of her office doorway and gently closed the door so not to cause any additional pain in her head.

The middle-aged man rushed over and started screaming in my ear. "Are you going to pay for the glass pieces that fool broke?"

"No, but hang on." I went outside to where Chris as sitting in the front seat, drinking a soda and munching on a bag of chips. "Where did you get the food?" He pointed at the convenience store across the street. "You need to go back inside and pay for the glass pieces you broke."

He gave me a sheepish grin, "Since we're partners, can't the agency pay for the damage?"

"What agency? We're not partners!" I shouted.

"I don't have any money," he replied.

"Fine." I took out my phone and the next voice I heard was Janice at Willy's shop. When I explained that I needed to speak to Denise, Janice asked if she needed to call her friend, who knew a friend, that knew a friend. I assured her, she didn't but it was temping. I told Denise what Chris had done, and she demanded I hand the phone over to him. Two minutes after getting chewed out, Chris got out of the truck and went back inside. Five minutes later he came out, handed me my phone, climbed in my truck and continued to stuff his face as if nothing had happened.

On my way to drop Chris off at his house, Jackson Fritz Pickett left a voicemail asking me to call him. The only thing I had learned while at the glass shop was that Leah had financial issues. Maybe on my next visit she'd be sober and we could talk. Chris started whining like a two-year-old when I pulled up in front of his house. When I pulled out a fifty and explained I had an assignment for him. He stopped his tantrum and eagerly snatched the bill from my fingers. I asked him to go back and stake out the glass blowing shop. If Leah left, he was to follow her and report where she went and what she did. It was a simple task for most people but for Chris I knew some how he would botch it, but for now he would be out of my hair.

I was about to call Jackson back when Chloe called and asked if we could meet. I suggested the dog park in thirty minutes. I quickly stopped by the house and got the guys.

While I sat under my favorite tree waiting for her, I returned Jackson's call. He asked if there were any developments to my investigation and if there was someone high on my suspect list that he should know of. He sounded disappointed when I said there wasn't much to report but I'd let him know if and when I had something that might help.

I'd only been at the park for about twenty minutes when Chris texted, letting me know he was bored and had run out of money.

Chloe arrived and released Grimm into the play area before sitting next to me.

"Chloe, I'm glad we could meet. After last night meeting both Leah and Ava, I was hoping you could tell me more about them."

"Okay, Leah spends most of her time drinking away her monthly alimony checks and trying to find someone to love, shower her with gifts and money like Trevor used too."

"Wait a minute, Leah gets alimony checks?" I questioned.

"Yes, no one else does but she claimed to know one of Trevor's darkest secrets and promised not to tell. So, he's paying her to keep her mouth shut."

"What about Ava?"

"She's a bossy old cow who tries to control my life like Trevor did. Whenever we get together, she blames me for messing up my marriage and the way I had treated Trevor. But then Leah blames me for messing up hers too. I try not to associate with them too much. They are always talking trash about me and Madison and how we ruined everything when we came along."

"When you were married to Trevor, did he ever talk about his two brothers?"

"I liked Robert. I met him once when he came to our house. He signed some papers and that was the last time I ever saw him or heard Trevor speak about him," she smiled when saying his name.

"What about Trevor's younger brother?"

"Tanner? No, the only thing I knew about him was that he was living in Alaska. I asked Trevor about him once and he told me to never mention his name again. I think they had a fight or something and Trevor was pretty mad at me for asking."

"What about your sister? Could you please..."

Chloe's eyes widen when she looked past my shoulder and a look of fear showed on her face. "Sorry, I've got to go." I watched as she raced over and retrieved Grimm from the play area and together, they raced back to her car.

I saw a large black SUV with tinted windows parked on the street. It looked to be the same one that was at Madison's funeral service where Trevor, Jake, Leah, and Ava got in and left. I tried to read the license number but it was too far away. When Chloe sped down the street, the black SUV followed. That explained a lot why she was afraid to be seen with me. I had to find out who and why they were following her.

I loaded Oz and Annie into the back seat. I had one more stop and that was back to the golf course. I wanted to talk to the course manager. "How can I help you?' she asked.

"The day of the charity event," I began.

"Please, don't bring up that subject. It has been nothing but a nightmare. First that poor girl gets murdered, then that nasty lady detective keeps showing up. If she comes here one more time, I'm going to scream. Then there's the press. Don't get me started on them, but the worst are the podcasters and crime buffs. Do you know this one group of kids tried doing a podcast while we were having another tournament. I had to call the police to have them removed. What a mess! Please, don't tell me if you're one of those. I just don't have the time or patience to deal with this mess anymore."

I handed her my business card and she eyed it with scrutiny. 'You're a private cop?"

"Yes, I'm investigating the murder of Madison Quinn and I represent the lady who the police are trying to pin the murder on. I've known her for a long time and I know she didn't do it. The reason why I'm here is because during the day of the charity event, I noticed a young girl walking around taking pictures."

"Yes, she works for "Big Daddy's Studio."

I smiled. "Thanks, you've been a big help."

"Is that all?" She questioned.

"Yes."

I called Big Daddy's Studio and we planned to meet in the morning.

Chris's truck was parked in front of our house, but he was nowhere in sight. After I unlocked the front door, the guys bolted inside and I could hear the TV playing in the living room. The kitchen counter was a mess, peanut butter and jelly spilled all over and an empty bread wrapper was on the floor. "How did you get inside?" I asked.

He let out a slight chuckle while focusing on the TV. "The patio door was unlocked."

'Why aren't you keeping an eye on Leah, like I asked you?"

"I followed her to the hospital, but then I was hungry and bored so I came here."

"And?"

"She met some guy wearing a long white coat."

He shoved the last of the sandwich into his mouth. "What did this guy look like?" I frustratedly asked.

"You know, he just looked like a guy in a long white coat. There were a lot of them there."

"Please tell me you took a picture of him with your phone."

"Nope, I was out of charge. It was boring just watching the glass shop, so I watched a movie and used up all my battery. I'm watching the end of the movie now. I rented on it your Prime account."

My patience was wearing thin. I grabbed the remote from his hand. It was all sticky from the jelly and I turned off the TV. "Hey, it was almost over. Why did you turn it off?" He cried out.

"Look, I paid you fifty to do one simple task. What did you do? You wasted it all on food and now all you can tell me is that she met some guy in a long white coat. You didn't think to follow them?"

"Wes, watching some lady is not exciting. I'm your partner. I should be by your side investigating the important stuff."

"Chris how many times do I have..."

An angry voice screamed from the kitchen. "Christopher Andrew Legget! Get your butt in here right now and clean up this mess." Marti appeared in the doorway and by the look on her face she was out for blood.

"Can't it wait until Wes gives me back the remote so I can watch the end of my movie?" He replied as he grabbed the remote out of my hand.

"Wrong answer," I thought. I've seen that look before, it's best not to mess with the bear.

I stepped out of the way as she stormed into the living room and wrestled the sticky remote from his hand. She pulled him off the sofa by his ear. He cried and whinnied not being able to see the end of the movie.

Marti stood with her arms crossed and a scowl on her face as she forced him to clean up the mess he had made. It took him an hour to do a five-minute job. Once he had finished, she escorted him to the front door. Before she shoved him outside, I calmly remarked, "Chris, just to let you know, it was the dude dressed in black that drove around on a Harley who killed the girl and her father."

"Wes, why would you spoil the end like that?" He cried out.

Marti slammed the door closed behind him and turned the lock. We high fived each other.

Chapter 12

Marti had left a note on the kitchen counter. "Had to go to work early today, see you tonight. Love you."

While I was rummaging inside the fridge for something to eat, my phone rang with a familiar sound. "Hey Cowboy, I hear you've gotten yourself in the middle of another hornet's nest. Meet me at the restaurant in thirty minutes."

Now that Rod was back in town, I was excited I'd no longer have to deal with Detective Sanchez. I was positive Captain Ross would assign him the case.

The smell of bacon and coffee filled the air as I stepped inside. I chuckled as I walked past the large round table in the center of the room where the same old white-haired men sat shooting the breeze and drinking their morning coffee. Rod was at our usual booth and I had to shield my eyes from the bright colored Hawaiian shirt he had on; his skin was dark brown from being out in the sun. Instead of his usual pale, pasty look, there was even a smile on his face. I stopped and looked around the room before sitting down. "What are you doing?" He asked.

"I'm to meet my friend who has bloodshot eyes and wears a wrinkled suit he has lived in for the past twenty-four hours. Instead of a smile he'd be scowling and drinking coffee instead of tea. So, who are you?"

"Cut the crap, Cowboy! Plunk your sorry excuse for a private investigator down."

He handed me a bag and inside was a bright Hawaiian shirt almost like his. "Wow, this is great! We could be Hawaii Five-O of the valley." I jokingly remarked.

"The one thing I didn't miss was your attempt to be a comedian. You should be arrested for impersonating one." He handed me a second bag and I started to look inside. "Hey, that's not for you. It's for Marti."

The waitress appeared with a large orange juice. "Where's Nancy? I thought she would be here."

"She's got the day off. I went ahead and ordered for us."

I'm glad to see you. Maybe now that you're back, you can take over Detective Sanchez's investigation. I'll be glad to get her off my back." I commented.

Before he could say anything, our waitress returned with two brain muffins and bowls of fruit. "What's this? Are you still on that damn heath food kick?"

He gave me his usual smirk and replied, "It wouldn't hurt you to make wiser food choices. I see you've been stuffing your face with Betty's apple fritters. You're getting a little pudgy around the middle."

"Hey, I'll have you know that is all muscle."

"Go on and keep telling yourself that, Pudgy."

As I struggled to swallow what must've been the week-old muffin, he talked about their time in Hawaii and all the things they had done and places they had visited.

Once he finished, I asked. "When do you start back to work?"

"Sorry, Cowboy, but the captain is sending me to Arizona. I've been enrolled in officer training classes."

"What? Does that mean you're not taking over Detective Sanchez's case? You can't do this to me. She's a real pain in the you know what," I asked.

"I've heard all about her from the guys in the department. She is a real ball breaker from what they've told me, and that she has her sights on yours if you keep interfering with her case. I suggest you'd be better off doing your fraud cases and staying away from her."

"Well, that's not going to happen. She has her sights on one of my friends as her main suspect," I commented.

Our waitress returned with the check and Rod nodded in my direction and placed it down in front of me. "Listen Cowboy, just let Detective Sanchez do her job without you interfering. See you in a month." His parting remark as he stood up was, "She's not going to have your back like I had in the past. Just stay far away from her."

I sat alone with a blank, dejected look on my face. He was my only chance to get that crap of a detective off my back. Now that wasn't going to happen. I needed some time to think, so when our waitress walked by, I ordered one of their warm cinnamon rolls with lots of butter.

Since I had talked to three of Trevor's ex-wives it was time to talk to the man himself. But first, I had to stop by Big Daddy's to pick up the photos.

As I walked into the office a strikingly beautiful young brunette asked, "Can I help you?"

"Big Daddy is expecting me. I'm Wesley Johns."

She escorted me into his studio. "He'll be right with you."

I glanced around the room checking out the walls lined with photos. There was one with Oz and Annie. "Hey, Wes, great to see you again."

Big Daddy was just that. He was a large, middle-aged man, with a dark brown beard, and his long brown hair was tied into a ponytail. I cringed when his large hand engulfed mine and squeezed like a vice as we shook. "I like your new digs. You even got a receptionist. Pretty impressive." I said.

He chuckled and slapped me on the back so hard that I almost fell over. "I owe it all to you. After that last case you had been working on, the word got out and now everyone wants Big Daddy's Studio for their events.

He led me over to the large table in the center of the room where about sixty photos were scattered about. "As you can see, not a lot of photos were taken since the golf tournament was just getting started. Opal, my assistant, was able to sneak a couple of shots of the murder victim before the police made her step back."

I scanned through the photos and a couple caught my attention. I pushed them aside and asked if he could make me some eight by tens. Also, on two of the photos I asked him to zoom in on my suspects. He said he'd have Opal drop them by the house on her way home from work.

The corporate office of Quinn Rentals had the top three floors of a five-story, nondescript brick building on the west end of downtown. The two floors below were an accounting firm and freight brokerage company. When the elevator doors opened, I stepped out into a very bright and stark looking lobby. The off-white walls and basic office furniture made the place feel sterile and cold. There were no plush chairs for visitors to sit in while they waited. Just cold steel straight back ones as if they had been here for decades. Instead of a large desk at the far end of the lobby where the receptionist would be sitting there was a wall with a small counter. A sign on the pebble glass window read, "Ring Buzzer."

I pressed the buzzer and when the frosted glass window slid open a young man appeared, "May I help you?" he asked in a brash tone.

"Yes, I would like to see Trevor Quinn."

"Do you have an appointment?"

"No." I showed him my press credentials. He gave them a once over in a nonchalant manner and said. "You must have an appointment."

He started to close the window when I replied, "How do I get an appointment?"

After an eye roll, he handed me a business card. "Call his secretary."

He closed the window leaving me standing there alone.

I rang the buzzer again. When the unpleasant man opened the window again there was a disgruntled look on his face, "Now what?" he shouted in an indignant tone.

I gave him my patented Wesley Johns smile and said. "How do I reach his secretary? There's no phone number on the card."

A huff came from his mouth, "Fill this out and put it though the slot when you're done. Now good day." He closed the window so hard I thought at first that the glass would shatter.

I was about to step out of the building when a voice said, "Mr. Johns?" I turned and was shocked to see Ava Quinn standing behind me. "What are you doing here?" she asked.

"I came to talk to your ex." A frightened expression showed on her face and she quickly grabbed my arm and ushered me down to the first floor without saying a word. The sign on the glass door read, "American Logistics." Once inside her office she closed the door.

"Are you crazy? If he finds out you're poking your nose into his business, who knows what he'll do?"

Ava Quinn sat behind a large wooden desk and clasped her hands together. "How is it that you're working in the same building?" I questioned.

"This company was here before Trevor's company took over the top three floors."

"Don't you think that is strange you both work in the same building?"

"Trevor is a very controlling and paranoid man. Once he heard I had accepted a job here, within a month he moved their whole corporate operations to this building."

"Why would he do that?" I questions.

"To keep an eye on me." Unlike the first time we met at Madison's Celebration of Life, Ava's cool and somewhat bossy attitude had changed to a frighten demeanor and kept focusing her eyes on the frosted glass door behind me whenever someone walked by.

"Tell me what you know about Madison and her marriage to Trevor."

It was like she flipped a light switch. She was back in control as she graciously moved to the edge of the desk and crossed her legs making sure that I noticed her short skirt. "What is it you want to know?" she asked in a sultry tone.

"Everything," I replied.

"Trevor came to me after their first date. He was smitten with her and wanted to file for a divorce from Chloe. I mentioned it would be a big mistake. She never loved him. The money grabbing whore just wanted his money. It was bad enough he had married Chloe, who was no different from her younger sister. I think they planned it to where Chloe would get a big pay out and Madison would clean out the rest of his money. Those two were real scam artists. Thank God, Jake was there to keep an eye on them. He saw what they were up to."

"Do you think Jake murdered Madison?"

Ava stood up and went back to her chair. "I wouldn't put it past him. The man is an animal. You be careful. I heard stories about him and people who suddenly disappear."

"Like Trevor's younger brother Tanner?" I commented.

A sudden panic expression appeared on her face as she looked past me. I turned in time to see a large shadow figure standing on the other side of the frosted glass door.

"Mr. Johns, I hope what I have told you is confidential and won't appear in the paper." She blew out a sigh of relief once the figure moved away from the door and you heard the floorboard creaking off in the distance. Ava stood up and went over to open her office door. She peeked down the hallway to make sure whomever stood outside her door was nowhere in sight. "I appreciate you coming in, but I don't think our company is right for your needs."

"Ava just one more question. Why did you and Trevor get a divorce."

"Talk to the wino, she's the one who wrecked our marriage. Another bitch out to get her hands on his money. Good day Mr. Johns." Just before she closed the door, she slipped a piece of

137

paper in my hand. I jumped when the glass door slammed hard into its frame.

I wanted to see what she had written but thought it was best to wait until I was back in my truck. I read on the back of the business card what Ava had scribbled. "These walls have ears. Meet me at Gigglies at seven tonight."

Trevor's ex-wives had painted a picture of this man whom I was starting to hate. I so badly wanted him to be responsible for Madison's murder. He needed to pay and spend the rest of his life behind bars if only I could prove it.

I had driven a block when I spotted a black SUV with tinted windows about two cars back. I turned left and so did the SUV, then I turned right and again, so did the SUV. Now I was paranoid that Trevor had Jake following me. I weaved in and out of the downtown core until I was sure I had given him the slip.

I had a feeling that every potential suspect had something to hide, even Chloe. Especially after Ava had told me she only married Trevor for his money. If she wanted me to find out who murdered her sister, she needed to come clean. Since I had hit a brick wall talking to Trevor, I thought I'd reach out to his older brother Robert. After searching social medias and the insurance data base I located him living and working in San Francisco. After the fourth ring a voice answered, "This is Robert."

"Afternoon, my name is Wesley Johns and I'm investigating the death of Madison Quinn." The phone went dead. I tried calling two more times and each time my call went unanswered. Great, I thought, another name to add to my suspect list. Was he in town the day Madison was murdered and if so, what would've been his motive to kill her?

I turned my attention to Tanner Quinn. I tried every database, public record, social media and it was as if he had fallen off the grid. No current address, credit card or phone activity, nothing. I even called the Alaska State Police and they had no record of him. The officer I talked to offered to do a little checking and would get back to me. The story was that Tanner, Trevor and Jake supposedly traveled to Alaska together but only Trevor and Jake returned. A knot grew in my throat which made it hard to swallow.

Marti stepped inside looking exhausted and handed me a large manila folder and remarked. "This was on the front doorstep." I glanced inside and saw the photos big Daddy promised he'd send over. "Hey, Nancy text me and said Rod gave you a package to give to me. Where is it?"

"I left it out in the truck. I'll be right back." No sooner had I stepped outside than I saw the black SUV parked down the street. Before I could closed the front door, Marti yanked the package out of my hand and disappeared into the bedroom. She returned wearing a sexy bright Hawaiian dress.

"Wow, you look great!"

"I like it. How about you take me out to dinner so I can show it off?"

"Okay, but first I promised to meet someone, then we can grab something to eat. Do you want to come along?"

"Does this have something to do with the case?"

"Yes."

She eagerly bounced up and down on the balls of her feet. "I'm all in. What do you need me to do?"

As we drove to Gigglies, a local gathering place, we came up with a plan for Marti to do some covert investigating. She sat in the truck while I went inside. Alone in a booth by the front door was

Ava sipping on a martini. I slid in across from her and noticed something different about her. Her hair was draped over her shoulder and her dress left nothing to the imagination. She pursed her ruby red lips and proceeded to slide around the booth until she was almost in my lap. "Would you be a dear and order me another one of these?" she asked in a very sultry tone. I let out a slight smirk when I noticed Marti in the next booth with smoke coming out from her ears.

"Wesley, I like the sound of your name. Are you married? Not that it matters."

"Yes."

"What a shame." She emptied her drink in one gulp. I signaled to the barmaid for another along with a club soda.

Things started to get awkward as we waited for our drinks. I tried to put some distance between us when Ava started running her fingers through my hair but she just inched herself closer. Marti looked as if she was about to climb over the booth and take matters in her own hands. I was so relieved when our drinks arrived.

"How well did you know Madison?"

"I didn't ask you here to talk about Madison, Honeybun. I thought it would be nice if the two of us got to know each other better. Let's not ruin the moment. Do you think your wife would be willing to share you?"

"If not Madison, how about your marriage to Trevor?"

Ava displayed a pouty look and in one gulp emptied her glass again and signaled for another. "Wouldn't you rather we go somewhere private instead of talking about my marriage or that Madison bitch?"

I was getting nowhere and if this continued on much longer, there might be another murder as I glanced over at Marti. "So, why did Trevor dump you?"

She let out a heavy sigh. "What the hell! He didn't dump me. I dumped that two-timing jackass. I found out he was seeing Leah behind my back and I got wind that he was going to file for divorce. Satisfied? Now can we change the subject, Honeybun?"

"Just one more question and then I will stop with the questions.

"Promise?"

"I promise. Tell me about Trevor's two brothers?"

After letting out a disappointing sigh, "Tanner was a cutie. If I had met him before I met Trevor, then I could see us hooking up. He was kind, thoughtful and fun. Trevor was all about the business, day and night, but not Tanner. The nights Trevor was working late or out of town, Tanner and I would go out for a drink, dinner or a movie. He was my best friend."

"Why not marry him after Trevor dumped you?"

Fire shot out of her eyes, "Look, I already told you! Trevor did not dump me."

"Do you know why Tanner went to Alaska?"

"He wasn't cut out for the business. He was a free-spirited sole that didn't like being confined to one thing. He hated the business."

"How about Robert?"

"He was just like Trevor, all about the business. At first, they worked well together but then something changed between the two of them and they fought and argued all the time. Trevor would come home at nights in a foul mood and just rant about his brother. Now are you finished? How about we talk about the two of us?" Ava shifted her body to where she was almost on my lap.

"What about us?"

She let out a slight giggle. "Men, sometimes you can be so dense. Here I am practically throwing myself on you. What do you say we leave this place? I know a good motel close by that's discrete. Your wife will never know as long as you don't tell her. It's for sure I won't." She leaned over and kissed me on the ear. "But first I could use another drink. Would you be a sweetheart and order me another while I go to the lady's room?"

No sooner had Ava slid out from the booth that I signaled for Marti to follow her. The barmaid dropped off Ava's drink and the tab. I started to get worried when twenty minutes had passed and neither one had returned. I was about to make sure everything was okay when Marti slid onto the bench next to me.

"Don't worry, Honeybun. She's not coming back."

"Why not?"

"Once inside the ladies' room she called someone. From what I could hear, she asked them to come pick her up."

"Did she say anything else?"

Marti reached for Ava's drink and took a couple of sips. "Oh yes, she had quite a lot to say. She told me she didn't buy the newspaper story, and she made it perfectly clear to stay out of her personal life!"

"Of the four ex-wives Ava seems the sharpest of the group. Unfortunately, she played us tonight."

"What do you mean us? She played you, Honeybun. Now how about that dinner you promised your sexy secretary is starving."

Chapter 13

I stomped on the brakes hard and came to a screeching halt. Parked out front was "The Lady," a nineteen forty-nine Pontiac Cheftain shimmering and shining in the morning sun as it cast its light upon her.

Denise, Janice, Stephanie, Marklynn and even Willy stood in a line with beaming smiles showing off their hard work to bring her back to life. I was so excited that I had trouble unbuckling my seat belt. Willy held out the keys and without hesitation I grabbed them. "The Lady" looked as if she had just come off the showroom floor. After my fourth trip around checking out every inch of the gleaming metal and chrome I hugged each and every one of them, including Willy. It was Janice who made me promise not to let Chris near or she'd make the call to a friend of a friend. We all laughed.

I turned the key and the engine roared. Chills raced throughout my body and my heart pounded hard in my chest. Denise promised to drive the truck home after she finished working on an old Chevy. I was disappointed when I found Marti in the bedroom getting dressed and not outside waiting for me.

After ten painstaking minutes of waiting, I opened the front door and her first words were, "Why isn't the Bird in the driveway? Who's car is that?" As she pointed toward "The Lady."

Beaming from ear to ear, I said, "Ours."

"What!" She screamed. Both Oz and Annie were already in the backseat hanging their heads out the window openings. "Wes, really, whose car, is it and why are they in the backseat?" I ushered her over and opened the front passenger door for her.

"Okay, I'm impressed. This is really a beautiful car, but why are we going to the show in this and not the Bird?" She remarked.

"Do you remember that night when we pulled into Willy's on a previous case and you made a derogatory remark about the rusted, old and banged up pile of junk parked up against the back fence?" I asked.

"Yea, so what?"

"This is that pile of crap! I rescued it from the junk yard."

She broke out in laughter, "No one in their right mind would throw good money down the drain on such a piece of junk. Okay, you've had your fun and games, come clean or else I'm going to call in one of those IOUs from Scrabble. Whose car is this?"

At the stoplight I reached over and took out a small photo album and a piece of paper from the glovebox and handed it to her. The light turned green, and my eyes moved from watching out the windshield to her. She slowly read the piece of paper, the title showing we were the owners. She carefully studied each photo that Willy's crew had taken throughout the restoration process. After she closed the book, I smiled as she blankly stared out the windshield.

There were seven neatly parked Detroit Steel beauties in front of Betty's. When I backed into a space, everyone stopped talking and were staring. I smiled at their shocked expressions as soon as I climbed out. Marti still sat frozen in the front seat still trying to put all the pieces together while I went inside to get our treats. Upon my return, everyone from our car group plus others were checking out our new ride. Doug and a few others had their heads under the hood. Doris, Lois, and Marsha were questioning Marti. I had pulled off the biggest surprise of them all. I stood there like a proud papa showing off his newborn baby.

Mike shouted, "Now that everyone's here, let's fire up these engines."

As eight classics cruised to the park, the initial shock had worn off and Marti became herself again. Parked at a light she reach out and punched me hard in the shoulder. "How could you keep this a secret from me?"

Today's car show was being held in a small town ten miles down the road where they blocked off the main street so we could display our cars. A crowd quickly gathered around to check out "The Lady". At first Oz wasn't sure what to do but he soon figured it out and took his place in front. Marti and Annie went off shopping as I sat back and enjoyed Betty's fried deliciousness while watching everyone marvel at the beauty parked before me.

Marti and Annie had been gone for two hours so Oz and I went looking for them. After an hour of searching, we gave up and went back to our classic. A crowd had formed around "The Lady" and people were taking pictures of Marti dressed in period clothing. She looked amazing. I grabbed my camera and snapped off a couple of shots of her and the guys posing.

Once the crowd dispersed, Marti explained she found a vintage clothing shop just a block over. She suggested we go back and look for an outfit for me. I had no intention of dressing up in a period outfit until she whispered something in my ear. With some remorse, I agreed and I cursed under my breath, "That damn Scrabble board." It was close to noon when we stepped out of the vintage shop. Marti draped her arm around mine and with both Oz and Annie out front on their leashes we strutted down the street looking as if we had just come out of a time warp. As soon as we turned the corner the men from our car group started giving me a hard time.

We posed in front of "The Lady" as cameras clicked away. I was about to return to my chair to escape the local paparazzi when a voice sang out, "Wes how about one more shot?" I turned to see Jackie, one of Royce's reporters from the paper. "This'll make a great story for the society section." I cringed at the thought of having my picture in the paper.

Today instead of the usual pizzas, Donavan was treating us to his new line of sandwiches. While we ate, I fielded questions about my investigation into Madison's murder. It was a relief when Doris thankfully changed the topic, suggesting all the club members dress up in period clothing to match the years of our classics. I wished I had my camera as Doris, Marsha, Lois and the other ladies from our car group dragged their men to be outfitted. Jeff, our club's somewhat bachelor, remarked, "Wes, now you see why I never married. I have no one to..." Just then his cougar of a girlfriend, Sunshine, pulled him out of his chair and they rushed to join the others.

Alone I closed my eyes for some peace and quiet. "How come you're dressed in those nerdy clothes? Where's your T-bird?" Fear raced throughout my body as he spoke. Standing before me was Chris.

"Chris, what are you doing here?"

"Denise and I thought we would come and check out the cars. Why are you sitting over here? Why is Oz sitting out in front of this old car instead of the T-bird?" I could see the gears in his head working overtime to figure out when it suddenly dawned on him. "Holy Crap! When do I get a ride?" He started to take a closer look when Denise sacrificed her body by placing it between him and car. He tried to push her aside, but when she whispered something in his ear, he quickly backed away.

When a street vendor walked by shouting, "Hotdogs" Chris raced after him. I asked Denise what she said to get him to back away so quickly. She giggled and jokingly remarked. "Janice would cut off his you know what if anything happened to your car." I broke out in laughter.

I closed my eyes for a second time when an unpleasant voice interrupted my solitude, "I didn't know it was Halloween. Who are you supposed to be, Clyde Barrow? Where's Bonnie?" Detective Sanchez snidely remarked.

"What are you doing here? Don't you have anything better to do than ruining my day? Go get yourself a hotdog or something and leave me alone."

She leaned down and put her face inches from mine. "You think you're so smart. Well..."

"Get out of my husband's face you tramp!" Marti shouted, as she stormed over and tossed her shopping bags on the ground and got into the detective's face. Her tone was sharp and to the point.

"What did you call me?"

"Maybe you should get yourself some hearing aids. I called you a tramp! You're a poor excuse for a police officer. Why don't you crawl back to Miami and leave us alone?"

Not fazed by my wife's attitude, Detective Sanchez dangled a pair of handcuffs and threatened to arrest her. I leaped out of my chair and placed my body between them and demanded she leave.

"Who are you to tell me what to do? I'm an officer of the law. I don't have to put up with you or her crap. Now get out of my way, I'm going to arrest her for threatening an officer."

A crowd gathered to watch Marti and Detective Sanchaz shouting at each other. Some took pictures, others were videoing them. "I'd like to see you try!" Marti defiantly said. "It'll be your ass that'll get in trouble not mine!"

Not willing to back down, Detective Sanchez made a big mistake grabbing Marti's arm. A deep guttural growl echoed from behind. "What you are hearing is Oz, advising you to gently let go of her arm," I calmly commented.

But Detective Sanchez didn't let go, instead, she tightened her grip causing Marti to whimper out in pain. Oz pushed his body to be between the ladies and showed the detective his pearly whites while letting out a deeper and more serious growl. If she didn't release Marti's arm soon, his massive body would pounce. The Detective released her grip and slowly stepped back all the while pointing her finger in Marti's face, "This isn't over between us. There will be one day when that mangy mutt won't be around and I'll....", her voice trailed off.

"You'll what?" I harshly remarked placing my body between the two of them. "I suggest you leave before..."

 Before I could finish my sentence, the detective commented, "Before what, you sick your doggie on me. Go ahead, then I'll arrest you both and send him to the pound."

I'd enough of her crap and threats. I pushed a button on my phone and after whispering a few words I handed the brash Chief Detective Sanchez my phone and said, "Someone here would like to speak to you."

The expression on her face was priceless as it turned a pale color. After shoving the phone in my hand, she gave me an eye piercing glare and remarked, "This is not over." Then stormed into the crowd shoving people aside.

"Who was that?" Marti asked.

"Her boss, Captain Ross." The was a long pause before we both broke out laughing.

Now that things had calmed down, for a third time I closed my eyes but Marti gave my arm a nudge and remarked, "Wes, look."

I broke out laughing as the others came waltzing around the corner dressed in vintage attire. The once reluctant men strutted as if they owned the moment. They all took turns posing in front of their classics as I took their pictures. Surprisingly, Jeff was having a good time all dress up in the sixties, wearing a leather head band, tie dyed shirt and multi color striped pants. But the best-looking couple was Eric and Lois. He had on a pin striped suit and she wore a flapper dress from the twenties. They looked great standing in front of their Model A.

I was relieved when they announced the trophy ceremony would be in thirty minutes. These clothes were starting to itch. Marti, along with the others, went up to see who won while I sat back and hoped for once I could close my eyes and relax.

Marti returned and proudly bragged, "Look, I won a trophy."

"You won a trophy? Don't you mean we won a trophy?"

"You got the Bird so I guess I get the Lady so in all reality, I won the trophy."

It had been a long and tiring day and I couldn't wait to get out of these itchy clothes. I went to work making enough room to park both classics in the garage. There would be some sacrifices to be made. The kayaks and a few other sport items were tossed into the back of my truck and the real trick would be to convince Marti it was time to part with them.

The walls of our bedroom were vibrating as the three of them were asleep on our bed. The noise was deafening. I settled for the recliner to watch an old western and I was almost off into dreamland when the patio door slowly opened. In walked our next-door neighbors. Carrie was holding a cake and Jack two bottles of wine. Marti must've heard our voices and staggered out from the bedroom sleepy eyed, "What are you two doing here?"

Carrie and Jack shouted in unison, "We're getting married!"

Marti rushed over and gave them a hug and almost crushed the cake. "When? Where? Are we invited?" Marti blurted out.

Carrie smirked over at Jack and excitedly said, "Right now!"

Both Marti and I shot each other puzzled looks before the front doorbell rang. Before I got a grasp of what was going on, Donavan, Irene, Jeff, Sunshine, Lois, Eric, Doug, Doris, and even Bruce and Sue all rushed inside, their arms filled with food and drinks. We all crammed ourselves in the living room and that's when I noticed a tall, pencil thin gentleman dressed in black standing by the patio door. The large black rimmed glasses and long black handlebar mustache gave me the impression of a cartoon character or an undertaker. "How did he get in our house and who is he?" I asked Donavan.

"Wes, relax, he's the minister."

We all watched in silence as he performed the ceremony. It was short and to the point. Once he said, "You can now kiss the bride," we all cheered, clapped and whistled.

After all the hugs and congratulations, it was time to eat. I froze when I saw Chris helping himself to the food. "What are you doing?" I screamed.

"I saw all the cars parked out front and thought you wouldn't mind if I joined in on the fun. Wow! Have you ever seen so much food? What's the big event?"

Denise rushed through the front door in a panic mode, "Sorry, Wes. He snuck out of the house. Come on, let's go home."

Chris fought to stay as she tried to pull him away from the food. When Denise yanked harder on his arm, the plate filled with food went tumbling onto the floor. Within seconds, Oz and Annie appeared and started vacuuming up the mess.

When Denise almost had Chris out the front door, to my surprise, Marti said, "Denise, it's okay if you both stay, the more the merrier."

I surveyed the room and couldn't find Sue or Bruce. It was Doris who said they had left right after the ceremony. Sue was having a hard time coping with everything that was going on in her life. It was close to midnight when everyone left. The new bride and groom were ushered off in a limo on their way to Vegas. The house was a mess, but I promised Marti I would help clean up in the morning.

We were too hyped up to go to bed, so Marti grabbed my hand and said, "Follow me."

It felt good to settle our bodies in the warm swirling water. She nestled her body into mine and we just sat in silence looking up at the stars. What a crazy day, I thought. Marti was the first one to speak, "My boss called this afternoon, and they want me to cover for a co-worker next week. I guess she fell and broke her leg. For now, I'll be gone for most of next week until they find a replacement." She leaned in and whispered," Will you miss your sexy secretary?"

Chapter 14

Royce, the editor from the paper sent a text and photo. "Wes, I thought you would enjoy this." On the front society section was the photo of Marti and me dressed in our costumes standing next to our new classic. I broke out laughing when I noticed Detective Sanchez dangling the pair of handcuffs. The caption read, "Officer tries to arrest Bonnie and Clyde." What made the photo priceless was the expression on the detective's face. I replied back, "I'd like an eight by ten."

"You got it. It'll be in the paper tomorrow," He replied.

Holding a cup of black gold in her hand and dressed in her uniform, Marti asked, "What's so funny?" After seeing the photo, we both had a good laugh at Detective Sanchez's expense. She reminded me of our dinner plans tonight and kissed me goodbye.

Now that things had settled down and was quiet, it was time to get serious figuring out who murdered Madison Quinn. Chloe asked me to find out who killed her sister and Sue wanted me to prove her innocence. As I waited for my computer to boot up, I thought back to when Ava had played us the other night and thought that maybe she had murdered Madison. But what would've been her motive? She claimed that both Chloe and Madison were nothing but a couple of gold diggers and only wanted to marry Trevor for his money and lifestyle. She made it perfectly clear she was the only one who had married Trevor for love.

My money was still on Trevor and his henchman, Jake. Even though they were my two main suspects, I wasn't counting out the four doctors until I had a chance to talk to each of them. Of all the suspects on my lists, three of them were the only ones at the charity event. As for the other, he could've been there and I hadn't noticed or wasn't in any of the photos Big Daddy's assistant had taken. The other thing that was running through my head was where was Tanner Quinn? Why hadn't anyone heard from him since moving to Alaska? That seemed suspect to me.

Although there were a lot of loose ends, it was time to take a deeper look into my two main suspects, Trevor and Jake. I typed their names into the insurance database website. This was where you'd go if you really wanted to know about someone's life.

Trevor Quinn was born in Arlington, Texas. His dad was in the military and as a family they moved around a lot. At the age of eighteen he enlisted in the army and did two tours in Vietnam as a supply officer. He was dishonorably discharged after serving two years in a military brig for stealing military supplies and selling them to black marketeers. After his time in the military, he moved back home and married Jennifer, his first wife. Two years later they moved to eastern Idaho where both Robert and Tanner lived. Together the three brothers started their rental business out of Trevor's garage. Public records showed that after being discharged from the military, Trevor led a clean life, not even one parking ticket.

Now with six equipment rental locations in eastern Idaho, the company then expanded their empire to be throughout the rest of the state as well as locations in Oregon, Washington, Utah, Montana, and Florida. They also had warehouses in Miami, Florida and Galveston, Texas. I paused and thought Florida, why there, none of the brothers lived there to oversee them. The more I thought about it, the stranger if seemed. I made a mental note to ask Trevor about them if and when he accepted my request for an interview.

Taking a closer look into his married life, what I found fascinating was that he took out a two-million-dollar life insurance policy on each of his wives. That meant, if Detective Sanchez or I were unable to prove he murdered Madison, the policy would pay him two million dollars. To this day, according to the insurance database website, he never cancelled the other policies on his previous ex-wives.

I text Catherine at the television station asking if she could have one of her reporters look into the company's financials. There might be a possibility they had a cash flow issue and needed the insurance money to bail them out.

I turned my focus on Jake Toleman. He was born in Boston, Massachusetts. He graduated with honors from West Point but for some reason they had blocked the rest of his military history. After his time in the service, it was like he had disappeared. No matter how much digging I did it was as if he didn't exist. No driver's license, no utilities or rent in his name, no tax returns, nothing. If I hadn't seen him in person or heard Ava and Chloe talk about him then I would've thought he was a ghost. The lack of information and what I had been told about him sent chills throughout my body. I sent an email to my buddy at the Pentagon to see if they could provide any additional information on Jake's military history.

As for Trevor's brothers, neither one served in the military. Robert currently resided in California and worked for a local manufacturing company. I'd like to know the reason he left the Quinn Rentals. I also thought it was strange when he abruptly ended our call when I mentioned Madison's name. It still bothered me that Tanner had disappeared from the radar. The Alaskan State Police had no record of him. The last time anyone had seen or heard from him was when he, Trevor and Jake went to Alaska. An alarm signaled about Tanner's sudden disappearance which gave me a queasy feeling.

Nothing really stood out when I started researching the four doctors. They each graduated with honors from medical school and residency. Only one of the four were married. It was time to pay them a visit. Before leaving the guys to guard the house, I grabbed the photos off the dining table that I had Big Daddy enlarged for me.

No sooner had I back out onto the street than I spotted the SUV that had followed me yesterday. I wanted to find out who the driver was, but without Oz by my side, discretion suggested I wait. Dr. Winston Lewis lived in an upscale condo near the hospital. After pushing the doorbell for a third time and no answer, I left him a note to call me. I had just stepped off the front porch when Dr. Lewis climbed out from a tan pickup. The man was strikingly good looking, his wavy black hair accented his facial features. He stood at least six foot five and there wasn't an ouch of fat on his body. If I didn't know better the man could qualify to be a model.

He gave me a puzzled look when he noticed me standing by his front door. I introduced myself as a reporter for the paper and there was a moment of hesitation in his voice before he invited me inside.

I sat at the kitchen counter watching him make up some kind of green juice concoction. I turned down his offer for a glass and instead asked. "Dr. Lewis..."

He interrupted me by saying, "Please, call me Win."

"Okay, Win, please tell me about your relationship with Madison Quinn. From what I understand it was more than just professional."

My question caught him somewhat off guard, but he quickly recovered by saying, "Who told you it was more than professional?"

I smiled, "You know us nosey reporters, we have ways to find out information."

After he swallowed down the last of the green juice, he stood at the kitchen sink looking out the window. "Tell me again why you're here?" He asked.

"I'm doing a story on Madison Quinn and the few people I have already talked to mentioned your name. I was hoping from what I had been told, you'd be able to give me some insight into her life."

When he turned from away looking out the window, he made sure to keep the counter between us. His facial expression had hardened. "I don't think it is any of your business. Like I told that lady cop, I worked with her on a few charity functions but that was all it was. I wish you people would quit poking your noses in my personal life. This conversation is over."

Without taking his hint, I slid over the photos of him and Madison at the golf course. He bent down to take a closer look. "To me, that looks like it was more than just a professional conversation. Take a closer look, and you can see the tears streaming down Madison's cheeks," I commented.

He abruptly looked up and said defensively, "I told her that I was upset about the way she was handling the event."

"Do you really expect me to believe that? Take a closer look at the way you're holding her hands. Both of your body languages suggest there was more than what you're telling me."

Dr. Lewis stared hard at the photos. The longer he stared at them the more deflated his attitude became. He moved around the counter still holding onto the photo and sat in the chair next to me. Not saying a word, I waited for him to speak. "Okay, okay, yes. Madison and I were involved. She was unhappy in her marriage and wanted someone to love her. Several times I tried to get her to leave Trevor. That day at the golf course she told me that we were over and that her husband had found out about us. She was worried that he would do something bad to me if we didn't stop seeing each other."

"How long were you together?"

"Six months. I pleaded with her to come away with me, but in the end, she just smiled. She told me she was only using me to make him jealous and that she never truly loved me."

"I bet you were shocked and heartbroken!"

"Yes, but you have to believe me. I didn't kill her!"

"So, after your breakup, what did you do?"

I watched as she disappeared into the crowd and realized she was just using me the whole time to get back at her husband. Those tears, those damn tears. She could turn them on anytime she wanted. I was furious and stormed off the course."

"You left before she was attacked?"

"Yes, and I can prove it. On my way home I received a text that I was needed at the hospital. They needed my opinion on a very sick patient. There were plenty of people who saw me there and they'll bear witness I couldn't have had anything to do with Madison's murder," he confidently remarked.

Dr. Lewis begged me not to print this in my article and I agreed just to keep up my cover. It wouldn't take much to check out his alibi, so I moved him to the bottom of my suspect list.

I had only driven a block when I spotted the black SUV again in my rearview mirror. After driving through a couple of subdivisions, I was able to elude them. Dr. Olrich Oslow was next on my list. He lived in a high-end neighborhood down by the river. His house was a modest two story modern and was about twice the size of mine. Within minutes a beautiful, tall middle-aged blonde answered the door. "May I help you?" she asked.

"Yes, my name is Wesley Johns, I would like to speak to Dr. Olrich Oslow if he's available?" I showed her my press credentials.

"May I ask what this is about?" She questioned.

"I'm doing a story about the murder of Madison Quinn. It was suggested by another colleague I talk to him."

She glanced down at my press credentials and said, "Sorry, he's not home." Before I could ask her to have him to call me, she slammed the door in my face.

Neither Dr. Andrew Burns nor Dr. Wayne Stewart were at home so I left notes for them to call me. It was close to noon and my stomach was letting me know I hadn't eaten anything all morning. Irene shouted as soon as I stepped inside, "Hi Wes, grab a booth. I'll be right with you."

It wasn't long after I had sat down that Irene placed a double cheeseburger with bacon, a side of tots and a large slice of coconut cream pie in front of me. I was halfway through eating my pie when the annoying man from Quinn's corporate office called and said, Trevor Quinn would see me at noon tomorrow. I was instructed not to be late. He also informed me that no cameras would be allowed and I was to come alone.

I was stuffed when Dr. Andrew Burns called and we agreed to meet at the small park next to the hospital in twenty minutes. When I stepped outside the diner, I spotted the black SUV in the parking lot across the street. So instead of pulling the truck out onto the street, I ducked down the alley behind the diner which led to the park.

Dr. Burns was sitting at a picnic table, dressed in surgical blues and wearing a long white coat. When I joined him, I noticed his lunch consisted of a turkey sandwich on wheat, some grapes and a slice of peach pie. The peach pie looked as if it had come out of a vending machine. "Dr. Burns, I'm Wesley Johns. Thanks for taking the time to talk. I'm doing a story about Madison Quinn's life and was hoping you could help me."

Just mentioning Madison's name caused him to lose his appetite and he wrapped up what was left of his food and placed it back in the bag. I could feel the slight chill in his voice when he said, "Why are you asking me about her? I hardly knew her."

I showed him a photo of them kissing in the woods at the charity event. He ripped the photo out of my hand and just stared at it. "It looks like you knew her more than just a little."

What he did next caught me off guard. He ripped up the photo and tossed it in his lunch bag. "I have nothing to say to you." He stood up, tossed the bag into the trash and stormed off.

Well, that didn't go as planned." I sat there watching nurses, doctors and other medical staff walk through the park coming and going. Why would he do something like that unless he had something to hide? I moved him up on my list of suspects along with Trevor and Jake. As for Dr. Lewis, he was high on my list until I confirmed his alibi. My phone lit up as Chris fired text after text begging for me to come by his house and pick him up. I ignored them.

I needed time to think and the best place was the dog park. I quickly stopped by the house and was able to get the guys into the truck and drive down the street without Chris noticing. They had a few friends to play with and while I sat in my favorite spot to keep an eye on them, I thought about that day at the golf course and tried to convince myself that Sue hadn't kill Madison. The real question was, if she hadn't then who and why. Any one on my list of suspects could be the killer, except for Dr. Lewis who claimed to have an alibi. Also, what was up with Dr. Burns? As soon as I mentioned Madison's name he panicked. When I showed him the photos of him and Madison, he ripped them up and tossed them in the trash. I needed to find out more about him. After an hour of playing, we headed home as soon as I turned onto our street there sat Chris in front of our house messing with his phone. I regretted the day he and Denise moved in down the street from us.

"Hey, Partner, I had texted you earlier but you didn't reply. I thought we could talk over the case. I have tomorrow off and I thought we could do some investigating. Whose our main suspect?"

"Chris when are you going to get it in that thick head of yours, we are not partners?" I harshly remarked.

I tried to open the front door without letting him inside but no sooner had I turned the knob than he pushed his way past me. Before I could unleash the guys he immediately started rummaging through the fridge. "Great! Leftover pizza."

Flustered, I went into my office and slammed the door. I needed to update my notes from my visits with Dr. Lewis and Burns, but mostly to get away from Chris. I flipped through the photos of the charity event hoping to find the missing piece of the puzzle so I could prove Sue hadn't murdered Madison. I examined one enlargement closely and asked myself, "Who are you? And what do you have to do with Madison Quinn?" I wondered if Detective Sanchez knew who he was? Fat chance she'd ever tell me even if she knew, unlike Rod if he was working on this investigation. I thought about paying Leah another visit, but when I heard the TV in the other room and remembered Chris would be lurking around and I didn't need him destroying anything else. It could wait until tomorrow.

I had just turned off the computer when Shawna Patton, AKA, the clown text for me to meet her tomorrow morning at six in the park. I replied with a thumbs up emoji.

Fortunately, Chris rushed home after receiving a text from Denise that dinner was ready. His parting comment was that he'd be here at seven to help with our investigation. I smiled knowing I'd be at the park.

Chapter 15

It was surprising the amount of people in the park this early on a weekday. Shawna was sitting alone on a bench along the river's edge. It was strange seeing her without her clown outfit. Her long red hair flowed in the breeze. "Hey," she remarked.

"Morning, I brought breakfast." Knowing Chris wasn't working today I made a quick stop by Betty's and got us some fried deliciousness. A pair of ducks sensing there might be some treats raced over squawking. Being the softy that I was I tore off a piece of my fritter and broke it in two.

"I come here a lot to think. It's so peaceful and I can relax." After taking a petite bite of fritter, she continued. "It's my down time after spending all day at the hospital. I hate seeing children struggle with their illnesses at such a young age." Her voice broke up a little as she talked about her kids in the children's ward. We both sat in silence and watched the dark, rushing water flow past us.

"Now that I've had time to think and put everything together after our last talk, I'll miss Madison. She visited the children's cancer ward almost every day. She also treated the children as if they were her own. There were days when she'd spend hours reading stories, pushing them around in their wheelchairs and watching movies. Whenever a new child was admitted, she appeared the next day with a teddy bear. The ward seemed a little brighter when she visited. Her smile was contagious and up lifting."

"It sounds like she had a heart of gold when it came to those children," I added.

After a long pause of staring into the water Shawna turned to me and said, "Wes, I liked her. I'll do anything to help you find out who killed her. The children miss her and keep asking when she's going to come back?" Shawna took a deep breath while wiping the few tears away. "I overheard the nurses at the nurse's station talk about how she was romantically involved with a few of the doctors. Everyone knew she was married but that didn't seem to stop her or them. One of the nurses commented that she had attended the event at the golf course the day Madison was murdered and saw her kissing Dr. Burns off in the trees. She also mentioned both Dr. Lewis and Madison were arguing about something. Shortly after that the poor lady was dead."

She pulled out a piece of paper and handed it to me. I raised my eyebrow when I read it. "There is one more thing I thought you ought to know. A couple of nurses wouldn't stop talking about this creepy guy who showed up at the hospital and started asking questions about Madison. He was wearing a dark suit, mirrored sunglasses and had a crew cut hair style. They got so creeped out that they called security. When security showed up it took three of them to usher the man out of the hospital because he was so big and resisted."

Shawna stood up, "Sorry, I have to go. I'm expected to be at the hospital by nine. One of my children is going home and I always like to be there to say goodbye. I'll let you know if I hear anymore. Thanks for the treats."

She had only taken a few steps when she stopped and turned, "I almost forget, the rumor around the hospital was that Madison was pregnant and that one of the doctors might be the father."

I sat there with my mouth wide open, "Could you please repeat that?"

She smiled, "She was pregnant."

There were still a few ducks hoping for some tidbits to come their way. After taking a couple more bites of my last fritter, I tore off what was left and tossed it to them. Once the treats stopped coming the ducks made their way down to an older couple tossing out treats.

The one phrase that kept running over and over in my head was, "She was pregnant." So, who was the father? Which one of the doctors? I knew after talking to Chloe it wasn't Trevor. What if he found out and sent Jake to kill Madison. I'll have to scrutinize the photos and try to find Jake at the golf course.

Before I reached my truck, my phone started going nuts, between texts it would ring. After the fourth call I answered, "Hey, Chris, sorry but I had to leave early."

"Why didn't you call me? Is this about our case? When are you going to come by and get me?"

"I need you to keep an eye on Leah Quinn. She's becoming our lead suspect. Do you think you can do that?"

"Awe, do I have to? I'd rather be with you. Maybe you could stop by and pick me up and we could get something to eat and then we could both stake her out together. I'm starving."

"Sorry, no can do."

"Could you at least stop by and give me some money?"

"Chris, you've got money, use your own. I have to go. I'll check in with you later and remember, wherever she goes you go. Understand?" I hung up before he started whining again.

I had just time to call on Dr. Oslow hoping to get a chance of asking about Madison before my meeting with Trevor Quinn. Just as I turned on his block, he was backing his black BMW onto the street. I followed him until he parked in front of a lawyer's office. It was Jackson Fritz Picket's office. I wanted to go inside but thought better of it and would talk to Jackson later. I parked down the street and waited. An hour and a half later, Dr. Oslow stepped out of Jackson's office with a grim expression. Now that Jackson was alone, I thought about asking him what was going on with Dr. Oslow but instead decided to follow the doctor. Unfortunately, traffic wasn't in my favor and I lost him.

Parked out front of the building of the five-story building was a non-descript black SUV. I took a photo of the license plate and shuttered at the thought of asking Detective Sanchez if she could tell me who owned the black beast.

The stark waiting room gave me the chills. I had second thoughts about meeting Mr. Quinn and his side kick Jake Toleman. I wished I had brought Oz along with me. I pushed the button at the window, and within minutes the same brass young man from the other day opened it. In an unprofessional tone he pointed to one of the old metal chairs and said, "Sit."

A small camera with a flashing red light was pointed right at the two chairs. On the outside I was trying to play it cool, but my insides were like a train wreck. Looking around the stark room, I decided it needed more comfortable chairs and maybe a plant or two and a couple of pictures on the wall. After sitting on this hard chair for thirty minutes my butt was getting sore. I was relieved when a door opened and the young man said, "Mr. Quinn will see you now. Do not attempt to shake his hand."

I was escorted down a long hallway, past several offices. As I passed by each one, I glanced inside, they were all vacant. The large wooden door at the end opened and there stood Jake Toleman. His hard, stern glare suggested this wasn't going to be a pleasant meeting. The black suit was tight on his muscular frame. The young man quickly disappeared into one of the offices we had passed.

"Stop!" Jake demanded.

"Why?"

"I need to make sure you're not carrying a camera or any recording devices. Place your hands on the wall."

"What if I don't?"

"Your meeting will be canceled."

Once he was convinced that I was clean he led me into a freezing office. It felt as if it was in the fifties. A window air conditioner was blowing out cold air. Just like the lobby, the walls were pale white with no pictures. In the center of the room was a large metal desk that looked to have been here when the building was built. Seated behind the desk was Trevor Quinn. He pointed toward the two metal chairs like they had in the lobby.

Before I sat, I glanced back to see Jake standing by the door with his arms crossed with a scowl on his face. "Mr. Quinn, I want to thank you for taking the time to speak to me after experiencing such a tragic loss."

After a long pause waiting for him to say something, I continued. "I was hoping you could give me some background for my story on Madison. How long were the two of you married," I questioned. Still not a word.

The silence was making me more uncomfortable and I hoped he would say something soon instead of staring at me with his beady little eyes. I did everything possible to keep my teeth from chattering as the room felt like we were inside a refrigerator. "Do you have any children?" I was hoping this would get him to open up, but no. "Tell me about how you and your brothers got into this business and if they are still a part of it?"

He raised his eyebrow and looked toward Jake before standing and walking around the desk. "Mr. Johns, let me be perfectly blunt. I don't like people poking their noses where they don't belong. If I feel they overstep then I must take action to make sure they understand it is in their best interest not to interfere any further."

The only noise in the room besides my teeth chattering came from the air conditioner. "Mr. Johns, I hope you get what I'm saying because…"

At the most inopportune time as usual, my phone rang. Before I could silence it, it went to voicemail. "Hey Wes, this is boring. She hasn't left the glass shop. Tell me where you are so we can meet for lun…" I shoved the phone in my pocket and smiled.

"This meeting is over Mr. Johns! Get him out of here." Trevor said in a harsh tone.

I felt a hand almost the size of a gorilla's grab my shoulder and lift me out of the chair. I was forcibly being escorted out of the room and was about to the door Trevor Quinn remarked, "Mr. Johns, for your sake, this is the last time we meet. If you continue to interfere with my business or life, then you'll make me act, and believe me when I say, you won't like it. Good day."

Before I could say a word, I was pushed down the long hallway and into the lobby. Once we were standing by the elevator, Jake spoke for the first time. "Don't ever come around here again." As soon as the doors opened, he shoved me into the lift so hard that my body went crashing into the other side. I couldn't believe how relieved I was when the doors closed.

It felt good to step outside and feel the sun's warmth. If I'd stayed in that office another minute, I would've been a frozen popsicle. I leaned up against the truck's passenger door and just looked up at the front of the building, trying to re-think what transpired in my meeting with Mr. Quinn. The man was cold, harsh and frightening, which made me wonder what was this other side he displayed to win over five wives. I knew for sure Trevor Quinn and Jake Toleman had my vote for killing Madison. Now I just needed to prove it.

I was about to get into my truck when out stepped Jake. He was wearing his mirrored sunglasses and an attitude of discontent. "I thought I told you to leave. Mr. Quinn will be leaving the building soon and I suggest you not be here when he steps outside," he harshly suggested.

Not sure where the courage came from but I smiled, "I'm on the public sidewalk so there is nothing you can do about it."

Talk about poking the bear. He stormed toward me with his fist balled up and a look that he was about to pound me into hamburger. He grabbed my shirt and lifted me away from the truck pulling my face within inches of his. His hot garlic breath made my stomach want to retch.

"This is the last time we talk. If I ever see you again, I will…"

From behind a voice said, "You'll what?"

Jake let go of my shirt and I fell back against the truck. He swung around to see Detective Sanchez standing with her arms crossed glaring at the man.

"Look, lady, this is none of your business. Now get the hell out of here before you get hurt."

She moved within a couple of inches from Jake's face. "Are you threatening a police officer? Because if you are, then you and I are going to have issues and I promise you, you will lose." She pulled out a set of handcuffs and dangled them in front is his face.

Without saying a word, Jake blew out a huff and angrily stormed back into the building.

I smiled at the detective until she started to unleash her fury on me. "Didn't I tell you not to poke around in my case? You're so lucky I saved you sorry ass before that gorilla beat you to a pulp. Do you know who you were messing with?"

"I was just standing here when this man came out of the blue and assaulted me," I started t explain.

"Right! You think I'm going to believe that? Maybe you and I should take a trip down to the station and have a little talk. What the hell's wrong with you? You solve a couple of homicides and think you are some master detective. Well, let me tell you, you need to keep out of my case. That man is someone you don't want to tangle with. Do you understand?"

"How did you know I was here? Are you following me?"

She let out a smirk, "Your buddy Rod asked me to keep an eye on you since he was off at the training center. So, get in your truck and go home and go back to investigating your simple little fraud cases."

Sanchez disappeared into the building as I got in my truck. On the drive home I wondered what I had gotten myself into. There was more to the story of Madison being the cheating wife. Both Trevor and Jake wanted to make sure I didn't poke my nose in their business. When I turned the corner, Chris was sitting on my front step playing with his phone and eating pizza.

"Hey, Wes, how come you didn't saying anything when I called?"

"Where did you get the pizza?" as if I didn't know.

"I thought since we were working on the case together, you wouldn't mind if I ordered one. I told Donavan you were okay with me putting it on your account. He followed me inside and went straight the fridge. After I fed the guys a treat, I reach for a root beer but there were none. Chris was drinking my last one. I opened the pizza box lid to see just the crust. The man was a human garbage disposal.

I went into my office and closed the door. After my morning with Trevor and Jake, the last person I wanted to deal with was Chris. I rocked back in my chair and closed my eyes. Shawna's words kept popping in my head, "She was pregnant." Did Madison tell anyone else, maybe her sister or one of the other ex-wives. Did Trevor find out and in a fit of rage show up at the charity event and kill her or did he send Jake? I couldn't remember ever seeing either of them there.

A pounding on the door brought me out of my trance. "Hey, Wes, I'm bored."

"Why don't you go home if you've bored?" I shouted back at him.

"There's nothing to do at home."

Then I had a brilliant idea. I opened my office door, shoved a twenty in his hand and suggested he go to the diner and get us a pie."

I waited for ten minutes making sure he was gone before I grabbed the guy's leashes and we headed to the dog park. Once they were inside their play area, I called Jackson Fritz Pickett and asked about his meeting with Dr. Oslow. He was caught off guard until I explained my suspicion about how he was possibly connected to Madison's murder. I left out the part that Madison was pregnant. He suggested I stop by his office in the morning.

With all this new information, I needed to touch base again with Chloe. Hopefully she could fill in some pieces missing from this twisted puzzle. She agreed to me at Sonny's BBQ Pit at six.

I raced home, dropped off the guys and fed them before making a hasty escape so not to run into Chris. My stomach growled when I smelled the wood fired smoke. Chloe was also early and she slid her body onto the other bench facing me.

"How is the case coming? Have you found out who murdered my little sister?" she asked.

"It's coming. Are you hungry?"

"Famished."

After placing our order, I remarked, "Chloe, did Madison ever confide in you about her marriage to Trevor or anything else?"

"I knew she was unhappy and wanted out. She told me not to tell anyone but she was seeing a doctor on the side."

"Did she tell you who?"

"No."

"Tell me about Trevor not wanting kids?" I asked.

"Before we were to be married, we had to agree to go to a doctor of his choice and I was to be placed on birth control pills. At the time I didn't think anything of it since we had never had any sexual relationship prior to being married. But I figured we'd be more intimate once we were husband and wife. Boy, was I wrong. Once married, we slept in separate rooms and never made love. Not once had we even slept together."

"Wow, didn't you find that to be strange? Then why the birth control pills?"

"Yeah! I questioned him about it, but he wouldn't give me a straight answer. He just demanded I continued to take the pills or else."

"Or else what?" I asked.

"I knew better not to ask."

"Do you know if this also happened to your sister?"

"Yea, and even Leah mentioned it happened to her too. I'm not sure about Ava. She never talked about the time she and Trevor were married."

Chloe looked relieved when our food arrived. She remained silent the whole time we ate.

I was still puzzled as to why they didn't have a sexual relationship. If it wasn't for sex, love or money then why marry all these women? Something wasn't right.

She got up and started to leave when I mentioned, "Did you know your sister was pregnant?"

Her body dropped like a rock onto the bench with her mouth gaping as she stared at me. "What did you just say?"

I repeated that her sister was pregnant, and she replied, "I thought that's what I heard. How do you know?"

"You didn't?"

"No, not a clue. She didn't say one word to me."

"Do you know if she told anyone else?" I asked.

"No. Do you think it was Trevor's kid?" She questioned.

"Not sure. It would be strange that she would be the one to have his child, don't you think?"

Chloe nodded her head and left without a word.

Chapter 16

Jackson's office was located in the old part of town near downtown. No sooner had I opened the front door when, "Come in Wes, I'll be with you in a minute. Have a seat in my office."

The wooden floors creaked with each step. Jackson appeared dressed all prim and proper as a lawyer should. "Tell me again how you think Dr. Olrich Oslow is involved with your investigation in Sue's case."

I gave him a short version about how he and Madison Quinn might've been having an affair and that he might've been her killer.

Jackson put his fingers together, leaned back into his chair and closed his eyes. There was a long period of silence before he spoke. "Interesting. Wes, all I can tell you is that a month ago, Dr. Oslow requested I start the paperwork as he wanted to divorce his wife. Then yesterday, it surprised me when he said he changed his mind and that they had reconciled their differences."

"Is the reason because he had been having an affair with Madison?" I asked.

"He didn't give me a lot of details for filing and then reversing the filing. It's interesting though about his timing on both. So do you have any proof that they were in a relationship?"

"Nothing solid. Did he offer up any reason why he had changed his mind?"

"No, just that he had changed his mind."

When his office front door squeaked open Jackson shouted, "Have a seat, I'll be right with you." Jackson then proceeded to write a name, address and phone number on a piece of paper. "Here, I use this agency from time to time on delicate divorce cases. Now if you'll excuse me, I have a client waiting."

After leaving Jackson's office, I called Dr. Oslow's office and was told he wouldn't be in today, so I went to visit him at his home. I had a lot of questions he needed to answer. One being, if he was the father of Madison's child? Since Madison and the child were no longer living there would be no need to leave his wife. I stood at the front door pressing the doorbell and after the fourth time and no answer I peeked through the front windows. The house was dark. I thought about paying the Dr. Stewart and Dr. Burns a visit next but instead I went home to think about where to go now in my investigation. I had so many loose ends and I wasn't any closer in proving Sue's innocents or finding out who really killed Madison.

My security detail was hard at work as they greeted me at the front door. Once they received their reward, they disappeared out to the back yard to chase squirrels. I started taking a closer look at the photos from the charity event examining each one closely trying to locate Dr. Oslow. My eyes were getting blurry and I was having had a hard time focusing when I felt a hand pushing on my shoulder. I screamed and leaped out of my chair. When I turned around to meet my attacker, instead there stood Marti's brother. "Jesus, Chris! What in the heck are you thinking sneaking up on me like that?" Once my heart stopped pounding hard in my chest I asked, "How did you get in? I'm sure I locked the front door."

He smirked, "But the patio door wasn't. Look, I brought some treats." He opened the lid and there were six of Betty's Southern Peach Fritters. She only made them on special occasions.

"Thanks, but I have a lot of work to do, so, if you don't mind, I'd appreciate it if you'd leave."

"That's why I'm here, Partner." He shoved the box of treats in my arms and started examining the pile of photos. When he picked up four photos, he held one up in front of me and said. "I've seen this guy before." I hadn't noticed but way in the back hiding behind a tree was my mystery man.

"Chris, how do you know him?"

"He's stopped by the bakery a couple of times."

"Did he ever say his name?" I asked.

He gave me a puzzled look. "Do you think he killed that lady?"

"Not sure. Call me the next time he shows up and try to stall him until I get there?"

"How am I going to do that?" Chris asked.

"I don't know. Give him a tour of the bakery or ask him to sign your guest book."

"We don't have a guest book."

"Chris use your imagination, think of something. You can do that, can't you?"

It was like talking to a rock. I just shook my head in disgust and walked away.

Once I heard the TV turn on, I slipped out the front door with the photo in my hand. Trusting Chris to do this one simple project was like asking me to stop eating Betty's apple fritters. It wasn't going to happen.

The bakery was quiet and Betty was in her office. "Wes, this is a surprise. What are you doing here?"

"I need your help." I handed her the photo and asked, "Have you ever seen this man?"

After putting on her reading glasses she took a long look and replied, "I've seen him come in here a time or two."

"What can you tell me about him."

"Not a whole lot. He asks questions about your car group. He asked about you before getting a cake donut with chocolate frosting, coffee and leaves. I just assumed he was interested in joining your club."

"Thanks. If you see him again, please call me asap. I need to talk to him."

"No problem. I have a few leftover fritters. You might as well take them home with you."

No sooner had I stepped out of the bakery than Betty remarked, "Wes, stop. That man you're looking for doesn't look like that anymore."

"What do you mean?" I questioned.

"The first time he showed was shortly after your group left for a car show. He looked just like the photo you showed me. Last weekend he showed up again, but this time he was all cleaned up, his beard neatly trimmed, nice clothes and drove one of those large boxy black SUVs. I hope this helps."

I was totally puzzled when I drove away. Who was he and why was he following Chloe and me? But what really gave me the shivers was why question Betty about me. Now that he cleaned himself up, I wasn't sure I could recognize him if he was standing next to me.

Paranoid, I kept an eye on my rearview mirror as I drove home hoping not to see a black SUV following me again. Just as I turned on my block my phone rang. I answered, "Wesley Johns."

"Mr. Johns?'

"Yes."

"I got your card. I'm Dr. Wayne Stewart."

"Ah, Dr. Stewart, thanks for calling me back. I would like to talk to you about Madison Quinn."

'Yes, I heard. What a shame, I really liked her. I'm at home now, are you able to come by so we can talk?"

Dr. Stewart sat out front when I arrived. He looked to be in his mid-thirties, wavy blonde hair, and a muscular frame. He started off the conversation with, "You're investigating her death? I thought the police were doing that?"

"I've been asked by a friend to also investigate. You're, one of the few doctors I don't remember seeing at the charity golf tournament that day?"

"Were you there?" He asked.

"Yes, I was going for the worst golfer trophy for a second year in a row."

He let out a chuckle. "If I played, I'd give you a challenge. I tried playing the game once and once was enough. No, I was out of town visiting my folks in Florida. Am I a suspect?"

I smiled, "Not that I know of. How well did you know Madison?"

"I worked with her on some of her charity events."

"So, it was just a professional relationship."

There was a slight hesitation. "Once after a meeting about one of the events, she asked if we could go out for a drink. She said she wanted to bounce some ideas off me. Later that night she hinted that we go somewhere more intimate."

"Did you?"

"We left the bar and promised to meet at a hotel. She was a no show. The next morning at the hospital this big scary looking dude came up to me and advised it would be in my best interest to stay away from her."

"Did you take his advice?"

"Are you kidding me? The man was a mountain, twice my size. From that day on I made sure to keep my distance from her. I even stopped helping with her charity events. Dr. Stewart made a point to show me his airline tickets and car rental receipts. After our talk I removed him from my suspect's list. That only left Dr. Oslow, Lewis and Burns.

I had just climbed inside my truck when I noticed the black SUV parked at the end of the block. It took me a while, but with some unexpected turns and running a few red lights, I lost them. I really wanted to know who was following me and why. I thought back about what Betty had said and started worrying it might be my mystery person, but what was his reason? How did he know me?

I stopped at a new sandwich shop in the area and went to the park to eat and think.

After removing Dr. Stewart from my suspect list, that still left a cast of suspects.

1) Dr. Oslow, who I had yet to question. Filed for divorce then changed his mind right after Madison had been murdered. Was he planning to divorce his wife to marry Madison? Did he kill Madison and now that she was dead, he cancelled going through with the divorce, or had Jake also paid him a visit.

2) Dr. Lewis admitted he and Madison were romantically involved. She asked him to take her away from her marriage from Trevor. He said she broke off the

179

relationship. Could it be that Trevor or Jake found out about them?

3) The elusive Dr. Burns. Ther was our brief meeting where he ripped up the photo and stormed off. Was their relationship serious, or did she go to him and say she was pregnant and that was the reason for her death?

4) Chloe. Even though she asked to find out who murdered her sister, I felt she wasn't telling me everything.

5) Leah Quinn. Our first meeting was a bust. She had a hard time focusing through her bloodshot eyes and pounding headache. The only thing I had learned about her came from either Chloe or Ava.

6) Ava Quinn. Maybe she should be higher on my list. Especially after the way she played us. I found it curious she continued to work in the same building after her ex moved his headquarters upstairs. Chloe mentioned in passing that she thought Ava still had a thing for Trevor.

After reconsidering each suspect, Trevor and Jake were still on top, now along with my mystery man. Who the hell was he and how was he involved with Madison's murder?

I peeked around the corner and blew out a sigh of relief, Chris had gone home. When I stepped into the kitchen I screamed, "Damn it, Chris, you could at least clean up your mess!"

After I cleaned the kitchen and the guys were fed, I was ready to crash in front of the TV. I had just sat down when the guys alerted me that someone was at the front door.

When I went to see what and set them off. I found a big envelope wedged between my front door and frame with just my name typed.

"Mr. Johns, I advise you to stop your investigation into the death of Madison Quinn. It's in yours and your wife's best interest." I was reading the message for a third time when my phone rang. The voice on the other end said in a harsh tone, "You've been warned." They hung up before I could say a word. I walked out to the street and looked both ways and sure enough parked down the street was the black SUV. They flashed their lights, then backed down the block and disappeared around the corner.

This was getting way out of hand and I wasn't sure what I had gotten myself in the middle of. I thought about calling Detective Sanchez but decided I didn't need her to lecture me. Maybe it would be in my best interest if I stepped back and suggest to Sue that she hire a professional. I needed time to think.

I shouted, "Who wants to go for a car ride?" I certainly wasn't leaving the house this time without my protection. I had just turned the corner when sure enough I spotted the damn black SUV in my rearview mirror. Once I got onto Main Street, I weaved in and out of the traffic hoping to lose them. When the light turned red, I quickly climbed out of my truck with my camera and clicked off a couple of shots. By the time I climbed back in, the light was green. It wasn't until the fifth light turned red; I was able to lose them.

I had an idea and drove to Willy's shop. It was quiet since most of the employees had gone home for the night. The only one left was Janice. The guys were happy to see her and so was I. "Wes, is there something wrong with the truck?" she asked.

"No, it's fine but I was wondering if you could do me a favor and loan me your rental for the night?"

She could tell by my expression that something had me worried. "Tell me what's happening?"

I gave her the short version and afterwards she went inside the office and brought a set of keys. She suggested I park the truck in the last empty bay to be out of sight. Once I had the guys loaded in the loaner, she commented, "Do you want me to make the call?"

It was a temping offer but I declined. I slowly turned the corner on my block and when I didn't spot the SUV I quickly parked in front of Carrie's and we hurried inside my house. I made sure every door and window was locked and the curtains were closed.

Even with Oz and Annie with me I had an uneasy feeling being alone in the house and almost wanted to leave and find somewhere safe to be. My thoughts turned to Marti. Maybe I should suggest she go and visit her folks for a bit. That would keep her safe until this mess got cleaned up. I knew she'd be home tomorrow so I had to come up with a plan and soon.

I had just settled in my recliner with Ruthie, my little league bat by my side, when the front doorbell rang. I jumped as the guys raced to the door barking. I peeked out our guest bedroom window and saw it was my worst nightmare.

I reluctantly opened the door and in stepped Detective Sanchez.

"So, what do I owe the pleasure of your visit?" I asked.

She walked in the kitchen and spotted my opened letter on the counter. I tried to pick it up and shove it in my pocket but she quickly ripped it out of my hand.

The silence was deafening as she read it over. Once she finished, she shoved it in her pocket and proceeded to glared at me. "This is why I insisted you drop this case. Not only do I have to find out who killed Mrs. Quinn, but now I have to babysit you. That is something I don't have the time for or want to do. Because of you, I now have to assign a patrol unit to drive by every hour for a wellness check just to protect your sorry ass. It's a waste of time and manpower. Stay away from this case before I have two homicides to solve."

Just before she stepped outside, she turned, stared into my eyes and pushed her finger into my chest. "I'm not your buddy who you can go running to every time you get yourself in trouble."

The house was quiet after she slammed the door. I thoroughly disliked that woman. Just as I sat down Ava called and wanted to meet her at Harvey Wallbangers in an hour. I almost declined thinking back to the last time we met and she played me.

The bar was nestled in the middle of a strip mall between a secondhand clothing store and vape shop. Ava sat at the table in the far back. She watched my every move with confidence as I stopped at the bar to order a double club soda with a twist of lemon.

Not wasting anytime, she said, "I talked to Chloe. We both agreed that you should drop your investigation into Madison's murder."

"Why? Is that why you asked me to meet you?"

"Yes." She reached into her purse, pulled out an envelope and slid it across the table.

"What's this?" I questioned.

She gave me a light smirk. "Payment for your services."

"Interesting. I never mentioned my fee to Chloe or that I would even charge her?"

"Nevertheless, take the money and get on with your life." She ordered another martini. "We need to put Madison's death behind us and move on. The police have their sights on the killer and I've been told an arrest will be coming soon." She quickly drained the glass and stood up. "Be a dear and pay the bartender. It seems I'm out of cash." She made a point to exaggerate her steps for the benefits of the two men sitting by the front door.

Not wanting to open the envelope I paid for her drinks out of my own pocket. I sat in the parking lot rehashing our conversation. Ava and Detective Sanchez both insisted I dropped the investigation. Something just didn't add up. I called Chloe but it went to voicemail.

Chapter 17

The bed shook violently as Oz and Annie leaped off and raced out their doggie door growling and barking. My heart pounded hard in my chest when I saw a shadow move across the bedroom window. I reached for Ruthie and slowly slid out of bed just as someone tried to open the patio door. I peeked out the bedroom doorway and suddenly heard a click, and the door slowly began to move. "Who's there!" I shouted.

A flash filled the room followed by a loud boom. I dropped to the floor after heard glass breaking. Another flash followed by a loud bang filled the room. My ears started to ring and footsteps shuffled across the floor. Where in the hell was my security team? Why weren't they barking? Did this intruder kill them? My body filled with rage thinking someone had harmed my guys. I had to act and act fast. I was about to leap up but abruptly stopped when a voice said, "Let's do this." There was a long pause before the other voice added, "Let's."

Before I could attack, something heavy slammed hard onto my chest. My arms were pinned and I struggled to free myself. "Get off me! Get off me!" I screamed. "When I get my hands on you..."

"Let's go to Huston, Idaho. It's that time of the year for their fun days event happening this weekend. There'll be a parade, a car show, fun activities for the kids, and best of all, lots of good food. Put it on your calendar. Starts early Saturday morning with a five K run. We'll see you there."

Slowly everything began to register. Another flash and boom echoed throughout the room. Looking up at two brown eyes staring at me I shut off the radio and turned on the light. Both Oz and Annie were giving me their puzzled looks as if to say, "He's almost on his way to the funny farm."

The rain pelted the side of the house and lightning filled the room followed by thunder that shook the house. The clock read five. I had forgotten to turn off Marti's alarm when she went out of town.

Both Oz and Annie's tails swayed from side to side with anticipation of breakfast. I had to admit I was kind of hungry too and since now I was wide awake, I decided to make my world-famous oatmeal, the perfect comfort food. I added sliced peaches, pecans, brown sugar, a touch of cinnamon, and lots of butter. By the time I added all the extras, there was more than enough for four people.

I had just dished up a bowl when someone started pounding on my front door. I glanced over at the clock and it wasn't even six-thirty. If it was that damn Chris, I'd either murder him or slam the door in his face. I was shocked to see a rain drenched, haggard-looking detective instead. Without saying a word, she pushed her way past me and went straight toward the kitchen. I watched as she shoved a heaping spoonful of my oatmeal in her mouth. "Gee, just help yourself," I sarcastically remarked.

Without much hesitation and between shoveling mouthfuls she asked if there was any coffee. I quickly pressed the button to start the pot brewing. The once cool and collected detective now had dark shadows under her eyes. Her makeup was a mess and her once neatly pressed clothes were soaked and extremely wrinkled. On one side of her jacket hung her badge and on the other side was her sunglasses. Her messed up hair looked as if she had been in a fight. After taking a couple of sips of hot coffee, she asked if there was any more oatmeal. I watched as she continued to shovel mouthful after mouthful until she emptied the bowl. "So, to what do I owe the pleasure of your company?" I asked.

She didn't answer, just stared into the half empty cup of black gold. I got up and fixed me a bowl when she finally spoke, "She's dead."

I turned and looked into her bloodshot eyes. "Who's dead?" I questioned.

She rambled on, "We got there too late. I haven't seen anything like that before in all my years on the force. The firemen did everything they could but in the end, it was too late. There's nothing left of the building but a pile of charred rubble."

"Who's dead?" I asked again.

With a blank stare, she looked up at me and said, "Leah Quinn."

"What! What happened?"

"The fire investigator thinks one of the blast ovens exploded causing the place to go up in flames."

"And Leah was inside?" I hesitantly asked.

"The firemen found human remains in the office. They were so badly burned, it was hard to identify who, but it must've been Leah Quinn. We won't know for sure until the coroner matches her dental records to confirm," she sadly spoke.

I stood there in utter silence, not sure what to say or think. All that kept going around and around in my head was that Leah Quinn was dead. When the detective's phone rang, we both jumped. "Yes, on my way." She then left without saying another word.

I had to go see this tragedy for myself. I loaded the guys in the loaner and we parked down the street from what used to be

Leah's glass shop. The concrete building was a shell from what it used to be, the charred-out roof had collapsed in on itself. Fire hoses were scattered about as firemen worked to clean up the smoldering mess.

First, Madison Quinn was murdered, and now Leah Quinn had died in an explosion in her shop. Something in the back of my head was telling me that this was not a coincidence. These two deaths were tied together, and I needed to find out who and why. I walked over to one of the exhausted looking firemen sitting by one of their trucks. "What a tragedy," I commented.

She slowly looked up at me and nodded her head. I could see where ash-colored tears had streaked down her cheeks. "What an ugly mess. This was my first time ever coming across a charred body and it will haunt me for years."

"What time did you get the call?" I asked

"The alarm rang at the station at three-forty-five. We got here just after four. The place was fully engulfed in flames."

"I heard from the police that one of the ovens got over heated and exploded," I added.

She slowly nodded her head. "That's what it looks like. We'll know more once the full report comes out."

"How long will that take?" I asked.

"Who knows. A mess like this could take weeks or even months. Look, I've got to get back to work." She struggled to stand as her body was exhausted. I watched as she joined the others.

I was almost to the loaner when someone shouted my name. "What are you doing here?" I turned to see a furious Detective Sanchez storming in my direction.

"I came to see for myself and take pictures for the paper."

"Where's your camera?" She demanded. The haggard, exhausted and mess of a detective that had come to my house was no longer. She was back to her arrogant and belligerent self. Neatly dressed and not one hair out of place. Her oversized sunglasses covered her once blood shot eyes and stained eye mascara.

"I left it in the car. I was on my way to get it."

She followed me to the loaner. "Where did you get this piece of crap?" she asked.

"My truck is in the shop."

"What's wrong with it?"

"Quarterly maintenance."

I wasn't sure if she was buying my story or not by the way she lowered her sunglasses and peered over the top. She was about to say something when another detective shouted, "Sanchez, we found something."

She opened the driver's door. "Leave!"

She walked toward the detective who called out her name. They were holding onto a slightly charred piece of paper.

I grabbed my phone and clicked off a couple of shots through the windshield.

We swung by the shop and picked up my truck. Janice handed me a piece of paper. "Just in case." I looked down at a phone number.

I called both Chloe and Ava. Neither one of them answered and I only left a message for Chloe to call me back.

The guys were chasing each other around the house while I sat rocking back and forth in my office chair trying to put everything in perspective. First Madison Quinn was murdered on the golf course at a charity event. Then mysteriously Leah Quinn's glass shop blew up killing her in the process. It just didn't make any sense. Nothing about this investigation made any sense.

A text from Shawna asked to meet her at the park in an hour. When I saw her sitting on the park bench in her clown outfit, I smiled. There was a long line of preschoolers eagerly waited for their balloon animal. "Give me a few minutes. I'm almost done," she remarked.

After the last kid went dancing off to join the others with her red balloon dog, Shawna turned to me and said, "Yesterday afternoon, I was called into the E.R. to help calm two children who were in a car accident with their parents."

"Are their parents, okay?" I asked.

"Yes, but what was strange was I overheard the nurses and doctors talking about how Dr. Burns was supposed to be covering the E.R. but he never showed. The hospital tried reaching him on his pager and phone but nothing. They called the police and requested they do a welfare check. The police said he wasn't at home either. It wasn't like him to miss a shift. Do you think he had something to do with that lady's murder?"

"I don't know, but right now it's looking that he might have."

She started to get up when she stopped. "Oh, I forget the juicy part. Two nurses overheard him arguing with Madison the day before she was killed."

"Do you know what the fight was about?"

"She claimed he was the father of her child. He argued that he wasn't and couldn't have been since she was on the pill. But she confessed she hadn't been taking birth control for months. She was insistent on keeping the kid and he argued she needed to get an abortion. He didn't want to be a father."

"Very interesting," I remarked. "Very interesting."

"Yea. One of the nurses jokingly remarked that they all thought it was Dr. Oslow's kid. Sorry, but I'm on my lunch hour and I've got to go. I hope this helps." She handed me a balloon animal.

My mind was spinning after listening to what Shawna had to say. This was unbelievable. One murdered wife, one ex-wife burned to death and now a missing doctor. Things were getting way out of hand. This might be a good time to step away from this case and go back to investigating fraud cases.

Before I could get back to my truck, Jackson Pickett called with more bad news. "Wes, are you sitting down?" I didn't like where this conversation was headed.

"No, but tell me anyway." I commented.

"I got a call from the D.A. early this morning. That crazy detective insist Leah Quinn's death was no accident but murder. To make things worse, she claims Sue is her number one suspect."

"I was told at the scene by one of the firemen the blast furnace over heated causing the explosion. They think it was an accident. Why would Sue want to murder Leah Quinn? That is crazy."

"Now they're saying it was deliberately tampered with and that it's no accident," he added.

"How can they say Sue had something to do with it?"

"The business across the street had a CCD camera that caught her leaving the place around six the night before. The camera showed Sue and Leah Quinn outside arguing. Do you know what that was all about?"

"Damn, Sue," I muttered to myself. "You're not making this easy."

"Have you talked to Sue about this?" I asked.

"I can't reach her. She's not answering her phone," Jackson commented.

"I'll drive by their house and let you know what I find out."

"I must talk to her A.S.A.P. before something else goes haywire on this case."

"I hate to break the news but one of the doctors Madison was involved with has gone missing."

"Can you repeat that?" Jackson harshly remarked.

"I just found out minutes before you called that Dr. Burns who was romantically involved with Madison, and who might've been her child's father has gone missing."

"Her what!" He exclaimed. "Oh, my God! Find Sue and get her in my office now before this gets so far out of hand that I won't be able to prove her innocence."

As I drove to Sue and Bruce's house I thought about the saying, "When it rains, it pours." Hell, I was in the middle of a hurricane. The house looked dark and there was no answer at the door. I called both their cell phones but they went straight to voice mail. I left a message for them to call me, urgently.

For now, until I got some answers, I moved Sue to the top of my list along with Trevor and Jake. I was having second doubts about Sue. She had not told me everything about what happened at the charity event. Why was she holding back information?

Marti had texted me last night reminding me to make sure there was plenty of gas for the grill for a party she was hosting later this week with her girlfriends. I picked up the tank and went to the closest Quinn Rental location to get it filled. Nick, the manager, rushed over and grabbed the tank and started filling it.

"Wes, it's been a while, not doing much grilling lately?" he asked.

"Not as much as I'd like to," I added.

Nick had been working there as long as I'd been stopping by to get the tank filled. He had to be in his mid-fifties with receding hair to the point where there were only a few strands left on top. His body looked frail but looks were deceiving. Under his uniform was nothing but muscle. "Seen the boss lately?" I asked.

He smiled, "Naw, he never comes by."

"Doesn't he come by to check on things from time to time?"

With the tank filled he one handedly lifted it into the bed of my truck with ease. "I can't remember the last time I've seen him, but we do get a visit from Jake every Monday, Wednesday and Friday. Around two P.M. like clockwork he stops by with a bank deposit bag."

"Don't you make your own daily deposit?"

"Yea, each morning I send the office manager to the bank across the street, but as soon as he shows up, we're instructed to stop whatever we're doing and drive clear across town to make his deposit. Is there anything else I can get you?"

"Just the gas."

I rushed home and dropped off the tank, got in Marti's SUV and returned to the rental store and waited for Jake to arrive. I had only been parked for fifteen minutes when he showed up and handed Nick the deposit bag. I took pictures of the drop off. The funny thing was that he didn't even get out of the black SUV. I followed Jake from a distance while Jake made stops at three other Quinn Rental locations. Instead of following Jake after the third stop, I decided to follow the manager to the bank.

As the manager stood in line, I made it look as if I was filling out a deposit slip at the counter. There were three tellers busy helping customers but when a teller came free, the Quinn manager waved the person from behind to go ahead. When it was her turn again, she approached a different teller at the far end and just dropped off the bag and left. There was no interaction between them or receipt given.

I was about to leave when another Quinn Rental employee stepped inside carrying a deposit bag. I watched as they waited for the same teller and handed her the deposit. Again, no interaction. Very unusual behavior for a banking institution. Before I stepped outside, I turned and took a closer look at the teller. I'd say she was in her mid-to-late thirties and it was as if I had seen her before but I couldn't remember where. I covertly took a couple of photos of her with my phone, making sure to capture her name on the teller window.

As instructed, I stopped by the store to pick up a couple of steaks and bakers for us. I couldn't believe my luck when standing in front of the meat counter was the blonde, blue eye and fair skinned, Dr. Olrich Oslow and the lady who slammed the door in my face the other day at his house. I followed from a distance hoping for the right moment where he might be alone. When she left him at the butcher counter I walked over and remarked, "Dr. Oslow, you're a hard man to get to talk to."

He gave me a puzzled look before asking, "Do I know you?" His thick Scandinavian accent made him hard to understand, especially here in the middle of the mega mart.

"No, I stopped by your house the other day to ask you a few questions about Madison Quinn. Your wife said you weren't home even though I thought I heard your voice in the background. My name is Wesley Johns and I'm investigating the death of Madison Quinn. Maybe now you could spare a few moments of your time while your lovely wife is finishing up her shopping."

"Are you some kind of reporter? I already told that lady detective everything I know. So, if you don't mind, I'm going to join my wife."

The butcher handed him a bag and when he tried to leave, I used my cart to block his way and commented, "I found it interested that you decided not to divorce your wife right after Madison's death."

He froze and quickly looked around for his wife. "Was it because you and Madison were having an affair and you planned to leave your wife? After Madison's death you suddenly changed your mind and went crawling back to your wife?"

He didn't say a word, didn't move, just stood there. "Would you rather that I talk to your wife?"

"Who are you?" There was fear in his voice.

"I'm Wesley Johns, I'm a private investigator..."

"You're what!" He shouted. "Look, I don't want any trouble. Yes, I knew Madison but that was only business." he nervously commented. "Now if you don't mind, please get out of my way."

"The rumors going around the hospital are that you two had a thing going on."

"That's the problem working in a hospital. Everyone tries to put their nose in other people's lives. I never once had any involvement with Madison outside of work. I only helped with her charity," he directly denied.

"I saw you at the golf course the day she died."

"No, I wasn't there. She asked a few doctors and nurses associated with the charity to talk to people hoping we could encourage them to open their wallets, but I had a previous engagement. Now if you don't mind, I must go and find my wife."

"So, why did you file for a divorce then change your mind? Does it have anything to do with Madison?"

"No, no, not at all. I found out that my wife had been secretly seeing another doctor at the hospital. My lawyer suggested I hired the P.I. to prove if she was or wasn't. I filed for divorce after seeing the photos of the two of them together. When my wife received the divorce papers, she begged me not to follow through. She promised she would never see him again."

"Do you have the name of the doctor your wife had been having an affair with?"

"Yes, Dr. Lewis. Go ask him. When I confronted him about sleeping with my wife, at first, he denied it, but when I showed him photos, he agreed to end it. Look, I've got to join my wife. I'd appreciate it if you didn't say anything to anyone, especially to her." Before I could ask any more questions, he hurried down the aisle.

I slammed on the brakes when I saw our front door was slightly ajar. I glanced down the street looking for the black SUV, nothing. I had just stepped inside when I heard Marti singing in the kitchen. She was opening up a bottle of wine. "Hey, I got a ride home so I didn't need to bother you."

While the grill was getting hot, I tossed a couple of bakers in the oven, tossed a salad and fed the guys. While I grilled the steaks, Marti sat out on the patio and told me about some of the crazy passengers she had encountered on this excursion. As we ate, she asked how the case was coming along. I gave her limited information so as not to worry her.

Marti vegged in front of the TV, I went into my office to find out more about my mystery teller. Her name was Donna Evans. She looked very familiar when I saw her at the bank but I just couldn't place from where. Searching through public records I found out that Donna had been divorced twice and was currently single. She had one child with her first husband. Donna's social media sites suggested she was obsessed with food. She posted almost daily some dish, whether she had made it or was eating out somewhere. There were no photos of her child. Digging a little deeper into the life of Donna Evans, I found her ex and child now live in Australia. When I tried locating her second husband, I found he was the guest of the state of California, twenty years for embezzling. Searching throughout her social media pages not once had she posted any photos of her or her family.

I asked myself, "Donna Evans what is your involvement with Quinn Rentals?"

I was about to crawl into bed when Bruce called. They had been staying with some friends at their cabin in the mountains and the cell phone service was spotty. When they had gotten to the small village near the cabin to get something to eat, he noticed that Jackson and I had left urgent messages. We agreed it would be best if they stayed there for a while until I could get things sorted. He promised to check in with me at least twice a day and I'd let them know when they needed to be home. I left Jackson a message advising him what was happening.

Chapter 18

Chris was leaning up against my truck when I stepped outside. "Hey, Partner, how's our case coming along?"

"Hey, Chris, I'm in a hurry. Your sister is in the kitchen and I'm sure she could use your help."

"She told me I should come with you when I text her this morning. I rushed over so not to miss you."

I cursed under my breath the day he rented the house down the street. "Look, I'm in a hurry. Maybe you can help another day."

"No can do, Partner. I'm scheduled to work for the next seven days."

"Oh hell, get in," I harshly remarked.

"Why are we taking Sis's SUV? What's wrong with your truck?"

"Nothing, now get in or go home. I'm in a hurry."

We sped down the street and I prayed I wasn't late. No sooner had I parked down the street from Trevor's office building that Chris started his usual whining that he was hungry.

We parked and waited. I used this time to call the P.I.'s number that Jackson had scribble on the piece of paper. Her name was Olivia Broadmore and we agreed to meet at her office at five.

It was half past ten when Jake stepped outside carrying five bank deposit bags. I kept my distance not to get too close to the black SUV and draw attention to myself. Chris was oblivious to what was going on while he played a video game on his phone.

No sooner had we stopped at a Quinn rental location than Chris leaped out of Marti's SUV and started racing toward the taco place across the street. I turned my attention back to the rental location in time to see Jake handing the manager the suspicious deposit bag. I quickly clicked off a couple of photos with my camera.

However, before Chris returned, the manager climbed in a rental truck and pulled out of the parking lot. "Crap!" I shouted. I looked over at the taco place and he was still in line. "Screw it," I remarked and followed the rental company truck.

I answered my phone on the sixth ring. Chris was in a panic after leaving the taco place and seeing my truck was gone. He wanted me to come back and get him but that wasn't going to happen. "Chris, hang out there and I will come back and get you." That had put him at ease. The only thing was that I didn't tell him when that would be. The manager drove to the same bank branch clear across town as the others did yesterday. From the street I had a good view of Donna behind her teller's window. After she accepted the deposit bag the rental manager, instead of putting it with others, she placed it under the counter. This got me to thinking if the bank manager knew what was going on or were they also in on the take.

Upon returning to the rental location Chris was nowhere in sight. "Where in the hell are you?" I angrily mumbled to myself. "Damn, if you weren't Marti's brother, I'd strangle you. Crap, I don't have time sitting here waiting for you to show up. You can find your own way home." Totally frustrated with the man, I drove back to Quinns corporate headquarters and parked down the street. The black SUV was parked out front. I wanted to go inside and ask Ava about Leah's accidental death but was hesitant that Jake could or would show up at any time.

I was relishing the silence when Chris started angrily pounding on the passenger side window of my truck. Fearful his actions would attract attention; I relented and unlocked the door. "Wes, what happened? You left me and didn't return!"

"How in the hell did you find me? I needed to follow my suspect while you were busy stuffing your face. Where in the hell were you when I returned to get you?" My tone was harsh but it didn't faze him.

After an hour of listening to him bitch and moan about the fact I had left him, I'd had enough and was going to drive him home when Trevor and Jake stepped out of the building. Trevor was carrying a large bag which meant more time with Chris. "Oh, lucky me," I thought to myself.

I followed them to a large Quinn Rental Industrial outlet on the other side of the airport. This time instead of the employees coming out to greet them they went inside. I really wanted to follow but knew that wouldn't be a wise choice.

I had only one option and prayed he wouldn't screw it up. I explained to Chris three times that I needed him to go inside and find out what they were doing. It wasn't until I bribed him that we'd get something to eat afterwards and that I wouldn't leave him this time that he agreed. With the lack of enthusiasm, Chris slowly took his time walking to the building.

I started to get worried when twenty minutes had past and he hadn't returned. When Trevor and Jake climbed in the SUV and sped off and I wanted to follow but instead, I made a promise and waited for Marti's Bozo brother to return. Thirty minutes had passed and still no Chris. I stormed inside only to find him laughing with some guy behind the counter. "Oh, hey Wes, meet Nighthawk. I found out he's one of the gamers I play against."

"Chris, we've got to go."

"Why, I just got here? Can you come back in an hour and pick me up. We have a lot of gaming stuff to talk about."

It was nice and quiet as I drove home. I left Chris with no promise to return. My thoughts were about how Jake would take a deposit bag to each retail rental location, then they would immediately take it to a bank clear across town and give the bag to Donna Evans. Why not just make the deposits themselves, unless they didn't want anyone to know what they were up too?

The guys and I went to the dog park so I could think. I settled under my tree and closed my eyes. Both Madison and Leah where married to Trevor and their deaths could not be a coincidence. They were connected but why and who wanted them both dead? Also, the mysterious disappearance of Dr. Burns gave me the impression he could've been the killer and was now on the run. One way or another they were linked to my investigation. The major players besides Sue were Trevor and Jake. Although not ruling anyone else out. There still were: Ava, Chloe, Dr. Lewis, Dr. Burns, and not to forget about Sue. What a mess.

I was sure Madison's infidelity and pregnancy was the key but who was the actual father. Why murder Leah, unless she knew who the actual father was and attempted to blackmail that person. It sounded like she was desperate for money from what she had let slip when I paid her a visit. I had so many questions and not enough answers. It was disappointing Rod wasn't working on the case, every now and then he'd toss me some information.

I allowed my mind to relax a little and thought about the upcoming car event and which car to take. I was looking forward to the distraction from this case.

"Hey, stranger," a familiar voice said.

There stood Chloe when I opened my eyes.

"Why aren't you answering your phone?" I asked.

"Sorry, but I've gotten so many calls from reporters, pod casters and just some sickos that I've turned it off. Did you hear about Leah? What a shock. She was so careful around those ovens. It doesn't make any sense."

"Maybe she'd had one too many drinks and lost her self-awareness around them." I commented.

"Mr. Johns, do you think you or that lady detective will ever find out who murdered my sister?"

"Yes, I do. Chloe, you were shocked when I told you the other night that your sister was pregnant. Why?"

There was a long pause. "When I told Ava, she said it was impossible."

"Impossible?"

"Yes, she explained that when Trevor was on his second tour, during a training exercise, he had gotten injured from a fake mine. The mines were designed to make a loud noise and emit smoke but the one he triggered malfunctioned and had an extra charge. He spent months in the hospital recovering. After a medical evaluation the doctors concluded he'd never be able to have children.

I stopped and paused and said, "Oh. That explains why the strict no kid's policy. Did Leah or your sister know?"

"I don't think so. I just found out from Ava, yesterday."

Chloe retrieved Grimm and as they walked to her car, I noticed there was no SUV today. I figured Trevor and Jake must be busy doing something illicit.

I closed my eyes again when my phone pinged. I had a message from my contact in the military. He sent a file about Trevor's military history, most of it I already knew. It was when I read about Jake, I started to get nervous. My informant typed in bold letters. "GREEN BERET. MEDICAL DISCHARED. STAY AWAY, VERY DANGEROUS. THE GUY IS A PSYCHO." Not only chills but panic raced throughout my body.

I called Trevor's brother, Robert, hoping he'd talk to me this time. Good afternoon, Robert. This is Wesley Johns. I called before about my investigation into the death of Madison Quinn."

"Look, I don't know what I can tell you. I haven't had any contact with my brother since I sold him my share of the business," he remarked.

"I have a few loose ends I'm trying to tie up. I'd greatly appreciate your help."

After a long pause, he agreed and explained how the three of them together started the business. In the beginning their inventory was an army surplus that Trevor had acquired while in the military. Well, so Robert had thought in the beginning before finding out about the truth of his brother's military past.

Robert insisted he had to go. "Please, just a couple more questions. Do you ever hear from your brother, Tanner?"

"No, not since he and Trevor and that jackass, Jake, went to Alaska together."

"How about Leah Quinn? Did you hear what happened to her?" I asked.

"No, and I really don't care. I have put that part of life past me and moved on. Mr. Johns, I don't know what else I can tell you. I've had no contact with Trevor and I'm at peace with that. So, please don't call me again."

I rocked back and forth in my office chair trying to make sense of all this. My brain felt like a bus station with people and buses coming and going. After some careful consideration, I decided to throw caution to the wind and pay Ava a visit at her office.

When I arrived Trevor and Jake were climbing in their SUV. Since I was still driving Marti's SUV, I was able to follow while keeping my distance. They drove to an old warehouse where some of the windows had been broken and the grass was growing between the cracks in the parking lot. At the far end of the lot was a white panel truck with two men standing in front. The black SUV parked next to the truck and I quickly clicked off photo after photo as fast as my camera would let me. One of the men went to the back of the truck, then handed Jake a large nondescript box, then the two men left.

Their next stop was to a trucking company where Trevor and Jake carried the box inside. For an hour nothing happened. I was about to leave when Jake came out and grabbed a large envelope out of the back seat of the SUV and went back inside. When they stepped outside my eyes bugged out and my jaw dropped. Detective Sanchez exited the building behind them. At first, I frozen but as soon as I pushed the button on my camera, it sounded like a rapid-fire machine gun. I screamed, "What the hell was she doing here?"

There was no tension in their faces, in fact they were smiling. Trevor handed the envelope that Jake had retrieved from the black SUV to Detective Sanchez. I was in total disbelief when she accepted it and placed it in her back pocket. I screamed again, "Oh my God, she's a dirty cop and I let her in my house!"

I sat there dumbfounded as they drove away. The more I thought about it, the more it started to make sense. Detective Sanchez had insisted I stay away from her case. Common sense told me to go straight to Captain Ross and show him the photos, but the only problem was that I had no evidence to prove they were doing anything illegal. I looked at all the photos I had just taken and there was no doubt about it. Something shady was going on between the three of them.

My head was spinning when the alarm on my phone started chiming. "Crap!" I forget all about my meeting with P.I. Olivia Broadmore. I drove like a mad man hoping not to be late. When I stepped out from the SUV I let out a chuckle and read the office sign by the front door. "C.S.I. Agency." Olivia Broadmore was not what I had pictured. She looked to be in her late fifties. When she stood to shake my hand, her short five-foot heavy-set body barely came up to my chest. I couldn't help but stare at her spiked purple hair, rings and studs lining her right ear, black lipstick, and dark mascara. But the clincher was the gold nose ring and the dark purple velour jogging suit.

"It's a pleasure to meet you, Mr. Johns. I've read a lot about you in the paper and how you've solved a few tough murder cases for the police." Her voice had a whinny pitch as she spoke.

"Thanks. "C.S.I. Agency?" I asked.

She let out a slight smile, "Cheating Spouses Investigation. Jackson called and said to give you whatever help I could about Dr. Oslow. So, why the interest in him?" She questioned.

"I'm trying to prove the innocence of a friend of mine on a case I'm working."

"Let me guess, it has to do with that lady who got murdered at the charity event."

"Yes."

She stood up from behind her acrylic desk and proceeded to sit in the chair next to me. Her perfume was strong and almost caused me to sneeze. She proceeded to show me the photos of

Dr. Oslow's wife with her lover. I smiled after recognizing him. "How long had you been watching them?"

"About four months. As you can tell, this guy is a real player."

She slid over more photos. Not only was Dr. Oslow's wife having a secret rendezvous with this man, but she had also taken compromising photos of him with Leah Quinn, Madison and a few other ladies. She handed me the photos and offered her assistance if I needed help. No sooner had I stepped outside than I commented. "Dr. Lewis, you've been a very busy man."

I hadn't taken one step inside my house when the first words out of Marti's mouth were, "Where have you been? My brother has been driving me nuts ever since I got home, whiny that you left him at some rental shop. Why did you leave him?" She stopped and paused after looking into my eyes. "Hey, are you alright? What's going on?" She pulled me in close and hugged me.

"What's he doing here?" I asked.

"Denise called and asked if it would be okay if he could come along with us to the meeting at Donavan's. She has other plans for the night."

"Crap. I'd forgotten all about it. Maybe it would be better if we didn't go."

"Wes, what's going on?"

"It's been a long day. This investigation has taken a few unexpected twists and the last thing I wanted would be to spend more time with your brother."

"What kind of unexpected twists?"

"I'll explain later when your brother isn't around."

The whole time we drove to Donavan's Marti kept giving me a worried look. Once at the pizza parlor, I was relieved Carrie and Jack were the center of attention since they had just returned from their honeymoon. After everyone had stuffed themselves, they turned the spotlight on me and wanted to know how my investigation was coming along. Before I could say a word Chris blurted out that we should have the killer behind bars soon. He then went into detail explaining how his hard work had uncovered the truth behind Madison Quinn's murder and that he had placed his life in danger to prove Sue's innocence. Marti and I weren't the only ones who rolled our eyes once he finished.

I was never so happy as when we dropped her brother off at his house. Just listening to him go on and on about how he almost single handedly solved the case was giving me a splitting headache. But when he remarked that he was thinking about leaving the bakery to come to work full time with me, I almost slammed on the brakes and was going to force him to walk home. Luckily Marti quickly came to the rescue and threatened him she'd call mom if he did.

Chris remarked, "You wouldn't?"

"Yes." When she took out her cell phone he quickly shut up.

I made sure the house was locked up tight before asking Marti to join me in my office. I showed her the photos of Trevor handing Detective Sanchez the envelope. After looking at them for a second time she blurted out, "I never liked that bitch! What are we going to do? I sure wish Rod was here and not off at some training class. Wes, I'm scared. What are we going to do? Do you think you should show these photos to Captain Ross? Do you think we are in any kind of danger?"

When I looked up and saw the frightened expression and the tears racing down her cheeks, I pulled her onto my lap, wrapped my arms around her and we sat in silence. I was just as scared too. But I wasn't going to let her know that.

Chapter 19

I had just gotten off the phone with Jackson after he had just gotten off the phone with Bruce. Jackson told them they needed to be back in town tomorrow by seven since they had a meeting with the D.A. Jackson asked me if Olivia was able to provide any information that would help clear his client, Sue. I wanted to tell him about Detective Sanchez's meeting with Trevor and Jake but thought it was best to keep it to myself for now.

I closed my eyes and leaned back into my chair and allowed the music from my office radio to help clear my mind when the DJ interrupted for a news flash. "City police have identified the man found dead along the riverbank late last night as Dr. Andrew Burns. They're asking anyone who knows anything about this man's death to come forward with any information that might help with their investigation."

"What the hell!" I shouted.

Marti came rushing into my office, "Wes, did you figure out who murdered those two women?"

After taking a deep breath, "No, they just announced on the radio the police discovered a man's body along the riverbank. It was one of my main suspects, Dr. Andrew Burns."

"Oh my God, how awful. Do they know if it was an accident or ...?"

"They didn't say but I have this unsettling feeling his death was no accident."

"How can you find out?"

"I could try calling Captain Ross, but after yesterday, I'm not sure that would be a good idea. I sure wished Rod was working this investigation instead of you know who."

"I have to rush to work, but text me when you know more. Wes, whatever you do, please be careful. These people you're investigating are very dangerous. I love you."

I gave here a light kiss on the cheek, "Don't worry, I've got Oz." I don't think my words gave her any comfort as she walked out of my office.

My thoughts were a jumbled mess. First Madison, then Leah and now Dr. Burns. This was starting to get out of hand. If the rumors going around the hospital were correct that Madison was pregnant with Dr. Burns kid, then that solidified Trevor Quinn and Jake Toleman as my prime suspects. Were they paying Detective Sanchez to look the other way? I really needed to know how the three of them were connected. The only thing I couldn't figure out was why they would have to murder Leah?

I about jumped out of my skin when my phone rang, it was Ava Quinn and she sounded frightened. "Wes, I don't know what to do. When I got to work this morning, there was a note on my desk, "You're next!" in big bold letters. I'm scared that I might be their next target. What should I do? Do I need to call the detective? Can we meet somewhere? Oh my God, this can't be happening."

"Tell me where and when and I'll be there."

There was a long pause, then she whispered, "There is someone standing outside my office door. I can't talk now I'll call you back when they leave."

"Why would someone threaten Ava and for what possible reason. None of this was making any sense. It was as if someone was targeting Trevor's wives. But why and how did Dr. Burns death play into all this? The more I tried to untangle the nightmare the more it looked plausible that my mystery man might have something to do with all the killings and threats. Who in the hell was he?

I panicked once the thought registered in my head, first Madison, then Leah and now Ava is being followed. That meant Chloe could be next on this killer's hit list. I called her but damn, it went to voicemail. I called Ava back but it also went to voicemail. "What was going on?" I thought.

I needed to know more about Dr. Burns mysterious death. I called Catherine, at the television station, but she was busy and they said they would have her call me back. I tried Royce at the paper, but he was in a meeting. I was getting frustrated at not getting any answers.

The longer I sat the more frustrated I got. Why weren't Chloe and Ava answering their phones or returning my calls. The way this investigation was going, I was worried that one of them might be the next victim. My head was swimming with thoughts and scenarios when my phone rang. "Mr. Johns, this is Chloe. I got your voicemail."

"Chloe, are you okay?"

"Yes, why?"

"Look, I need to see you, like now. It's important. Be at the dog park in thirty minutes."

"I just sat down with my friend for lunch." Her voice became strained. "What's going on?"

"I'm worried about your safety."

There was a long hesitation before she agreed to meet after her lunch. For now, I felt she was safe being around friends.

I had just loaded the guys in the truck when the black SUV appeared at the end of the block. It gave me a slight relief knowing it wasn't following Chloe or Ava. For now, I felt they were safe. It took me twenty minutes of weaving in out of subdivisions before losing them. Then instead of parking in my usual place at the park, I parked down by the fountain.

I sat on the other side of the enclosed dog area under the cover of trees where I could watch the road. It felt like an eternity when Chloe's little car finally pulled into the parking lot. I waved at her and she came over and sat next to me.

"Mr. Johns, what's going on? After we talked, I couldn't enjoy my lunch so I left."

"Chloe, did you hear the news?"

"No, what news?"

"They found Dr. Burns's body down by the riverbank."

"Oh no! How awful! What happened to him?"

"I don't know, but I'm worried about your safety."

I could see the frightened look in her eyes as she spoke. "Why? I didn't have anything to do with him. I never met the man or even knew who he was."

"Chloe, first your sister was murdered at the charity event. Then Leah's so-called accident at her studio and was burned to death. Now Dr. Burns's body was found. Plus, Ava called worried because someone left her a threatening note at her office."

Her voice was shaky. "Oh my God! And now you think someone will try to kill me?"

"Yes, both you and Ava."

"Why would anyone want to kill me? I haven't done anything. What are we going to do? Maybe you should call that lady detective and ask for her help. Do you think someone is at my house waiting to kill me? I need to get home and check on Grimm." She leaped up and started racing to her car.

I tried to chase after her but she was too fast. I quickly gathered the guys and ran to my truck. The whole time I thought what a stupid idea of parking so far away. As I left the park, my phone rang. "Wes, I got your message. You called?" Catherine said.

"Yes, thanks for calling me back."

"You sound out of breath. Are you okay?"

"I took the guys for a run." Once I caught my breath, I asked if she had any more information on the death of Dr. Burns.

"The police just released a press report. Dr. Burns's body was found at one A.M. along the riverbank by the water park. He had been stabbed numerous times in the back."

"So, it was murder!" I commented.

"Why are you so interested?"

"I have a feeling his death is tied to the death of Madison Quinn. Catherine, I've got to go but I'll call you back later." I hung up before she responded.

I parked on the street in front of Chloe's place. The front door was wide open. Oz and Annie leaped out of the truck after hearing Grimm's barking. I found Chloe on the middle of the floor sobbing. Grimm was trying to comfort her. She looked up at me and said, "I'm so scared. I don't know what to do?" She then handed me a piece of paper. "This was slipped under the front door."

"If YOU WANT TO LIVE, TELL THAT NOSEY NEWSPAPER REPORTER TO BACK OFF OR YOU'RE NEXT."

I had to act fast and made a call. Once I got Chloe to trust me, she raced around the house throwing things into a backpack. I explained for her to drive to the mega mart and park next to a white minivan. There would be two elderly people inside. I couldn't help but not laugh as poor Grimm did his usual dance to struggle to get his large body into Chloe's little car. After she drove away, I loaded the guys into the truck and started to pull away from the curb. I stopped when the black SUV turned the corner. Thankfully, Chloe's car was out of sight. I made sure they followed me home.

Just as I stepped inside, I received a text, "Package arrived safely."

I called Ava but no answer. I left her a message to call me asap hoping she had found a safe place to hide until we got this mess figured out. After an hour of waiting, I step outside and looked down the street. The black SUV was nowhere in sight. Not taking any chances that I might be followed, I drove all over town before arriving at Chloe's safe house.

Lois was standing by her front door, with a rolling pin in hand looking as if she was about to whack someone with it. "Wes, about time. Where have you been?" She demanded to know.

Thank goodness I had left the guys at home since Grimm was wreaking havoc inside. A frightened and scared Chloe sat at the kitchen table trying to hold a conversation with Eric while nibbling on one of Lois's sugar cookies.

She looked up at me, "Mr. Johns, what are we doing here?"

"Trust me, for now you're safe. Lois and Eric will take good care of you. I just need time to get things sorted."

"How long will that take?" Chloe muttered.

"It shouldn't be too long."

Grimm had found a new buddy in Eric who gave him bites of cookies and ear scribbles. Lois rolled her eyes and shot him a disgusted glance. Lois turned to me and said. "Wes, maybe Grimm would be better off at your house where he could play with Oz and Annie."

Chloe revolted at the thought. "He's my security blanket. There's not a night that he doesn't sleep with me on the bed."

"On the bed!" Lois exclaimed. "Oh, my Lord. You poor girl! You must wake up covered in dog hair."

"I'd feel a lot safer if he was here with me."

Eric gave Grimm another bite and commented, "So would I. Maybe we should think about getting a dog for protection."

"We're not getting a dog. Wes what have you gotten us into?"

"If this is going to be a problem, I'll find somewhere else she can stay."

Lois picked up her rolling pin, crossed her arms and glared at me. "Over my dead body."

I started to leave when I turned and asked Chloe for her phone.

"Why do you need my phone?" She questioned.

"The killer could use your phone to track you. I'll take good care of it, trust me."

She dug into her purse and at first hesitated to hand it to me, but when Lois mentioned that if she needed to talk to someone, she could use theirs.

It was time to turn up the heat on my shrinking list of suspects before another one of Trevor's wives was murdered. I pushed past his receptionist and stormed into his office tossing the photos P.I. Olivia Broadmore had given me onto his desk. "You've been a very busy boy, haven't you Dr. Lewis?" I harshly remarked.

"What do you mean barging into my office? Get out!"

As soon as he looked down at the photos, the arrogance and defiance left and was replaced with bewilderment. "Where did you get these?"

"That's not important. What is important is your relationships with these woman."

"What is it to you?" His cocky attitude returned.

He smiled and ripped up the photos and tossed them in the trash. "What photos? Now leave my office before I call security."

I just shook my head, "Really? Are you that stupid? I have copies. Now cut the crap. I want to know about your relationships with Madison, Leah, Dr. Oslow's wife, Dr. Andrew Burns and the other women in these photos. Right now, you're a prime candidate to be spending the rest of your life wearing a bright orange jumpsuit."

The office was silent after he swiveled his chair around and stared out the window. I slammed my fist on the desk which caused him to jump. "Look, you can either talk to me or the police. It's up to you."

I took out my phone and started dialing. "Alright! Alright! Hang up the phone. I'll talk."

I quickly ended the call since Donavan was on the other end asking for my order.

"I met Madison at a charity event. That night we went out for a drink and ended spending the night at a hotel."

"Did she tell you she was married?"

"Not until a month later. Once she told me I ended the relationship."

"Did you know she was pregnant?"

"Yes."

"Did she also tell you who the father was?"

"No. She just asked me to hook her up with a doctor friend who performs abortions. She was afraid her husband might find out."

"That's strange because I heard she was planning on keeping the child." The expression on his face suggested she hadn't told him that she had changed her mind. "Did you question her if the child was yours?"

"I had a paternity test done and it turned out the baby wasn't mine."

"If it wasn't yours then any idea whose it might have been?"

"She didn't tell me, but I had my suspensions it might have been Dr. Burns. You see, shortly after she broke it off with me, the rumors around the hospital were that she was seeing him."

"Why didn't she go to him instead of you?"

"I don't know."

Why were you two seen at the charity event arguing?"

"Because I still loved her."

"Look, I have patients in the outer office. Can't this wait until I've seen them?"

"No! How did you know Leah?"

"I met her through Madison."

"How long were you two seeing each other?"

"For a couple of months."

"Why only for a couple of months."

"I started seeing Teresa, Dr. Oslow's wife. Look, I know what you think of me, but I'm telling you the truth. I didn't have anything to do with Leah's death. I was out of town with one of the nurses. You can ask her or the friends we were with."

"Tell me about Dr. Burns?"

"Why?"

"Really, you're going there right now?"

"Look, I didn't care much for the man. Yes, he and I got into a couple of heated discussions about Madison. Whenever he could, he'd throw out some derogatory comment how she dumped me for him, or that I was only half the lover that he was. The man was an arrogant bastard. The night before he disappeared, we had a very heated argument over the care of a patient to the point he threatened to hit me. It took another doctor and two nurses to get him to back off. That was the last time I saw him. I'm telling you the truth. I despised him but I had nothing to do with his death. Now get out of my office before I call security."

The doctor sitting behind the desk looking up at me was a sleazeball. Until he provided me with the names and phone numbers to prove his innocence, he remained high on my suspect list. When I started to leave his office, I turned and said, "Just so you know, we'll talk again.

I looked over at the young receptionist in the outer office. She was also in one of the photos and I just negatively shook my head. I was halfway down the long hospital corridor when the elevator door opened and out stepped Detective Sanchez strutting her way toward Dr. Lewis's office. I quickly ducked down the stairwell.

On my drive home I received a text from Ava, getting out of town for now. I will text you later."

Marti was making dinner and the guys were at her feet hoping something would accidentally drop their way.

"Something smells good." I commented. I looked into the pan and there was enough to feed a small army. "Whose coming to dinner?" I questioned.

She gave me a sheepish grin, "Chris and Denise."

"What! Why?"

"Did you forget? It's our weekly scrabble night."

"Crap!"

Chapter 20

I contemplated the situation. Over the past two days of watching, trailing and taking photos of Trevor and Jake I hadn't found one shred of evidence that proved they had anything to do with Madison or Dr. Burns murders. Nor could I tie them to Leah's suspicious death. Nothing, a big fat nothing.

I began to worry I might not be able to prove Sue's innocence. I was standing over the stove stirring the oatmeal while trying to put all the pieces together when the front door opened. Oz and Annie rushed out of the kitchen alerting we had company. There stood an exhausted-looking Bruce. "Wes, sorry to barge in like this but I needed someone to talk to."

"When did you get back into town?" I asked.

"Yesterday morning per Jackson's request."

"Coffee?"

"Yes, and a lot of cream if you have it," he replied.

Bruce looked as if he had aged ten years since the last time I had seen him. The black puffy circles under his eyes, the unshaven face and blood shot eyes told it all. No sooner had I placed a steamy cup of coffee in front of him, he remarked, "Wes, what am we going to do? That lady detective and her crew came by our house around five yesterday with a warrant. They spent hours tearing our house apart. It was close to midnight when they left. Our house is in a total disarray and my wife is distraught over the way that detective had kept badgering her to confess."

I had almost forgotten the oatmeal and rushed over and took it off the stove.

"Did they tell you what they were looking for?"

"No. They just left with bags of Sue's clothing and a few other things. Thankfully, when Jackson showed up, he put an end to that detective's abusive behavior toward us and sent her and her team packing. May I have some of whatever you're cooking? I haven't eaten since yesterday afternoon."

I had just dished up the oatmeal for Bruce when the guys rushed to the front door barking. Before I could go see who it was, in walked Chris. "Why aren't you working?" I asked.

"Betty gave me the rest of the day off since I finished all my baking. Is that your world-famous oatmeal?" He grabbed my bowl and sat next to Bruce. "What are you guys talking about? Is it about our case? I have all afternoon to help with our investigation."

I cringed at the thought.

"Wes, I want a straight answer. Do you really think Sue had anything to do with the murder of that lady at the charity even?" Bruce asked.

Before I could say a word, Chris chimed in by saying, "No, we don't and with us on the case, I can guarantee we'll soon find the real killer."

Bruce and Chris were having a deep conversation when Betty called and reported my mystery man had just walked through the front door of the bakery. She was trying to stall him by having one of her other employees giving him a tour. She asked me to hurry over before he left. No sooner had I stepped inside the bakery than Betty gave me a disappointed look. "Sorry, we did my best."

"Did he say anything?"

"He asked if Chris was working and I said he had already gone home for the day. When we tried to show him around the bakery he just ordered a bear claw and coffee and walked out."

"Why would he be interested in Chris?"

"I don't know. You'll have to ask your brother-in-law. All I know the last time the man stepped into the bakery, he and Chris talked for twenty minutes or so."

"Did you happen to see what kind of car he was driving?"

"No, I was busy helping another customer."

"I did, it was a black Chevy Suburban with tinted windows." Standing next to Betty was a somewhat heavy-set young man, I bet in his late twenties.

"Wes, sorry, meet Frank, my new employee."

"Did you happen to get the license plate number?" I asked.

"Sorry, I didn't pay that much attention."

Knowing Bruce and Chris most likely had eaten all my oatmeal. I grabbed a couple of fritters and headed home. It puzzled me not knowing who this mystery person was and why he kept showing up at the bakery. One thing for sure, Chris and I needed to chat.

I was right, the oatmeal and Bruce were gone and the kitchen a mess. "Hey, Wes, where did you go?" Chris asked from the living room while shoving a handful of chips into his mouth. Both Oz and Annie sat impatiently hoping he'd share.

I turned off the TV and stared down at him. "Chris, did you ever talk to anyone about this case?"

"What? No way."

"Betty tells me she has seen you and this guy talking?" I showed him a photo of the scruffy looking man I had taken at the church. He nonchalantly glanced at it while trying to get the remote out of my hand. "Well?" I asked.

"Yes, I've talked to him before, but he doesn't look like that now."

"What's he look like?" I questioned.

"His hair is much shorter and the beard is gone."

"Do you know his name?"

"No. Now, can I have the remote back?"

"What do you guys talk about?"

"Fine, he heard you were a detective and he wanted hire you. Why I told him I was your partner and we busy trying to solve a murder case."

"Did you tell him who was murdered?"

Sheepishly, he grinned. "Yes."

"And?"

"He just asked me how the case was coming along and if we had any suspects."

"Damn it, Chris! You might've been talking to the killer."

Unfazed by my remark he just sat there with his usual blank look. I tossed the remote at him and stormed out the front door to escape before I wrapped my hands around his neck. The whole time I was seeing red. Damn him!

The man was a nuisance and now he had possibly come in contact with the killer and had given him information about my investigation. Who in the hell, was this mystery person. At the light I tried to piece together what would've been his motive behind the murders. If he was the killer, then the other question to ask was what's going on between Trevor, Jake and Detective Sanchez. As for Dr. Lewis, I was still waiting for proof he had nothing to do with the murders.

By the time I parked out front of Trevor's office building, I was still stewing about Chris and his big fat mouth. I was having a hard time focusing on the task at hand as my mind was trying to sort all the pieces of the puzzle out. I just hoped today something would break loose where I could end this nightmare of an investigation. I'd been parked for thirty minutes when Trevor and Jake stepped out of the building. Just as I started the engine my phone rang. I was surprised to hear his voice. "Hey, Cowboy, how's it going?"

"Just peachy. When are you going to get back here?"

"Soon. I just wanted to let you know that I heard through the police grapevine that your friend Sue has also been connected to the murder of that Dr. Burns."

"What!" I screamed.

"Right now, they're running tests on the murder weapon. Detective Sanchez thinks the knife that was used to kill him came from her house."

"That's nuts!"

"Look, that's all I know, I've got to go. I'll be back next week. Nancy and I have some exciting news to share with you and Marti."

"What the hell!" I screamed. What in the hell made Detective Sanchez think Sue had anything to do with the murder of Dr. Burns let alone with both Madison and Leah's. The news just kept getting better and better, not. I followed Trevor and Jake to an old warehouse when Jackson called and wanted me to meet him at the county jail at eleven. I sat there with a blank expression on my face and my head hurt from all the thinking. Sitting here wasn't doing me any good. I called and a tired Bruce answered, "Hello."

"Great, you're at home, I'll be there in twenty minutes."

As soon as he opened their front door, I said, "We need to talk. Jackson called and I'm to meet him in an hour down at the county jail. Bruce, this is the time I need straight answers from you if I'm going to help prove your wife's innocents. I've received information that the knife that was used in the murder of Dr. Burns came from your house." Looking at him was like I was looking at a deer frozen in the middle of the street about to be hit. He didn't say a word. "Bruce, where were both of you that night. You said you were at the cabin." Still nothing. "Do you want to see your wife sent to prison for something she didn't do? Snap out of it and talk to me."

Finally, when he opened his mouth, the words came out broken and at first it was hard to make any sense of it. "Why, why, why, why would they think that?"

"Bruce, focus, I don't have a lot of time. How did a knife from your kitchen end up being the murder weapon?"

"I don't know. I have no idea."

"Well, something fishy is going on. I want to know everything about the night the doctor was murdered. You were staying in the cabin up in the mountains, right?"

There was a long pause. "Not exactly."

"What do you mean, 'Not exactly?'" My patience was growing short for the run around he and Sue were giving me."

"I didn't want to tell you but we had to come into town to get Sue's meds. But honestly, it was only for a short time. I went to the store to stock up on groceries while she went to get her meds. I'd been home for an hour when she arrived. I asked what took her so long and she told me there was a long line at the pharmacy."

"So, there's someone who could prove where she was?"

Bruce fidgeting with his fingers. "Wes, I don't understand. As soon as we got home, she hurried into the bedroom and changed clothes before we left to go back to the cabin. It was close to midnight by the time we got back to the cabin."

"Why did she change clothes?"

"You know women, they're never happy with what they've got on."

"Do either one of you know this Dr. Burns?"

"I don't, not sure about Sue."

"Show me the clothes she changed out of the other night."

I followed him into the bedroom. The laundry hamper was empty. I proceed to check the washer and dryer, nothing. My only assumption was Detective Sanchez's crew found them before me.

I left a shaken man, who could barely speak or walk. He was pondering that his wife of many years might actually not be the person he thought she was.

The drab grey walls, the worn white and black checkered floors and the fluorescent lights made the jail a depressing place. Jackson was waiting for me in the lobby. After making it through security, we were escorted to a small room and waited for Sue. As we waited, Jackson filled me in, "They've arrested her for the murders of Madison Quinn, Dr. Andrew Burns and now Leah Quinn's murder. She's to remain here until her hearing in front of the judge the day after tomorrow."

"Whoa! Wait a minute! You said Leah Quinn. I thought that was an accident?"

"The police and fire marshal have determined she was murdered prior to the killer setting the oven to explode and burn down the place."

"How can they think Sue was involved with her murder?"

"They found the murder weapon outside next to the burned-out shell of the building with Sue's fingerprints. CCD TV from a business across the street from the glass blowing studio showed Sue being the last one to leave the building. Plus, the knife from Dr. Burns murder had her fingerprints on it."

"I can't believe a word of what you just said. This is crazy. What does Sue have to say about this?"

"That's why we are here. I hope she'll tell us."

Sue entered the room and sat across from us. Her face was a drab gray to match the color of the walls. Her eyes were blood shot and streaks of dried tears stained her cheeks. Her hair looked as if it hadn't seen a brush or comb in days. She just sat slumped and defeated, focusing on her shaking hands and not on us. "

In a soft tone I said, "Sue, if you want us to help, you must tell us what's going on. Why were you at the glass shop? I also talked to Bruce and he explained how you came into town to get your prescriptions on the night Dr. Burns was assaulted and murdered."

That was too much. She put her head in her hands and started weeping. Jackson leaned across the table and put his hand on hers trying to give her some comfort. Once she calmed down, she talked for the first time since entering the room.

"Bruce and I got in a big fight about coming to town. It was late afternoon and Bruce thought we could wait until the morning. I told him if he wasn't going to take me then I'd drive myself. That's when things blew up between the two of us and we said words I think we both wished we could take back. In the end, he drove us and not once did we speak to each other. As soon as we got home, I got in my car and drove to the pharmacy. I lied. There was no line." She paused and wiped off her tears. "After picking up my meds I drove to the river park and walked along the riverbank crying. When it started to rain, I rushed back to my car and my pants got snagged on one of those thorny bushes. When I got home, I rushed to change out of my wet clothes and tossed them in the dryer."

"Sue, why didn't you tell me this before when I asked you?" Jackson said.

"Because I'm afraid I'm going to lose the only man I ever loved. Bruce wouldn't even talk to me and once we got back up to the cabin, he went into the other bedroom and closed the door. I'm afraid he's starting to believe I really did kill those people. But you've got to believe me when I said I didn't."

"Why were you at the glass blowing shop?"

"I had commissioned them to make a special vase for my parents' fiftieth wedding anniversary. I was there to pick it up. It's still in the back seat of my car."

"Was there anyone else in the place when you left?" I asked.

"No, just the lady who helped me."

"How did your fingerprints get on the weapon they claimed was used to bash in her skull before the fire was started?"

"I don't know. I entered the store and heard glass breaking in the back. When I peeked through the doorway, she was smashing beer bottles with a metal bat. Wait, I know, I know. When she saw the stressed-out expression on my face, she smiled and asked if I would like to give it a try. I used the bat to smash a few bottles, but I never thought of using it to hurt her. I didn't even know who she was. I thought she was just an employee."

"So, you were the last on to see her alive?"

"Yes, I guess so. She walked outside and opened my car door. Then she went back inside and locked the door."

I glance over at Jackson and commented, "Then the CCD video will show Leah was still alive when Sue left."

"Sue that was the last time you every saw Leah Quinn, right?" I asked.

There was a long pause. "Well, no, as I started to leave the parking lot, I saw her by the back door, bent down crying. I got out of my car and went over to see if there was something I could do. She was so distraught about something. I offered to call someone for her but she declined. Then her face grew in anger, she grabbed a bat leaning up against the building and started pounding the side of the building. When I reached for it, at first, I thought she was going to hit me but, instead she gave it to me and stormed back inside locking the door behind her."

"What did you do next?"

"What could I do? I leaned the bat up against the building and left."

"Sue this is important, are you sure there was no one else there but you?"

Just as she was about to reply the guard notified us our time was up. Jackson and I were about to get up when Sue turned and said, "Wait, I remember now. I looked in the rearview mirror as I waited at the light and saw a large Black SUV parked next to the glass studio's back door."

"Did you see who was inside?" Jackson asked.

"Sorry, no. The light turned, and I drove off. At the time I didn't think anything of it." The guard ushered her out of the room.

As we walked down the drab gray hallway, it was a shame our time with Sue had ended before I could question her about the night Dr. Burns was murdered.

Outside the county jail, Jackson's grim face and tone suggested that his client and my friend was in trouble, deep trouble. "Wes, it doesn't look good."

Before I could agree, from behind us Detective Sanchez commented, "If it isn't my least favorite private copper and his attorney friend. You're wasting your time, you know. There's enough evidence to lock your client away for the rest of her life." I badly wanted to do something about the smug look on her face.

Jackson replied, "Good to see you again, officer. We'll have our day in court."

"Counselor, I suggest you and your client work out a deal with the D.A. before she goes to trial. There's enough evidence to put her away for life." I wasn't sure if it was the arrogance, the rudeness or the half-hearted comment but I wanted to smack her.

"So far from what I've seen, your case is circumstantial at best. Once the jury sees all the evidence, you'll have no case." I smiled as the Jackson Fritz Pickett I knew returned to his cool and confident nature.

The detective's nostrils flared. She removed her oversized sunglasses and placed her face inches from Jackson's. Her intimidation tactics didn't faze him one bit as he stood his ground. She shoved her finger into his chest and in an abrasive tone said, "I don't like slimy lawyers who twist the facts to get their guilty clients off. I especially don't like you."

Jackson gently removed her finger from his chest and remarked, "I don't like lazy cops who take the easy way out. I can't wait until I get you on the stand and rip your case apart. Now good day, Detective." Jackson walked away leaving just me and her.

"As for you, you'd better hope our paths never cross again." She threatened as she put her sunglasses back on and started to walk away.

"No can do. Why don't you go back to Maimi where you can bust some little old lady for jaywalking. That's the only thing you're good at."

She abruptly spin around and declared, "I don't ever want to see you again or I'll..."

"You'll what? You'll have your buddy Jake do something? Yes, I know all about you being in Trevor Quinn's back pocket. I haven't put all the pieces together yet but when I do, I think you'll look good in jail house orange." Damn, me and my big fat mouth, I had let it slip, now she knew that I knew she was a dirty cop.

As I pulled out of the county parking lot I saw the black SUV behind me. I figured now that Detective Sanchez made Sue the scapegoat for the murders, Jake had no more need to follow. She had made sure he was in the clear. However, I had this tingling feeling in the back of my head that this wasn't quite over yet. What if it wasn't Jake but that mystery person that had been following me. He was also at Madison's funeral, Celebration of Life, and kept showing up at Betty's pumping Chris for information. I called Lois and let her know what was happening and to still keep Chloe under wraps.

In my heart I knew Sue was innocent and I just needed that one piece of evidence that would show Trevor, Jake, my mystery man or even Dr. Lewis was responsible for the deaths. But which one. The one thing that puzzled me after talking to Sue was the bat at Leah's glass studio. When I drove to see the fire damage right after Detective Sanchez broke the news and left my house, there was nothing left but ashes. The bat would've burned up in the fire. That just didn't make sense. I went into my office and reviewed my notes, photos and videos trying to find what I was missing. My phone rang.

"Mr. Johns, is it true they arrested the killer?" Ava Quinn asked.

"They think they have. Where are you?" I asked.

"I flew to Miami and I'm staying with a friend. I'll be here for a couple more days. What do you mean, they think they have?" She questioned.

"Let me know when you get back into town. Then we can talk. I've got to go. I'm in the middle of something."

I was excited to see the love of my life enter my office. We sat out on the patio and I gave her a play by play of my day, and we went over the pros and cons and dismissed if we were wrong and Sue did actually commit those murders. We both agreed she hadn't but how to prove it was the question.

Our side gate opened and both Carrie and Jack appeared. "What the hell's going on?" Carrie blurred out. "We just heard on the news that they arrested Sue for those murders. There's no way Sue could have done that. Wes what are we going to do?"

Marti suggested we order pizza and maybe with the four of us go over all the evidence I had collected. Hopefully we could figure out who the real killer or killers were. I suggested we'd be better off going to Donavan's, so as to not be interrupted by Chris. Everybody that that was a great idea.

Donavan and Rose were happy to see us and when Marti broke the news about Sue, they offered to help. The six of us sat at a large table in the back room and went through the photos from the golf course and I showed them the videos I had collected of Detective Sanchez, Jake and Trevor. We all agreed it was either Jake or Trevor who murdered both Madison and Leah. We didn't have a motive but we felt they were involved. The wild card was Dr. Burns. Why would someone want to murder him? The one thing we agreed on was that Detective Sanchez was dirty and had something to do with these murders.

The one missing player I didn't bring up in our discussion was my mystery suspect. I wasn't sure what his interest was in my investigation but in the back of my head, there was the nagging thought he could be the killer. Thanks to Chris's big mouth, he knew more about my investigation than I wished he had.

Chapter 21

I called the station and asked for Captain Ross. It was time that he knew there was a dirty cop on his team, and her name was Detective Vera Sanchez. Unfortunately, he was out of the office, so I left a message for him to call me back. Marti was at work and I needed to think. While I sat under my favorite tree watching the guys chasing their friends, I realized I had no clue about who murdered Madison, Leah or Dr. Burns, and I wasn't sure if I'd ever find out. I only hoped it wasn't my friend. Trevor and Jake were my main suspects but my mysterious person was up there too. As far as I knew, because of Detective Sanchez's tainted investigation toward Sue, they had gotten away with murder. Make that three murders.

My phone pinged, the text read, "Meet me at the old theater on Wilson Street, Rod."

I was relieved he was back in town. Now maybe he'll be able to make some sense out of this twisted mess I had gotten myself into. "Sorry guys, we'll have to cut play time short today. How about a movie instead?"

On my drive over, I thought it was strange he asked me to meet him there instead of our usual place and the text didn't come from his usual phone number. Maybe his phone had crapped out and this was a new one. I was just glad he was back in town and I no longer had to deal with you know who.

The old theater was surrounded by a makeshift chain link fence. The large wooden sign out front said, "Coming soon, Quinn Rentals." There was a lot of heavy equipment in the parking lot and the unmarked police cruiser that Rod used.

We sat in the theater's parking lot. I was hesitant to climb out of the truck. The hairs on the back of my neck stood on end as an uneasiness crawled up my back and sweat moisten my shirt. The more I thought about it the more I began to think this was a bad idea. I re-read the text Rod had sent and something was odd about it, but I couldn't place what. I was about to reply to the text asking Rod to meet at our usual spot when Sue's lifeless expression came to mind. The thought of her spending the rest of her life behind bars for a murder or murders she didn't commit made me quiver. I slowly opened the truck door and thought this was still a bad idea. Oz and Annie excitedly tugged on their leashes dragging me along toward the theater's front door.

I stopped and looked out at the vertical theater sign. I was going to miss this place. I had seen many movies here, most of them with Marti. I stepped into the lobby and the only light came from the dust covered front windows. My stomach churned and not in a good way. Both my legs went weak and my brain was telling me to get out. As I turned to leave, I heard voices from inside the theater.

A slight smile crossed my face when I noticed the candy boxes in the concession stand display case. No telling how long they'd been there. The lobby walls were covered with movie posters and the one that caught my eye was of the last Friday the 13th. You know the kind where you're not supposed to go into the basement when there's a killer around but you do anyway.

I pulled the guys back outside and we went to retrieve my micro camera and pocket recorder. Before entering the theater for a second time, I unhooked the guy from their leashes and they quickly disappeared inside. With each step the silence and uneasiness started to creeped me out. Common sense won out and I realized it would be in my best interest to find the guys and leave.

I slowly walked past the concession stand and stepped into the large theater room hoping to find Oz and Annie, but instead I saw two shadowy looking fingers upfront by the screen. I couldn't make out their faces in the darkness since the only light came from a few holes in the roof, but from what I could tell, one of them looked like Rod.

Now that my eyes had almost adjusted to the darkness I looked around for the guys, but nothing, not even a sound. I had only taken a few steps toward the two figures when Detective Sanchez asked, "Mr. Johns, is that you?"

"What in the hell is she doing here?" I whispered to myself. I stood there frozen while trying to put all the pieces of the puzzle together when I realized this was a trap. A lump formed in my throat and I wanted to call out their names but my mouth was so dry that if I did call for them nothing would come out anyway.

"Mr. Johns please come forward, I have new evidence that'll prove your friend Sue is innocent," the detective commented. Not trusting her, I turned to look for the guys and get the hell out of here. "Were waiting," she shouted so loud that her voice echoed throughout the empty cavernous room. I thought it was strange it was her who spoke and not Rod. I took out my micro camera and switched it on and placed it on one of the few remaining theater seats.

"Mr. Johns, we don't have all day."

With each step, I kept whispering to myself, "Wes, this is not a good idea. Let's get the guys and leave." After taking two steps, I decided it would be my best interest to listen to my gut feeling and leave. We could have this meeting outside where I'd feel much safer. But when I started to back away, I felt a push from behind. "Good morning, Mr. Johns. Glad you could join us." My body almost went limp hearing his voice. This was definitely not good. I pushed my lips together and tried to whistle for my protection but nothing. When I didn't move something hard and small was pushed up against the center of my back. "Move!" Slowly he pushed me toward the stage. I stopped when the carpet changed to plastic. Not good.

When we got within ten feet of the stage, I could now make out the other figure, it was the snotty young kid from behind the glass window from Quinn's corporate office. What in the hell was he doing here?

I felt the pressure stop from the center of my back. The plastic made a crunching noise as Jake walked past me and joined the others. That's when I saw the small dark object in his hand. I made a hard gulp and wanted to run. "Mr. Johns, you've been a thorn in our operations. Today it's going to stop," Jake commanded. He turned toward the young snotty kid and told him to go outback and make sure we weren't interrupted.

"Yea, I have a habit of doing that. How much did you have to pay this bitch to look the other way?" I asked.

Jake smirked, "It's always good business to have the law on your side."

I glanced over at Sanchez who had a self-satisfied look on her face before saying. "Let me guess. It was the money?"

"Always the money."

"From the start, you had no intention on investigating Madison's murder, let alone the others. Plus, that time when you threatened Jake with the handcuffs in front of Quinns corporate office, that was for show. Wasn't it?"

"I have to give you credit." The detective blurted out. "You're not as dumb as you look. You're a persistent bastard."

"Why pin the murders on Sue?" I questioned.

Jake remarked, "Enough of the small talk." He raised the gun until it was pointed at my face.

I glanced around the large room hoping my security would rush to my rescue, but they were nowhere to be seen. Stalling for time, I asked, "So, why kill Madison and the others?"

The silence was deafening. Neither one of them answered me.

My knees buckled when Jake handed the gun to Detective Sanchez and said, "You kill him."

Without hesitation she grabbed the gun and pointed it at my head.

Right now, I was cussing out my friend Rod for not taking this case. Why did he have to go off to training and leave me to deal with this crooked cop and psycho? When I glanced around the building trying to look for a way out, Jake was quick to spot my attempt and pulled out a second gun.

My heart pounded hard in my chest and I felt my body about to crumble onto the plastic. It took all my strength and concentration to keep my legs locked in place. "What did it take to convince her to switch over to the dark side?' I asked.

Jake smiled, "It wasn't hard. She was our police informant in Miami. She made sure we didn't have any issues when product came in from South America and Asia."

I glanced over at Sanchez, "So you've been working for them all along."

She nodded her head and smiled.

It never failed, at the wrong moment, the sound of Frank Sinatra's voice filled the empty theater singing, "Fly me to the moon."

Both Jake and Sanchez froze until they realized it was my phone. I let it go to voicemail. When he started singing again, I quickly answered. "Hey, I can't talk right now. I'll call you back soon."

"That was a nice touch," Jake commented. Give me the damn phone. No more interruptions. He stomped the crap out of it until it was nothing but pieces. "Now get on with it." He said to Sanchez. "The construction crews will be here in two hours and we need to dispose of the body and be far away."

Detective Sanchez raised the gun and her finger was on the trigger when it sounded as if there were footsteps on the other side of the theater. She lowered the gun. After scanning the darkened room and realizing no one was there, she pointed the gun back at my face. Jake was getting impatient with her and demanded she pull the trigger or he'd do it.

"Jake, what really happened to Trevor's brother Tanner?"

"It's none of your business."

"Come on, you're going to kill me so what's the harm?"

"Tanner poked his nose where it didn't belong, just like you. He found out we were fencing stolen goods and drugs. The rental was just a front for us to launder money. When he threatened to go to the police, well, something had to be done! Big brother convinced him it would be in his best interest to move to Alaska and connect with nature."

"What about Robert, how come he got out of the business so clean?"

"The man was dumber that a doorknob. He didn't have a clue. When the stupid fool fell in love and wanted to move to California, he needed extra cash. Trevor bought out his share of the business."

"Out of curiosity how many people have you killed since getting out of the military?"

He smiled to the point where his teeth showed. "Counting you and her. Over a dozen."

Fear raced across Sanchez's face. She struggled to get her words out. "What do you mean, me?"

"Look Honey, we've appreciated your help but you're nothing but a liability now. Sooner or later someone else will connect you to us and that's something we can't have."

"Every cop will be looking for you if you kill me," She stammered.

"I don't think so. They'll never find your or his body after this place is demolished. You'll both be buried under two feet of concrete."

In a flash, Sanchez pointed her gun at him and pulled the trigger, "Click, click, click, click."

Jake chuckled, "You don't think I'd be stupid enough to give you a loaded gun."

The detective struggled to get the words out. "No, wait! I thought you loved me. Why are you doing this?"

"Sorry, but it was only about the sex. You're pretty good, not the best but I made it work."

His snide remark caused her to confess, "I've taken the precautions. There is an envelope in my locker at work with enough evidence to put you away for years."

Jake smirked, "That has already been taken care of. You have nothing."

Tears ran down her cheeks. "But, but, but you can trust me. I won't say a word to anyone. I'll, I'll quit the force and move back to Cuba. Please, you don't have to do this."

"Sorry, Babe, you're a liability and liabilities are not good for business."

"When you asked me to take care of that doctor, I did what you asked. I promise I won't tell a soul."

I started to slowly back away, but when the plastic below my feet started to crinkle Jake said, "Don't get any ideas." As he pointed his gun toward me.

"The problem is that you talk in your sleep. We can't take chances that if you ever shack up with another man, he might overhear something he shouldn't."

I would've enjoyed this lover's spat a lot better if there wasn't a gun pointed at me. "So why did you have her kill Dr. Burns?"

Jake hesitated but it was her who goated him along. "Go ahead and tell him. What do you have to lose since you're going to kill both of us?"

"Having gotten Madison pregnant, he demanded money from Trevor to keep the scandal quiet, and we couldn't have that."

Just as Jake started to raise his gun at me, a voice cried out from behind the stage. "Boss, you'd better hurry, someone just pulled up out front."

"Sorry you two, this is the end of the line." A bright flash of light caused me to squint as the loud boom echoed throughout the theater.

I watched in horror as his pant leg started turning a dark crimson red. The man was a rock and didn't scream out in pain. "You shouldn't have done that?" Jake harshly said to her.

Unfortunately, I couldn't say the same for Detective Sanchez when he pointed his gun at her and fired. The bullet disappeared into her chest and blood quickly soaked her shirt. She let out a blood curdling scream as her gun fell from her fingers and her body crumpled to the ground.

I went for her gun but Jake pushed me away. I closed my eyes and prayed it would be quick, but instead I heard Jake cry out in pain followed by metal hitting the plastic. I watched as he tried to wrestle Oz's grip off his leg, but Oz had no intention of doing so. His teeth held on tight to the bullet blood-soaked leg.

Jake reached for his gun but suddenly cried out in pain when out from behind me a foot stomped hard onto his hand. When he looked up his face turned a pale white. "Jake, you look like you've seen a ghost." The young man remarked.

"Tanner! I thought. How in the hell?"

"You thought what, Jake? After you shot me and left me to die out in the forest that day that you'd never see me again. What do you think my big brother is going to say when I show up at the office? Will his face turn as white as yours?" Tanner bent down and picked up the gun and pointed at the puzzled expression on Jake's face. "God knows I should pull the trigger but I'm not like you or my brother."

When Jake tried to remove his hand from under Tanner's foot, a flash followed by a loud boom that filled the room causing Oz to release his grip and rush to my side. A metal clicking sound echoed as the gun dropped to the floor and Jake turned his head in time to see the last puffs of smoke escape Detective Sanchez's gun before it fell to the floor. Her eyes closed and body slumped up against the stage.

Jake's body went limp as he laid still on the plastic. Tanner fell back into one of the empty theater seats as his face showed the horror of what had just happened. Oz and Annie stood over Jake's body daring him to move. From the back of the hall a voice sang out. "Hey, Cowboy. I see you've gotten yourself in another mess."

I was never so relieved to see Rod as he and others raced down the aisles. Soon the theater was filled with police and first responders attending to both Jake and the detective.

A female officer escorted me and the guys out to the lobby. Sitting on a bench was a shaken Tanner Quinn, my mystery person of interest. His leather face and sunken brown eyes surrounded by dark grey circles gave me the impression life had been hard for him. Even the pants and shirt hung from his body as if they had come from a second-hand shop. Tanner struggled to get the words out as he tried to explain to the officers what happened. I could tell he was in shock.

When they wheeled Jake's lifeless body past me on a stretcher, his haunting eyes sent chills throughout me. But it was when they wheeled out Detective Sanchez's body under a cover the reality of what happened sunk in and I nearly fell onto the lobby floor. It was both Captain Ross and Rod who caught me and helped me to a bench. When I looked up Rod, he was holding onto my camera. Captain Ross bent down and scratched both Oz and Annie behind their ears. "Wes, go home." He said. "You know the drill and we'll see you in the morning."

Rod put his arm around me as he walked me out of the theater. The bright light cause me to squint and when we walked past one of the patrol cars, I smiled. In the back seat sat a deflated young arrogant man from the Quinn's headquarters.

Rod asked, "What made you come to the theater?"

"Your text," I replied.

"I never sent you at text."

I showed him the text and after reading it for a second time he smiled, "I never sent that, Cowboy."

As soon as he said, "Cowboy," I should've known it was a trap.

"Okay, two can play at this game. How did you know I was here?" I questioned.

"Guess." He then pointed toward a tearful-looking Marti with her arms open running toward me. After a hard hug, Rod commented, "Get him out of my sight. I'll have an officer bring your car by the house later." She tossed him the keys.

Once we got the guys loaded in the truck, she pulled me aside and squeezed me hard. "I got so worried when your phone went dead. I called the station asking for Captain Ross and told him you were in trouble. I was never so relieved when Rod called to say you were okay and for me to hurry to the theater."

After giving the guys an extra couple of treats for a job well done, Marti joined me out on the patio. She handed me a root beer and I smiled when I saw the bottle of wine in her other hand.

Neither one of us spoke. I enjoyed the silence as I tried to wipe away the nightmare from my brain. It was Marti who spoke first with tears gently flowing down her cheeks. "Wes, is this how our lives are going to be from now on? You'll put yourself in danger trying to solve some murder while I live in fear that one day you might never come home?"

I didn't answer but just sat and watched the guys chase each other around the yard. Neither of them seemed the events of the day had affected them as it had us. After some time I replied, "Do I stop helping our friends when they need me?"

"No, but... I don't know. I just worry too much about losing you."

Before I could say another word, she leaped up and raced over to my arms. "I love you and I never want anything bad to happen to you."

We hugged and cried until we had no more tears left. The stress of the day had taken its toll on our emotions and bodies. When Oz and Annie raced to the front door barking, we assumed it was the police officer returning Marti's SUV, but as soon as I opened the door. Chris snapped, "Why is there a police car parked out front?" as he pushed his way past me.

The officer handed me the keys and remarked, "Good job."

"What does she mean, 'Good Job?'" Chris questioned.

It was Marti who said, "Wes just solved the case. We now know who killed Madison and Leah Quinn as well as that doctor."

"He what?" Chris shouted. "I'm your partner! I should've been there! Wes, why didn't you call me?"

"If you don't mind, your sister and I would like to be alone." But instead of getting the hint, he went straight to the kitchen looking for something to eat. No sooner had I attempted to close the door, than Eric pushed it open and in stepped Lois, and Chloe.

Chloe hugged me tight and long. "We heard on the news. Thank you so much. Now Madison can rest in peace."

Being alone with my wife wasn't going to happen, but then surrounded by friends was what we needed. The patio door opened, as usual Jack had two bottles of wine in his arms and Carrie held onto bags of chips. Once the wine was poured everyone was seated out on the patio, except for Chris who sat in the living room alone pouting. I started to tell them my story, but Lois stopped me. "Wes, stop! Wait until the others get here."

"Others?" I questioned.

"Yes, after seeing you on the news, I made some calls."

Marti, Lois, Carrie and Chloe went inside to do something in the kitchen, leaving me alone with Jack and Eric. Jack asked, "Wes, now that it's just us, what was it really like? We don't want the usual sugar-coated story that you'll tell in front of the ladies."

I took a deep breath and replied. "Hell! I hope to never go through anything like that again." I had just finished when Donavan and Jeff joined us. "Wes, I brought sandwiches and pizzas."

I was never so happy to hear laughter as we all gathered around listening to Jeff complain about how Sunshine had taken over half his closet with her clothes and most of the bathroom counter with her makeup. Donavan added the same thing happened with him and Irene.

Marti popped her head out the door and suggested we'd better hurry and grab something to eat since Lois wouldn't be able to restrain Chris much longer. There was enough food for a small army. Pizzas, sandwiches, chips and Irene's special pies covered the dining room table. I was thankful that Marti made sure to keep the conversation away from what had happened this afternoon.

It was late by the time we got our house back to ourselves. Marti nestled her body into mine under the sheets and we laid there in silence as I gently stroked her hair. "Wes, it really scares me every time you get yourself involved with these kind of cases. Just the other day, I noticed I'm starting to get gray hair. I worry so much that one of these days you're not going to come home to me."

"I know, I promised not to get involved but if I remember correctly, it was my sexy secretary who said we needed to help clear Sue's name."

"Oh, shut up. Sure, blame me for almost getting yourself killed." She then climbed on top of me and with her tear-soaked brown eyes looking down at me. "If this is going to be our lives, then promise me you'll get some help."

I gently placed my finger on her lips. "Maybe you're right, I need some help besides Oz and Annie."

"Don't tell me my bother?"

"That'll never happen." I pulled her body close to mine and felt her tears on my neck. We never said another word as we fell asleep in each other's arms.

Chapter 22

A gloomy-looking Chris stepped out of the bakery carrying four boxes of fried deliciousness. After he handed the boxes to his sister, he begged us to let him come to the station. It was Betty who came to our rescue and requested that he get back inside and finish up a special order that was going to be picked up soon.

Two officers met us in the parking garage under the station. One insisted on carrying the boxes. The other held onto both Oz and Annie's leashes. No sooner had we stepped into the detective squad room that mayhem broke out as everyone rushed over to help themselves to what was inside. You'd have thought they had never tasted Betty's bakery treats before. With her quick thinking, Marti rescued the box marked "For Captain Ross Only." As one of the detectives with a donut half shoved in his mouth started to open it.

In the past when we would visit the station after solving a murder case, let alone three this time, officers would take Oz and Annie for a walk and Marti would have gone to replace my phone. However, this time Marti insisted she join the meeting. I whispered into her ear, "Is this what you meant when you said you needed help?"

"I'm your sexy secretary and your partner in crime," she replied. "Don't you think it would be best I was here to take notes?"

Before I could answer she entered the room and sat next to Captain Ross and opened the box of treats for him to choose.

After the introductions had been made, the room filled with applause and laughter when I mentioned that Chris wouldn't be joining us today.

"Wes, you got yourself in a hornets nest this time and you're lucky to come out of it alive," Captain Ross commented. Marti reached out and grabbed my hand under the table. "You see, the F.B.I., Maimi Police, the Florida State Police along with other federal agencies have been trying to get enough evidence to bring down Trever's Quinn's illicit organization for a long time. Detective Miller wasn't in a training class in Las Vegas but instead in Maimi working with these organizations. As of this morning, the Florida State Police raided three warehouse, five rental locations and arrested over twenty suspected persons involved. Here in the valley, we raided the Quinn headquarters, one warehouse and five rental locations."

A man from the Police Internal Affairs office explained how they arrested the Deputy Chief along with two other high-ranking officers in the department. The group came under suspicion after they ignored HR hiring procedures and hired Detective Sanchez. It was the Deputy Chief who insisted Detective Sanchez lead the investigation into Madison Quinn's murder to help steer everyone away from the Quinn organization. That's when Internal Affairs became involved and started investigating.

"Why send Rod to Miami in the first place? Couldn't he have helped with the investigation here?" I asked.

"We felt it was in the departments and public's best interest if we isolated Detective Sanchez. The relationship between you and Detective Miller could've hampered our investigation. With his help he was able to expose the corrupt officers in both the Maimi Police and ours that were tied to Trevor Quinn's illegal operation," Captain Ross added.

"Did Nancy know about this?" Marti asked when she turned to Rod.

"No. All she knew was he was in Vegas for training. She had some time off coming to her and spent the time visiting her folks."

For Marti's sake they didn't show the video I had recorded in the theater. I was glad not to relive the nightmare all over again. "What about Jake?" I questioned.

"He died on the operating table from his wounds," Rod added.

"What about Sue?" I asked.

"We'll be meeting with the D.A.'s office later this morning. With Detective Sanchez's confession she'll be cleared from Dr. Andew Burns' murder, but she'll still be held liable for Madison and Leah Quinn's deaths, that is until we can prove otherwise. Now that there is some doubt on this case, we're going to suggest she'd be let out on bail. Once we locate and interrogate Trevor Quinn, I'm betting she be exonerated from all charges."

"When will that be?" I asked.

"Unfortunately, he disappeared before we were able to take him into custody. But don't worry, I'm sure it will be only a couple days." Captain Ross added.

"Did you ever find the letter Detective Sanchez claimed she had written in her locker?" I asked.

"We didn't find one, but we're sure the Deputy Chief or one of the others beat us to it and cleaned out any evidence that would link them to her or Quinn's organization."

As we stepped out of the conference room I asked Rod, "What's the story with Tanner Quinn. It's kind of strange he suddenly showed up out of the blue."

"His brother and Jake took him elk hunting in Alaska. When they had their chance, Jake shot him and to hide the evidence, they left him for the bears. It was by some luck when a hunting party from the Tanacross tribe came across his wounded body. They took him back to their village where he spent a year with them while they cared for his wounds."

"Why didn't he report this to the police?"

"Come on Wes, use that thick head of yours. It would be his word against theirs. After what happened at the theater we reached out to the local police and they had no record of him. During our interview with him, he said they flew up in Trevor's private jet and Jake was the pilot. There were no witnesses."

"How did he get from Alaska to here?" I asked.

"He hitched a ride with a trucker. Once he got back to town, he re-established his bank account."

"What about..."

"Stop right there. I suggest you talk to him to get the full story. Now if you don't mind, Cowboy, I have some paperwork to do."

"Well, I'm glad you've returned so you can have my back." I jokingly remarked.

"Cut the crap, Cowboy. I'm serious when I say, you need to stop getting involved with these kind of cases and let us do our job. Both Marti and I are afraid that one of these days you'll be in over your head. Understand!"

"So, you really do care about me?" He just shook his head and walked away.

Chloe and Grimm joined Marti and me at the dog park. Without saying a word, the three of us sat and watched our four-legged family members play together. When tears raced down Chloe cheeks, Marti pulled her body into hers. "I miss my sister. She didn't deserve to die." Chloe leaned over and hugged me.

"Thanks for everything. I really appreciate how you looked after me. I'll never forget your kindness."

"We're glad we could help. Maybe now you can move forward with your life."

"Yes, that'll be good. I've got to go to my new adopted grandparents' house and gather my stuff."

"Grandparents?" Marti questioned.

"Lois and Eric. They were so kind and comforting. I owe them a lot."

Marti gave me a questionable glance. "So, when were you going to tell me she was staying the them?"

"I was afraid if I told you then somehow your brother would find out and mistakenly blab it to the world." As soon as those words escaped my lips, I knew I was in trouble. "Are you hungry? What do you say we get lunch?"

"I can't believe you don't trust your sexy secretary to keep a secret. No hot tub fun for you tonight, Buster, and you can definitely forget any snuggle time in the near future."

"Oh really?" I said as I kissed her.

"Okay, maybe this time, I'll let it slide. But it better be one heck of a lunch. I'm starving."

We had just gathered the guys when an elderly looking couple showed up with the cutest puppy. It was a miniature Australian Terrier. Marti got down on her knees to play with it, which made our guys jealous.

That gave me an idea and after getting a phone number I quickly made a call. We dropped the Oz and Annie off at home then drove to a small white house on the other side of town. Marti asked, "Wes, what's going on? I thought you were taking me out to lunch."

"Come on, you're going to like this."

A middle-aged man opened the front door holding the cutest brown and white little furball puppy. Marti quickly melted and grabbed her out of his hands. "Wes, she's so cute. Is she ours?"

The moment I told her no tears formed in her eyes. "Then why are we here?"

"Carrie."

A smile grew on her face. "She'll be perfect."

Carrie was in one of her brightly colored jumpsuits watering her plants out front when we pulled into our driveway. When Marti climbed out of the truck holding the little furball, Carrie dropped the hose and rushed over to hug her. "I can't believe you got this little cutie," she excitedly exclaimed. "What does Oz and Annie think?"

Jack stepped outside and shouted. "Hey, what's all the commotion?"

Carrie quickly replied, "Come check out Wes and Marti's new family addition."

"What are you going to name her?" Both Jack and Carrie said in unison.

"We haven't, but I'm sure you'll come up with cute name for her."

Carrie froze and stared at us. "You didn't, you wouldn't, you shouldn't. Are you kidding me?" Water welled up in her eyes and she blinked away the tears. "Thank you! The house has been so quiet and not the same without Dolly."

The tearful Carrie, held on tight to her new friend and commented, "I'm going to call her Nelly."

Marti wrapped her arms around my neck, kissed me and said. "You've done a good thing today." It had been a long time since we'd seen Carrie smile like that. "Now don't you still owe me lunch?"

U-Stackum Burger and Brew was packed with the lunch crowd but we were able to find a table in the back. After placing our order Marti mentioned, "I have the next six days off. Are you working on any fraud cases?"

"Nothing that can't wait. What did you have in mind?"

"Vegas Baby, Vegas."

We checked with Vern who agreed to watch the guys. After lunch, I dropped Marti off at home to make reservations while I went to the mega mart to stock up on food for a growing teenager. No sooner had I stepped inside our house, with my arms filled with groceries that I noticed a guilty expression on Marti's face. "What's going on?" I asked.

She took a deep breath, "Sorry Honey, I might've messed up. Please don't be mad at me. It was an honest mistake."

I squinted my eyes and was about to ask when I heard the TV on in the other room. Chris burst into the kitchen and started rummaging through the bags of groceries. "Wes, guess what? We're going to Vegas with you! Isn't great?"

"You're what?" I shouted as I slapped the bag of cookies out of his hand.

"I'm sorry. I didn't see him come in the house; I was on the phone trying to book our airline tickets when he overheard me. Before I knew it, he was on his phone telling Denise they were coming to Vegas with us. I tried to stop him but you know my brother."

"Well, we'll have to un-invite them."

"We can't."

"Why not. Because Denise already got the time off and told everyone she was going to Vegas. Her co-workers pooled their money for her to gamble on their behalf. I didn't have the heart to tell them no."

I slumped into one of the counter chairs. "Let me guess, we're also paying for everything?" I despairingly commented.

Chapter 23

Jackson called to advise the D.A. agreed on bail and that Sue was released late last night. I replied, "That's great news. Sorry, but we're in a rush to catch our flight to Vegas. I'll talk to you next week." I replied.

I honked the horn three times before Denise popped her head out the front door. "We'll be ready in five."

Twenty minutes later out stepped Denise with a small carrying on and Chris had a large black trash bag filled with clothes. "What are you doing with that?" Marti questioned him.

"I don't have a suitcase, so I packed everything in this bag."

"Why didn't you say something last night?" Marti frustratedly asked.

He gave her his usual sheepish grin. We rushed back to our house, got the spare carry-on out of the garage and stuffed the bag and his clothes inside. By the time we arrived at the airport we had an hour to spare.

It took Chris four times to make it past security. I sat at the gate enjoying the circus of people as they rushed in a panic to make their flights while He, Denise and Marti were ordering coffee.

I felt my phone vibrate in my pocket, but before I could say a word, the voice on the other end asked, "Mr. Johns?"

"Yes," I hesitantly answered.

"This is Robert Quinn. I just got off the phone with Tanner. I also talked to Detective Miller yesterday and he told me the F.B.I. has seized all Trevor's property and closed down the rental locations.

It could be months or years before they finish their investigation."

I replied, "Once all the investigations are done and Trevor is spending the rest of his life behind bars, do you think Tanner will have any interest in becoming the new boss?"

He let out a slight chuckle. When I questioned him about why the chuckle he remarked, "Trevor never ran the operation. He doesn't have the brains."

"Why do you say that?"

"I know my brother. He barely made it through high school. The man doesn't know the difference between a spreadsheet and bed sheet."

"So, it was Jake who controlled the business and not Trevor?" I questioned.

"No, his job was to make sure my brother didn't do anything to mess up their operation."

"Then who was the top dog?"

"Her, the bitch. Before she came along, their operation was nickel and dime at its best. She had the brains, the talent, and connections. As soon as she became involved, things changed as well as got messy. If you didn't do what she demanded then God help you if you saw the next morning's sun rise above ground. She was the reason I left, as I feared for my safety and life. I tried to tell Tanner she was no good and to get out, but he idolized my brother."

I sat there stunned as I ran through a list of possible names. Then I said, "Ava", out loud.

"I've got to go, but thanks again. My only advise, watch your back as long as she's around."

"Before you hang up. Tell me this, if she was so smart and running things, why did your brother divorce her?"

"All I know, it was her idea. Trevor never confided in me as why."

Now my mind was racing, trying to put everything together. I'd never suspect Ava as the boss. She played me well as the poor frightened divorced wife worried for her life.

I was in the middle of collecting my thoughts when Chris plopped his body next to mine, disrupting my train of thought. I leaped up out of my seat after he spilled his hot coffee on my pant leg and it started to burn my skin. "Chris you're a walking disaster!" I shouted.

I was in the men's room cleaning up the stain when a terrifying thought raced through my body. If Ava was the boss, she could've had Jake murder both Madison and Leah or maybe she did it. But why? I quickly dialed Chloe's number but it went to her voicemail. I then tried both Bruce's and Sue's numbers and the same thing. Something was wrong. I called Rod, but damn, I got his voicemail too.

I joined the others waiting for our flight nervously hoping someone would call me back soon. "Wes is everything alright? You seem that something is bothering you?" Marti asked.

Before I could tell her what, Robert had said, my phone rang, "Mr. Johns, you've got to come, she is threatening to kill us if you're not here in an hour. Please hurry," a frightened Sue pleaded.

I leaned over and whispered to Marti that something had come up and to go ahead without me and I'd catch the next flight to Vegas. Seeing the panic in my eyes. "You're not going anywhere without me," she remarked.

We told Denise to go on without us and we'd meet them in Vegas. When Denise questioned if something was wrong, we made the excuse that Vern had called and Oz was sick. We raced down the terminal and into the parking lot. As we left the airport Marti asked. "Wes, now can you tell me what's going on?"

"Bruce and Sue are in danger and possible Chloe!"

"How? Both Detective Sanchez and Jake are dead. Do you think Trevor might try to kill them?"

"No! It was Ava all the time. Ava is threatening to kill both of them if I don't show up at Sue's house."

"Wes, you can't! She'll kill you. Call Rod."

"I did and it went to his voicemail."

"Are you sure it's Ava? The last word we heard was that the police were still looking for Trevor. Maybe he's behind the killings."

"Or worse, they both are." I added.

Marti tried Sue's phone again and still no answer. She dialed Bruce's number and he answered on the second ring. Trying not to sound alarming she asked, "Hey, Bruce is Sue with you? We heard the good news."

"No, she's at home resting. I'm at the cabin cleaning up, I should be home in a couple of hours." He replied.

"Thanks, I'll try her at home."

When the tires squealed to a halt, I noticed the black SUV parked in front of Sue's house. I tried calling Rod again, crap, I still got his damn voicemail.

We watched as the front curtain moved slightly and I could see Ava looking out. My phone rang, "Mr. Johns, why don't you come inside and join us?"

I started to open the door when Marti exclaimed, "What are you doing? You can't go in there! Wait for Rod!"

"If I don't, it might be too late. Call 911 and get help. I'll try stalling her until they get here."

"Oh, no you don't! I'm not letting you go in there alone."

We waited until she reached dispatch and gave them the address.

The front door was slightly ajar. Marti clung to my arm so tight that I was starting to lose the feeling in it. "I didn't give you enough credit," Ava commented as she stood in the hallway waving a gun at us. "I see you brought your wife with you. How nice."

"Do you really think you'll get away with this? I called and the police are on their way." Marti remarked.

"Shut up Honey and go sit next to them." She pointed toward Sue and Chloe who were nervously sitting in the middle of the living room. Their mouths gagged and their hands and feet tied together.

Now I wished I'd stopped by the house to get my protection. "Mr. Johns, you go over there and sit in that chair."

Stalling for time I said, "Why? Why murder both Madison and Leah? Killing the four us will only make things worse for you."

Ava let out a haunting chuckle, "Just three, the fourth, now that you had brought your wife, she will come with me as a hostage until I no longer have a need for her."

I strained to listen for sirens, but nothing. "You killed Madison at the charity event, but I don't remember seeing you there."

"I was there you just didn't notice me in my blonde wig and large sunglasses."

My mind flashed back to the stack of photos on the dining room table, no matter how hard I tried I still couldn't picture her, even in her blonde wig.

"Why kill her? What did she do to you?"

She smirked, "That bitch went and got herself pregnant."

"So?"

"You don't understand. Trevor was fine with fostering any kid but, I couldn't let that happen. It would've messed up everything."

"How?" I asked. I still couldn't hear any sirens.

"Because it should've been my kid, not hers."

Her strong demeanor started to waiver. "You're still in love with him, aren't you?"

Marti interrupted, "I bet the two of you are planning to escape out of the country."

An evil chuckle escaped Ava's lips. "I had everything well planned out where your friend here would take the fall for the murders of Madison and Leah, but then that stupid fool went and messed everything up. Instead of coming to me he arranged to have that stupid lady detective kill that doctor. Then to make matters worse he arranged Jake to have her kill you at the theater. Once Jake told me of Trevor's plan to have you killed, I knew it would only be a matter of time before the detective became a liability.

She had to go. Things would've worked out, until she shot Jake and Tanner showed up."

"So, where's Trevor?" I asked.

"Somewhere where nobody will ever find his body."

"Body? "I questioned.

Again, with the haunting chuckle, "He had become a liability, no loose ends like the four of you."

"You do know the police and the F.B.I. have seized all the assets from the company?" I remarked.

"Not all. My sister, Donna, cleaned out the special bank account we had set up at the bank before the F.B.I. tried to seize the assets. She's already out of the country and in a place where no one can touch her."

"I thought I noticed the family resemblance when I followed one of the rental managers making their special deposit at the bank."

"Enough with the small talk." Ava forcibly grabbed Marti's arm and yanked her up off the floor. "You're coming with me."

I started to get out of the chair in protest but she waived the gun at Marti and I quickly sat back down. "Why kill Leah?" I asked.

Ava lowered the gun and gave me an evil grin. "That drunk! Every time she needed money she went crying to Trevor. He felt sorry for her and she knew what to do to get whatever she wanted from him. But I'd had enough of her leaching off my money. I threatened Trevor if he gave her any more money. When he told her no more, she threatened to go to the press and tell everyone about our little side business. She had to go."

Off to my right where Ava couldn't see, a shadow slowly moved across the curtain covered window. I blew out a slight sigh of relief knowing Rod had gotten the message. I just needed to buy him more time before he was in place to rescue us. "Why Chloe?"

Ava smirked and glanced over at her. "She hired you, instead of letting that worthless detective do her job. We had everything in place for this one to take the fall." Ava pointed her gun at Sue. "But when you found out Sanchez was on the take, well things started to get messy and it was time to clean house and run."

"Let me get this straight, Madison was pregnant with another man's child, Leah was threatening to go to the press to expose your little secret, Dr. Burns attempted to blackmail Trevor. After I found out Detective Sanchez was on the take, she had to go. What about Jake?" I asked.

For a moment, I thought I saw Ava let down her tough demeanor as water welled up in her eyes. "You were in love with him? Weren't you?" Marti added.

I quickly used this opening to help keep her distracted. "You both were lovers. I bet after Jake had killed both the detective and me, you two planned to run away together leaving Trevor to take the fall."

"Well, you've got it all figured out. But you are only half right!" Fire in Ava's eyes ignited, "I found out last week, not only was that bastard sleeping with me but also with that bitch. No one does that to me and gets away with it. Once we were safely out of the country, I had made plans for him to have an accident, but thankfully that detective grew a backbone and took care of the problem for me. I've wasted enough time. I have a plane to catch."

"I don't think you'll get far. They'll be watching the airport."

Ava snickered, "Who said anything about going to the airport? Twenty miles east I have a buddy who has a private air strip and plane. He owes me a big favor. I'll be out of the country and the authorities won't be able to do anything about it."

There was a long eerie silence in the room, except for Chloe and Sue's whimpering. Just then a noise came from the kitchen and when Ava turned to investigate. I said, "Sue, I bet you forgot to feed Dory today?"

"Whose Dory?" Ava questioned.

"Their cat."

Holding tightly onto Marti's arm Ava asked me, "Are there any last words you would like to say to your wife?"

The panic look in Marti's eyes made me sick inside, especially when she attempted to free herself from Ava's tight grip. I thought about rushing Ava but she was too far away.

Off in the distance I heard sirens, "Thank God, but they'll be too late. Where in the hell was Rod, he was cutting this a bit too close for my comfort," I thought.

Ava also heard them, "Well, that's my cue to leave. Don't worry, Honey, you'll be seeing your sister soon." She pulled back the trigger and suddenly an extremely loud explosion echoed off the walls and smoke filled the small room.

Ava cried out in pain and let go of Marti as she dropped to her knees crying. I rushed to get the gun as two officers burst through the front door screaming, "Drop the gun! Drop the gun!"

It was a total bedlam in the house. One officer picked up the gun Ava had dropped while the other grabbed the gun out of P.I. Olivia Broadmore's hand. Marti rushed over and her body collapsed on mine as she burst in tears, her body shaking violently as she wrapped her arms around me. There was a puzzled expression on my face as I watched the circus unfold before my eyes. The officer was handcuffing Olivia who was standing in the kitchen doorway. "Where in the hell did, she come from and how did she know to be here?" I thought.

Ava sat in the corner handcuffed crying in pain. Two officers towering over her watching her every move as a first responder attended to her wound. Two other officers were about to escort Olivia out the door when Detective Miller entered the house and said. "Officers, take those cuffs off her." The officers turned and gave him a questionable glance but did what they were told. "Hello, Olivia. It's been a while." Rod commented.

"You could say that Detective. I heard you had gotten married. Good for you, now maybe you won't be such a tight ass." She chuckled.

I watched as the two of them talked as if they were old friends. Finally, I had to ask. "Do you two know each other?"

Rod commented, "Olivia was my captain before Ross. She was a damn good officer. It was a shame she left the force."

"Oh, my God, Wes, I thought she was going to kill you when she pointed her gun at you." Marti tearfully said.

Two officers took Sue and Chloe out onto the back patio to get their statements while the first responders attended to Ava's wound. Olivia came over and remarked, "Lucky I came along when I did."

"Yes, it was." I said. "Marti, this is P.I. Olivia Broadmore. Olivia, this is my wife."

Marti wiped the tears from her eyes, released herself from my grip and gave Olivia a hug. "Thank you."

"What are you doing here?" I asked.

"I got a call from Jackson. He wanted me to keep an eye on Sue after she was released on bail. He wasn't quite sure if she would try to skip as she was still the main suspect of the two murders."

As two officers escorted Ava out of the house, she turned her head and gave us a scowl and remarked, "I have friends. You'd better watch your backs."

Olivia chuckled and replied, "As if I haven't heard that before. Bring them on." Both Marti and I gave Olivia a stunned look. "She's all smoke and mirrors. Any connections she might have won't have anything to do with her now. They'll stay as far away from her as they can."

"You used to be a police officer?" Marti questioned.

"Yep, twenty-five years on the force."

"Why did you leave?" Marti questioned.

"I wanted to do something different. Besides, police code wouldn't allow me to have purple hair and rings or more than one stud on my ear."

Rod pulled me aside. "Okay Cowboy, we need to talk."

I started to follow him into the kitchen when Olivia remarked, "Cowboy!"

After Rod lectured me for getting myself in this messy situation, I joined Marti and Olivia out front. By the look of their body language, you couldn't tell they had just met. "Cowboy!" Olivia commented.

"Long story," I answered.

"You'll have to stop by sometime and tell me how he gave you the nickname, Cowboy," she snickered.

Chloe walked over and gave both Marti and me each a hug, her body was still shaking. She squeezed her body hard into mine, "Lois told me you were one of the good ones. I agree. You're my knight in shining armor."

"Do you need a ride home?" I asked.

She smiled, "No, my adopted grandparents are coming to pick me up. Grimm and I are going to stay with them for a while until my parents return. Thanks again."

Two hours had passed while we gave our statements when Bruce's car came to a screeching halt and he rushed inside. The street was still lined with police cars, first responders, news crews and want-to-be crime solvers.

I asked, "Do we still have time to catch a flight to Vegas, today?"

Marti wrapped her arm around mine, "Yes, but how about we talk about it over lunch?"

"Did someone say they're buying lunch?" Olivia jokingly remarked.

"Would you like to join us?" Marti asked.

"Only as long as, Cowboy, here is buying."

Chapter 24

Instead of going home, we stayed in a boutique hotel downtown and ate at a very expensive steak house. Vern was watching the house and guys and we wanted to be by ourselves. Marti called Denise and explained what happened and that we wouldn't be joining them. I wasn't surprised to hear they had visited three different buffets so far. She sent us photos of the piles of food on Chris's plates. For now, our tip to Vegas was out of the picture.

After a quick stop at Betty's, we drove to the police station. Olivia was already seated at the large table when we entered the conference room. No sooner had I put the donuts on the table that she reached for one of the special sprinkled donuts reserved for Captain Ross. When he gave her a dirty look, she commented, "You don't want me to tell June, do you?" After a long pause of silence, they both broke out laughing.

For everyone's benefit who weren't at Sue's house yesterday, we took turns recanting our statements. Olivia being an ex-officer, gave a precise point of view of the events from the moment she had parked down the street to shooting Ava. She explained there wasn't enough time to negotiate with Ava. She was close to pulling the trigger. Captain Ross advised Olivia she would have to appear before a review board before being cleared of firing her weapon with the intent of doing bodily harm. But with four witnesses, he was confident she would be cleared of any wrongdoing.

The D.A., who was also in the room, said Sue had been cleared and all charged had been dropped after reviewing the statements given by Marti, Chloe and me.

Captain Ross added that Ava had been charged for the murders of Madison and Leah Quinn. When I asked about Trevor, he replied, "We're hoping she'll tell us where his body is buried, but at the moment she's not talking and has lawyered up."

Before the meeting concluded, Rod informed the group that this morning the Miami task force had arrested Donna Evans attempting to board a cruise ship headed for the Dominican Republic. They also confiscated the two offshore bank accounts where Donna had hidden the money as well as a one-way plane ticket to Argentina from the Dominican Republic.

Once the meeting was over, the detectives in the squad room rushed over to talk to Olivia. I asked Rod, "So does this mean, you're back here at your old job to watch my back?"

"You'd like that, wouldn't you, Cowboy?"

Marti gave him a big hug, "I don't think that'll be necessary. I've found him a new guardian angel." She pointed toward Olivia.

Just before we left, Marti went over and whispered something in Olivia's ear, who smiled and gave her a wink.

Bruce and Sue were out in the hall, and as soon as Sue saw the two of us, she rushed over and gave us a tight embrace as tears streamed down her cheeks. "I don't know how to ever thank you?"

"Just don't invite us to join you at next year's golfing charity event." I jokingly said.

Once we were alone in my truck, I commented, "I have a new guardian angel?"

"I've come to the realization you'll always come to the rescue of people in need. It's the knight in shining armor in you. I love that you care. It's just that I'm afraid there's going to be the one time when Oz or Rod won't be there to save you and you may need an angel to step in. her named is Olivia Broadmore."

"What are you trying to say?" I asked.

A smile crossed her face. "Yesterday at lunch while you had stepped away, she and I decided you needed someone to watch over you. She agreed to keep an eye on you if ever you come across another body."

"You what? She what? I don't need her following me around everywhere I go. I've got Oz, and besides, if I remember correctly, I wasn't the one who found the last body."

"That's beside the point. You can't expect Rod to continue to do it. He's married now and he has Nancy in his world."

"Are you going to be the one to tell your brother about Olivia?" I asked.

She smiled and leaned over and kissed me on the cheek, "You are, but let him down easy, remember he's, my brother."

We drove to the airport to get our bags, we had decided after yesterday's excitement we weren't in the mood for Vegas. I thought it was strange when Marti asked me to park in the long-term parking lot instead of waiting out front.

As we made our way inside, Marti wrapped her arm around mine and said, "I made alternate plans."

"What kind of plans?"

"I got us booked on a flight leaving shortly to Arizona where I have reservations for the next five days at a ranch, just the two of us. Just think we can sit out on the porch at night watching the sun set behind the mountains."

"I like the sound of that." I replied.

Once we got settled on the plane and they closed the door and we were about to take off, she handed me a pamphlet describing all the activities at the ranch.

It wasn't until I read the second page when I turned and said, "You didn't?"

The smiling slowly crept across her face, "Yes, I did."

"You didn't say it was a working ranch and I would have to be doing ranch stuff. You can count me out." I started to unbuckle my seatbelt, "I'm getting out of here."

"Sorry, too late, we're about to take off." She produced a piece of paper and after reading it for a second time I said under my breath, "Curse that damn Scrabble game." I looked over to see a smile creep across her face.

"I love you, too." She said.

I hoped you enjoyed their latest mystery as much as I enjoyed bringing it to you. Wes and Oz will return in their seventh mystery in 2026. The title is still undecided. I'd appreciate it if you would recommend their series to your family members and friends. Thank you and happy reading.

S.B. Biddinger